The Hatton Garden 8

Andrew Darragh

Copyright © 2017 Andrew Darragh

All rights reserved.

ISBN: 1542604664
ISBN 13: 9781542604666

During the robbery, you're running on pure adrenaline, immediately after the robbery, there's a gradual decline, and in my particular case, I felt empty. It was almost anticlimactic.
Bruce Reynolds (1931 – 2013)

For my mate, Oliver.

AMETHYST

In the April of 2015 a gang of thieves pulled off one of the most daring heists in British history. It shocked the establishment, ruined lives, initiated one of the biggest investigations the Flying Squad had ever undertaken, and gave certain media executives and newspaper editors a field day. As insurance firms were eventually inundated with claims and film studios battled for production rights, eight people made life-changing decisions.

Karl Brant BOX 18

Dwight Shunter BOX 113

Juliette Roux BOX 286

Sean Murphy BOX 375

Massimo Alessi BOX 492

Gavin Foble BOX 767

Ralph Wilson BOX 801

Yuri Tavlenko BOX 971

Although all of them rented a deposit box, none of them had the contents stolen. They were however, left with a calling card that brought them to the attention of the Metropolitan Police and the Flying Squad. This is the story of how they were left with no option but to act.

CITRINE

The flight from London Heathrow to Khartoum International Airport had been an uncomfortable one. Nine hours in cattle class with a chorus of screaming kids nearby wasn't his idea of fun. Neither was the arid climate he walked into, the whacky race exchange to the nearby Regency hotel and the bed of nails he was expected to sleep on. The shower was welcomed but room service wasn't. He had fond memories of the food on offer so stuck to the water and sandwiches he had brought. After switching on his laptop and spending almost one hour trying to get a signal he gave up and attempted to settle down for the night. The noise outside was relentless, the air conditioning inside came and went, and the morning couldn't come quick enough.

After checking out of the hotel it took him forty-five sweltering minutes to get to the offices of the man who had summoned him. After signing into the building and enduring a further fifteen minutes of chaotic shouting and bawling from a staff that went about its business like the final scene of a Bollywood movie, he eventually found himself sitting before the Sudan's answer to hell on legs. She was a no nonsense solid lump of a woman who went by the name of Nadima, and although she stood just four feet from the ground she strutted around as if she were six feet tall. In between barked orders at office staff and a short yet in-depth interrogation of the visitor, she eventually allowed him to pass by her desk and walk the final ten paces to his destination.

Mahendra Bavishi was a sixty-nine year old thickset affable entrepreneur who watched every penny and knew the finest details of everyone under his employment. That's why the man before him had been associated with the firm for eight years. Mahendra had many rules and the four at the top of his list were; must be good at the job, must be honest, must be cheap and must come recommended. If you got past those four, then you stood a chance with him. On paper the employee currently sitting before him did just that, and as the initial recommendation had come from his son Manish, then it was an arrangement that suited him well.

"Pleasant flight, my friend?"

"Yes sir."

"The accommodation?"

"Delightful."

"Only the best for my people. I have prepared your office as usual."

The visitor looked around to see the usual sparsely decorated fit for purpose shoebox of a room before smiling a faked satisfaction.

"Did you bring all the required accounts from Manish?"

The visitor tapped the bag perched on his lap.

Mahendra retrieved a file from a nearby safe and handed it over. He checked his watch, the day was already seven hours old. "Ok, time is money my friend, you have a flight to catch." The visitor nodded and retreated to the prearranged workspace. He took a laptop and file from his bag and within minutes began to audit the company records. For four hours, he worked at a thunderous pace interrupted by just two small breaks for water. With what concentration levels remained he went over the files one last time. Satisfied that everything was in place it was now all down to timing and routine. He looked over to Bavishi and noted that in between checking his watch he was punishing a keyboard and squinting at a monitor. Not far away, and in between screaming down a phone, Nadima was busily ordering people around. The visitor smiled, it was time to make his first move. Collecting a pile of papers, he went across and tapped on the office door.

"Come in, come in, how can I help?"

"Sir, I have completed the forecast and budgetary checks you set out last year and Manish has come in ahead of schedule and had changed a deficit into an eighty seven-thousand-pound profit."

"So, my son is doing well."

The employee nodded, the files were placed on the desk and after a brief review they were signed. At exactly 11.23am he retreated out of the office and ten minutes later he was back.

"And this one is?"

"Tax returns, the reclaim value is twenty five thousand pounds."

They were signed with a broad stroke of the pen and an even broader smile. At 11.45am they were replaced with a summary of why three large amounts of funds had to be shifted into the required offshore accounts or be lost. It took Manish just five minutes to complete the transactions. At exactly 11.55am a spreadsheet was placed on his desk with the account details of four people. He checked his watch and scanned the details.

"So, all four have defaulted on payment of their deposit boxes?"

"Yes sir, there are no partnerships involved, we have been unable to track down any next of kin so as per procedure we have notified the treasury and the required independent inspection authority. We have booked a proposed date to open the boxes in their presence so all we need now is your approval." At that the employee left the room and said a silent prayer for routine.

Mahendra hammered at a few keys, stuck his face into the monitor and began clicking away at the mouse. The employee checked his watch, it was 11.59am. Moments later the old man hit 'control alt delete', got to his feet, locked his office door and exchanged words with Nadima before sweeping out of the office. As soon as he was out of site she followed suit. The employee knew where they were both heading and knew that he had exactly fifteen minutes to complete the main reason for him being there.

Taking a DX4 Data Logger from his bag he connected it to his mobile phone and made his way to Nadima's desk. In the top drawer, he found the key he needed and moments later he was sitting in Manish's chair. He plugged the logger into one of the available USB ports, fired up the required application on his phone and let it run. It took just two minutes to find the first set of keystrokes used on the board which were logged at exactly 6.15am. They consisted of seven letters and two numbers. The employee was now looking at Aalllih41so he opened up a second anagram application and set it away. Of the twenty-three options given only one made sense. He knew it to be the name of the biggest football team in Sudan so he guessed that the numbers with it where just for the year so he typed in Alhilal14. The screen flickered for a moment and then he was in. He reopened the last file worked on and was met with another password screen. The logger was put into play and ninety seconds later he had six letters and four numbers, they were ttHoan0898. He shook his head, there would be no need for the app. When he typed in Hatton8890 and the address of Mahendra's safety deposit building in London, a spreadsheet appeared on screen. There were three tabs, the first was marked 'Costs' and listed the set-up charges for the company along with the annual upgrade and repair expenditure. The second was marked 'Profit and Loss', it was mostly in red but it ended with a few lines in black. The third tab was just marked 'Sheet3' but it was completely blank. That's when the employee began to panic. He rechecked each folder several times looking for hidden columns or code but there were none to be had. He checked his watch, it was thirteen minutes past midday, and he had two minutes left. He returned to the third tab. It had no specific name but it was there. Why? He selected the whole sheet, clicked on the font selector and chose black. Suddenly the data he was after appeared on screen. "You crafty old bugger," he whispered before exporting the file to his phone. He then quickly logged out of the PC, darted out of the office, locked the door, returned the key to the required desk drawer and shot back to his chair. As soon as he was seated Mahendra reappeared with Nadima in his wake. They were both laden with bags of food and drink. What he witnessed next he had seen several times before and even now it still never ceased to amaze him. It was finely co-ordinated eating at full speed. For the next ten minutes he looked over to the tops of two heads and their owners as they performed a front crawl through the pool of food spread out before them. The drinks were emptied in four minutes flat and at exactly thirty minutes past midday they were both back to work.

The employee stopped for a glass of water, and as he made his way back to the desk, he got the raised hand he had been looking for. The requests had been signed and they were handed over with the question he needed.

"How was the file I gave you?" asked Mahendra.

"I'm afraid to say that there are a few anomalies but I will need a while longer to be sure."

"How much longer?"

"Two hours, possibly three."

Mahendra checked his watch. The employee knew that he was calculating the cost of a missed flight and another night in the hotel against what might be discovered. After tilting his head from side to side for a few moments he suddenly went still. "Bring what you have to me in one hour and I will do the rest."

The employee nodded and returned to desk. He spent the next hour on a report requested by Manish before returning to his father with a file he had completed some two hours ago.

"So, what have you found?"

The employee placed several pieces of paper on the desk. "As you can see, these invoices have been paid for the same manufacturer for a variety of amounts. I have checked them against the relevant purchase orders and in each case the fabrics requested have all been of the same quantity. When you check the higher amounts they all carry the same signature."

"Is it someone in their accounts department?"

"No, it's someone in your materials control department."

Mahendra looked up in disbelief. "Can you prove it?"

The employee placed a batch of timesheets on the desk and circled the signatures. He then placed them against the invoices. "He has been using a false name but if you look at the formation of the lettering it's all by the same hand."

Mahendra began to nod. He then quickly logged into his PC, went into the required personnel file and then scribbled a date on one of the pieces of paper. "Could you do a quick check on the figures for the same manufacturer going back six months from that date?" The employee nodded and fifteen minutes later he was back with a nod of the head.

"And he was supposed to be a friend of a friend," muttered the old man. As he sat there in silence the employee let a polite cough escape. The old man broke away from his thoughts and checked his watch. "I'm sorry, thank you for all the hard work, tell my son I appreciate everything and have a pleasant flight."

"Thank you, sir." At that the employee collected his things and left the building. Three hours later as Mahendra was raging at around thirty thousand feet with one sorry-looking department head standing before him, he was cruising at an altitude of twenty-eight thousand feet with a glass of white wine in his hand. Once back at Heathrow he took a taxi to Holborn and handed his report into Manish along with his own invoice. They chatted about his visit, he got a firm handshake and a single signature as well as the usual offer of a full-time position at the firm. As ever, the employee gave the usual polite refusal as contracted work with various clients suited his needs better. The only time the two men weren't in the same room was when Manish left to complete an agreed bank transfer. Whilst he was away the employee took that time to make copies of three keys that sat within a ringed cluster on a nearby desk.

With the business concluded he made his way to Twickenham and called into a print shop he had used on several occasions and obtained a single large size print of a spreadsheet. He then went to a key cutter, called into a nearby café for breakfast and walked the final mile to his destination. The man he met there took the print and keys from him and handed over a large brown envelope full of cash. As he then took a taxi home, had a shower and climbed into bed, the recipient of the print had already worked his way through the first batch of names he wanted.

The pain in his chest and the burning sensation had been with him all day. Four indigestion tablets hadn't managed to shift it. To take his mind off it he poured himself a glass of beer, lit up a cigarette and pulled his favourite read down from his bookcase. It wasn't the tome of some notable wordsmith, and it wasn't some fictional escapade of some young wannabe. It was all his own work and it was all fact. The pictures and clippings outnumbered his scribbles. To him it was pure memory, to others simply a scrapbook. It was just over fifty years old and ran to one hundred and seventy-four pages, six of which were heavily sellotaped. It contained two hundred newspaper clippings, eighty-one photographs and five handwritten letters.

After taking a mouthful of beer and blowing smoke into the air he began to flip through some of the pages. He stopped at a bold headline that read 'BALACLAVA AND THE 40 THIEVES.' It was in *The Daily Sketch* next to a supporting story 'I drove in handcuffs – Driver Mills.' Both stories were dedicated to the notion that it had been an inside job. The reader smiled and lifted his glass in toast. On the opposite page was the front page from the *News of the World*. The headline 'HOW THE GREAT ROBBERY WAS PLANNED' sat over a story that began with detectives and country bobbies looking for a wisp of smoke coming from buildings that hadn't smoked all summer in order to find the gang's hideout. As he read on the acid taste that now filled his mouth was taken care of with more beer and a headline in the *Daily Mirror* 'THE HOODED MEN IN HANDCUFFS.' Below it was picture of three men with blankets over their heads, being guided by three police officers. The story was all about the first breakthrough arrests. The clipping below it was from the same paper and carried the story that one of the train robbers wanted to give his money back. Beside it was a picture of a moustached Bruce Reynolds. Across the page were two clippings from the *Evening Standard*. The first story was on possible sightings and carried the headline 'TRAIN GANG ALERT IN SOUTH AMERICA.' The second article had a sub-headline of 'Watch for four men on holiday beaches.' According to the report four men with suspected links to the robbery had been seen in the sunny gambling and yachting resort of Montevideo, Uruguay.

After rubbing his chest in order to help some gas escape from his lungs he turned to a full page spread that was from the *Sunday Times Magazine*. The picture made him smile. It was a crumpled glove wrapped over a lightbulb within a signal box and carried the phrase 'How to stop a train and make two and a half million pounds.' After a long drag on his cigarette he flipped over a few pages to the photographs. He had taken most of them and they never ceased to lift his spirits no matter how many times he looked at them. There was one with his old work colleague, Paddy. They had both started working on the trains on the same day and had hit it off from the start. There was one with Buster Edwards at his flower stall. There was one of him sharing a drink with Ronnie Biggs at a bar in Spain. It was signed *'Thanks for everything.'* The pics that followed were taken at his early retirement party. All the motley crew were there. As his eyes ran across their faces his heart was filled with both sadness and joy. If only he could have told them. Then there were the letters. His favourite was one he had received from Bruce Reynolds. There was no date, location or name on it. It ran to a few paragraphs and was ended 'Be lucky, I'm still getting away with it, your old mate B.'

He laughed out loud and that's when the pain ran across his chest. The scrapbook slid to the floor as he tried to get up. Gasping for air he dropped the glass and the cigarette. As they hit the floor his legs buckled and he fell. As he attempted to rub his chest his lungs struggled to say open. What air managed to pass through them entered the room accompanied by a terrified howl. His body then went into spasm as every nerve ending seemed to be on fire. As he attempted to move he could see the scrapbook. The cigarette had just ignited one of the pages. His mind went back to the train. He thought about his old mate Paddy one last time. He thought about what they had started. As the scrapbook caught fire and burnt its way into the carpet he thought about the deposit box. As the air in his lungs began to disappear he scrambled to his feet. He swayed for a moment and then looked down at the scrapbook. As he reached for it everything just went black.

He met her in a car park in Dartford, Kent that was just thirty minutes' drive away from his target's used car business. She was from an agent he had used before and she had come highly recommended from the owner friend. She was wearing a long blonde wig that wrapped a striking face which needed very little makeup. The bust was ample and, as requested, looked like it was about to topple out of a little black outfit that just about touched in all the right places. The heels were high, the jacket was leather and the provided script had been committed to memory. He was dressed in a dark blue Canali suit beneath a distressed brown Himalayan sheepskin coat. The Rolex watch was Yacht-Master gold and the slow burning cigar was Stradivarius Churchill. The E-Class Mercedes he was using had been leased under a false name.

After a brief chat, he drove to the forecourt of 'Pentire Cars' and parked up. When he got out she quickly took up position on his arm, gave him a kiss on the cheek and guided him towards the showroom. He stopped at the smoking area just off from the entrance to draw on his cigar and she went inside to buzz around the available vehicles. With the company secretary, out to lunch that left two salesmen on shift and she had the attention of them both. As she swayed around the vehicles on display, he focused on the only private office in the building and the seventy five-year old face he was after could be seen through the window. It was a face that had seen war and the bombed-out streets of London, it had seen petty crime fine tuned into no nonsense hard burglary. It carried a tired look beneath thinning grey hair set back on a high forehead. It seemed to hang over a slight frame that looked as if it was being held together by the clothes that creased their way around it. It was the face of criminal that came with a record that began crisp, collected a few creases and was now looking tattered around the edges.

He blew smoke from the cigar and waited for her to step outside; he patted her on the bum and that was the signal for her to go ahead with what had been planned. It took her just one minute to find the red BMW parked in the specified location and begin to wave. Both of the salesmen reacted but when the quickest one shot out of the door the slowest one just looked across to him so that they could share a smile and a shake of the head.

A mobile phone rang and as the face in the window answered it he stubbed out the cigar, reached for the phone in his own pocket and made his way towards the toilet facility. He hit the required button and the phone on the showroom switchboard began to ring. The salesman picked it up and as he did so there was an almighty scream from outside. He ended the call and disappeared into the toilet, leaving the door ajar. He then looked on as the salesman replaced the phone and ran outside. He pushed the saved number on his phone once again. He waited for the voice to answer before the screams coming from the forecourt got louder. Seconds later the line went dead and the required face shot across the showroom and ran outside. He quickly nipped into the vacated office and found the mobile phone on the desk. It took him just ninety seconds to plug in a portable sim reader and download all the contacts. Moments later he was outside looking at a red-faced salesman denying that any contact had took place. Harsh words were exchanged, tears flowed, and apologies were made. Fifteen minutes later he dropped her off in the same cark park they had met in. She walked away with an envelope containing five hundred pounds and the details of what she would be doing tomorrow.

His second target was sixty-seven years old. He was grey, he was light on his feet, he had a shape women classed as content and although his face had that lived in look, the apartment he was looking to rent out had not. It was situated in Canonbury Square in Islington, North London and at one time was home to such disreputable art types such as George Orwell and Evelyn Waugh. On the outside, it was Georgian fantasy with blue plaques and stunning formal gardens. Inside it was blazed with gleaming alabaster, creamy leather furniture, deep carpets and a state-of-the-art kitchen that was overflowing with glossy units and snazzy appliances. There was a sunken bath amidst marble and stainless steel and the bedroom was minimalistic with a double bed wrapped in crisp white linen.

The view was verdant and very easy on the eye. He had informed the target that he was looking for somewhere to house one of his company executives that he was going to relocate from Texas for one year whilst they put together a massive bid for drilling rights in Kazakhstan. He knew that the oil and gas tag meant money and that's why he was assured of the personal touch. Well he wasn't but his company secretary was. She was dressed in a deep blue suit over a cream blouse. The hair was tied back, the glasses hung from a chain around a smooth neck that ran down to just the right amount of cleavage that always got a second look. The smile was pleasant and the notepad and pen were at hand.

The sales pitch was allowed to run its course and when the nod was given the secretary broke off to inspect the bedroom on her own. He then led the target into the kitchen and enquired about the paperwork aspects of it all. As soon as it was laid out he reached into his pocket for the phone. Seconds later the target's phone began to ring. The target said a few hello's to a connection that had already ended before placing the phone on a worktop in order to answer a few quick questions. That was quickly followed by a shriek coming from the bedroom. When the target went to investigate, he found that the secretary had somehow trapped herself inside a walk-in wardrobe. The drama was quickly sorted and moments later all three of them gathered in the kitchen to share a laugh about it. The showing ended there and a decision was promised before the end of the week. The target left with a good feeling and went to visit a friend who lived close by, the secretary left with another envelope and went to visit her favourite shoe shop. He left with the contacts of another mobile phone.

As his third target was a withering seventy five-year old creature of habit he was going to deal with him solo. That meant that he had to be in the North London Olympia gymnasium on the following Wednesday by 9.00am. He paid the required visitor fee and signed in under a false name. After a quick change, he entered the exercise room with a locker key, a bottle of water, a towel, a mini pouch containing his phone, a sim reader, a set of headphones and a handwritten regime he had used many times. He then spent the next thirty minutes doing cardio on bikes and rowing machines. He then moved down to the free weights section and carried out various vertical and horizontal push and pull routines to work his shoulders, biceps, triceps and chest. At exactly 9.55am he moved to the mats to do some stretching and cool down exercises. At the top of the hour the target entered and took up a position on the very next mat. After a polite acknowledgement, the target went into his usual limbering up routine. It would be followed by a forty five-minute routine with his personal trainer. He had no need to see any of it, he just needed to make sure that the target was using the usual locker and the key on the mat besides him proved that. A few stretches later he left the room and returned to his own locker. The target's locker was one place to the left. He had used that very same locker on previous visits and that's how he had a copy key in his pocket. He looked around the room and found it to be clear. He inserted the key into the lock and thirty seconds later he had his hand on the phone he needed. He connected it to the reader in his pouch and let it run. Just as it was about to complete the routine a towel wrapped steamed out coughing pensioner opened a locker just a few feet away. He never reacted or shifted focus away the phone reader and as soon as he got the transfer confirmation he needed he replaced the phone, locked the door and retreated to the nearby washroom. He gave it a few moments and then made his way back to his own locker. He then ended the session with a steam, sauna and shower.

Upon returning to his apartment he switched his laptop on and connected the sim reader. After opening the required software, he opened up the three files he had obtained and set the application away. Three hours later he not only had all the shared numbers of private contacts and who they belonged to, he had all the numbers and names of companies the users had been in touch with. He spent another two hours cross-checking the data and then sent three text messages. To the three recipients it looked like the messages had come from each other. It was time for all four of them to meet.

In Islington, North London there is a small gastropub owned by Geronimo Inns that goes by the name of 'The Castle'. It's a place where young professionals from nearby businesses such as Ticketmaster, the Crafts Council and staffers from the local shopping outlets go for a post-work beer and put the world to rights. It's also where two pensioners had found a table in a quiet corner away from the group gathering menu boards and television sets that were showing the specials of the day and reruns of old comedy classics.

Seventy five-year old gym user John Kenneth Collins was sat reading a newspaper opposite a sixty seven-year old phone twiddling property landlord by the name of Terry Perkins. Both men were there because of a text that had been sent by the man they were waiting to meet.

"Anything interesting in that comic?" asked Perkins.

"Well," began Collins, "on the entertainment front that talent show called 'The Voice' has been won by an Indian called Gerupto Sing and in the ads column a new speech therapy group has been set up in Islington. If you have a problem that needs sorting just call D-Dave on f-five, f-four, three t-two, one."

As Perkins began to laugh, seventy five-year old used car salesman Brian Reader entered the bar and made his way over to their table. As soon as he sat down one of the bar staff brought over a gin and tonic and placed it before him.

"Cheers," he offered before taking a sip.

Collins and Perkins shook their heads before the latter announced, "We never bought it." He then looked at the drinks already on the table and when he looked to Collins he was already shaking his head. "Who the hell bought these?" All three of them looked around the room before returning their puzzled gazes back to each other. Reader then placed his phone on the table and said, "Right then, where is the fire, Kenny?"

"Don't look at me pal, I'm just here in answer to your text."

"Me too," added Terry.

"But I never sent..."

"Good evening, gentlemen," offered a tall red-haired figure now standing by their table. "Sorry about the phone stunt but I just had to make sure."

"Make sure of what? Who are you? What's your game?" asked Reader.

The figure took a seat opposite him. "For at least two years you have been planning to rob the safe deposit facility in Hatton Garden." He then paused just enough for effect before turning to Collins and Perkins and whispering, "And you two are in on it." There was a moment of silence as one of the bar staff placed a vodka and coke on the table and the figure lifted it in toast before taking a drink.

"You must be mistaken," replied Reader. "Now if you don't mind we have business to discuss."

The figure pulled an envelope from his pocket. He then placed a series of photographs on the table. "That you, Brian, isn't it? Casing the joint under a variety of disguises? And then we have you, Kenny making a visit to the vault on the pretence of opening a box. I believe the false name you used was a neighbour that died several years ago. Last but not least we have you, Terry. Why would you be buying several pairs of overalls in a variety of sizes along with numerous pairs of white fabric gloves as well as a few copies of *Forensics for Dummies*, 2004 edition at a cost of fifteen pounds each? You could have got them on Amazon for thirteen pounds forty-eight pence apiece. You could have even got Kenny's dead neighbour to pay for it."

"Don't let the door hit you on the way out," said Reader.

"On my way to the Flying Squad you mean? Those pics and your phone records should be enough to get you all a tug and put an end to your little caper." The figure got to his feet and was about to turn away when Perkins spoke up. "Hang on a minute, mind if I ask a few questions?" The figure shrugged and lowered himself back to the chair.

"Are you on the take?"

"With the law you mean? No chance."

"Are you affiliated to any mob in Hatton?"

"Luckily for you, no."

"Kenny," interrupted Reader.

"He knows man, he can ruin it all, and I'm just trying to find out what he's after."

"I want in, well just not in, I want it to be done my way," answered the figure.

The three pensioners reeled back in shock.

The figure slowly moved forward in his chair. "I've had that place in mind for eight years on and off. So, while you three have been dithering around with bits and pieces I have managed to get to the essential stuff. I know how to get into the building, I know to get down to the vault, I know how the alarm can be isolated, I know the easiest way to the boxes and I have a bloody good idea on the best ones to hit."

As they all sat in a stunned silence he reached into his pocket and pulled out a small black velvet pouch. "Right, let's get to the point. We all want this job and for that to happen we have to trust each other. To do that you have to make sure if I'm genuine or not." He then slid the pouch over to Reader. "You know Freddie the Fence?"

"Everybody on the right side of the manor knows Freddie."

"Give him that. Ask him to shift it and offer him eight percent. He will ask for twelve, you agree on ten. Once he sees it he will ask about me." The figure then lifted the sleeve covering his left arm to reveal a three-inch scar. "When he asks how just tell him knife wound from a grass. It will take him a week to complete his end and I will give you a further week to make up your minds. I will call in here two weeks from today at the same time. If you are all here, then I'll assume we have a deal."

"If not?" asked Reader.

"Buy yourself something nice with the cash."

"And the job?" enquired Collins.

"Won't be an issue for you as I will move long before you ever will."

As the figure got to his feet a ripple of laughter filled the bar as the television showed a certain Spanish hotel waiter in one his usual confrontations with his manic boss.

"You've got a lot on your mind, we didn't want to bother you."

"What like a health inspector, coming after a twenty four-hour warning and a rat loose in the hotel?"

"He must have escaped and come back."

"Back."

"They home."

"Oh, I see he's a homing rat is he?"

"We'll find him."

"Well if you could, that would be lovely before they close us down."

He took one last look at Reader. "Hope you managed to sell that red BMW." He left him with a puzzled look on his face and as he was about to walk away, Perkins spoke up.

"Have you got a name?"

"Basil," came the reply.

As he left the pub the penny dropped with Reader.

"Aw for fuck's sake."

The others looked on.

"A few days ago he came into my showroom with a busty sort and pulled a stunt that left one of my salesman shaking like a shitting dog. He must have done my phone then."

Perkins laughed. "The twat did me at one of my apartments, probably the same bird." They then both looked at Collins.

"What? What...?"

"Thanks ever so much for your help. Have a very nice Christmas." And with that sign-off six armed robbers made off with twenty million pounds worth of gold bullion in one of the biggest robberies in British history.

It all began one early Saturday morning on 26th November 1983. At exactly 6.30am security supervisor Michael Scouse opened the door to Unit 7 of the Brinks Mat warehouse on the Heathrow International Trading Estate near Heathrow Airport in West London. He was followed into the building by four members of his team in Robin Riseley, Ron Clarke, Richard Holiday and Peter Bentley. Whilst one of the lads made the tea the rest gathered their paperwork together and looked at how they were going to transfer gold bars that collectively, were the weight of a fully grown hippopotamus. The consignment had been delivered to the warehouse in seventy-six boxes on pallets and so calculations had to be done to ensure that the team could do their required jobs in the time allocated using the transport that had been provided. As the team began to discuss possible procedures the doorbell to the warehouse rang and Scouse broke off to give usual latecomer and final team member, Tony Black, access to the building. Shortly after joining the team he began to act strange and then advised those present that he needed the toilet. Moments later the security team found themselves staring down the barrel of a gun being held by a menacing figure wearing a balaclava under a trilby hat. Scouse, who was in his office with Black, was then confronted by another similar figure. All of the guards were then forced onto the floor, their hands were tied behind their backs and bags were placed over their heads. Scouse and Riseley were then singled out for a beating for good reason.

The warehouse was a class one security building that housed three of the world's strongest safes that were currently holding three million pounds in cash. To get to them, access was via an alarmed vault door that needed two sets of keys and combination numbers. The safes could only be opened by further sets of keys and combination numbers. Somehow the robbers knew that Scouse and Riseley were the key and combination holders. It took just two minutes of threats for the robbers to get the information they needed to get through the vault door. Once they were at the safes it became a different matter altogether. As the combination numbers were constantly being changed and had to be committed to memory, Riseley, who was in total shock, could not remember the numbers. Even when Scouse and he were dowsed in petrol and had matches struck near their faces he still couldn't recall the numbers. The gang began to get desperate and then looked around to see what else they could take. That's when they began to open some boxes that had been stacked on pallets at the opposite end of the room.

Moments later they started to pick up some of the six thousand eight hundred solid gold ingots, each weighing just under four hundred grams and worth three thousand pounds each. Soon afterwards, Tony Black was ordered to open up the warehouse shutter doors and then a van was reversed in so that the boxes could be loaded. Ten minutes later the van screeched away from the warehouse. Five minutes after that, Peter Bentley broke free from the cuffs on his wrists and then helped everybody else. The call was made and the Flying Squad, led by Detective Inspector Tony Brightwell, were called into action. He quickly ascertained that the fifteen-minute blag must have been executed with help from someone on the inside and so all six members of the security team became prime suspects. Their clothes were taken for forensic checks, their homes were searched and they were interrogated. Michael Scouse was arrested but that was before the police began to focus on another member of the team.

Investigations had highlighted that the sister of Tony Black was the common-law wife of known criminal Brian Robinson. When Black was then made to reconstruct his actions on the day of the robbery it became apparent that items in his statement just couldn't have happened. When the police then checked his diary, they noticed a routine change and obvious false entries. Black eventually cracked under intense investigation and admitted his involvement. He then named Robinson along with Michael McAvoy and Tony White and what detailed information he had passed to the robbers. When Black had to pick them both out of an identity parade, McAvoy punched him in the mouth. When it came to court Black was sentenced to six years in prison. Robinson and McAvoy were both sent down for twenty-five years each, while White was acquitted on a technicality.

Now that the Flying Squad had names they turned more of their attention to getting the bullion back as they knew that if it wasn't recovered it would be used to finance other criminal activity in the city. After several enquiries they received a tip off about a known money launderer by the name of Kenneth Noye. They put him under surveillance and discovered that had had recently taken a trip to Jersey to purchase eleven gold ingots for one hundred thousand pounds from the Charterhouse Japhet Bank. He had then placed the ingots in a nearby TSB safety deposit box on the island before returning home with the paperwork. He then used an associate to take eleven ingots from the robbery along with documentation he had obtained in Jersey along to Scadlynn Bullion

Limited, a melting company based in Bristol. They would exchange the bars for cash and then mix the ingots with copper and brass so that its pure signature would be lost and it then could be sold back into the market and couldn't be traced back to the Brinks Mat robbery. Ironically, a lot of it was purchased by Johnson Matthey Bankers Ltd, the original owners of the gold.

The Flying Squad now had the laundering run under constant surveillance but the one thing they didn't know was where the haul was actually stashed. Their attempts to find that out turned to tragedy when DC John Fordham was discovered by Noye and his associate on his property and was stabbed eleven times. When he was rushed to hospital he succumbed to his wounds and died. The police were left with no choice but to arrest all those known to be involved in the robbery. At Noye's property police found eleven gold ingots and bundles of fifty pound notes that all contained the serial number 'A24'. When they were checked out it was found that a branch of Barclays bank in Bristol had issued them to a local company by the name of Scadlynn Bullion Limited. Noye and his associate had two dates in court. The first was for the murder of DC Fordham, but thanks to a stern defence put up by John Matthew QC, the jury acquitted them both and somehow put down Noye's frenzied attack against an unarmed man as self-defence. The second was for laundering the gold and VAT fraud and Noye was sentenced to fourteen years in prison, his associate got nine years as did Garth Chappell, the boss of Scadlynn.

The fifty pound notes were now becoming key to whole operation and when a courier on his way to a Swiss Bank was stopped on the Belgian-German border with a case full of them in the boot of his car, the investigation widened. The money was quickly linked to bent solicitor Michael Relton, shady property developer Gordon Parry and taxi firm-owning, prostitute-running wise guy, Brian Perry. The latter was a known friend of McAvoy and he had been the one entrusted with the money. When police informed McAvoy that his friend was now living in a mansion and he and his newly acquired friends were buying property and enjoying a lavish lifestyle off the back of the proceeds from the job, he wanted to do a deal. McAvoy chose Tony White to act as the go between in a money exchange that would get him a reduced sentence but on the day in question White foolishly turned up with Perry and he told the police that all the money had gone. Now the police knew that Perry had been involved in it all from day one. Further investigations followed along with further arrests, and in the years that followed, the heist became a curse to many of those found to be involved.

In 1984 the gold trading wing of Johnson Matthey collapsed and was taken over by the Bank of England. In 1987 Brinks Mat detective Alan Holmes shot himself. In 1990 Great Train Robber, Charlie Wilson, who had been involved in laundering some of the money from the Brinks Mat job, was shot dead on the front door of his hacienda in Marbella, Spain. In the same year heist grass Nick Whitting was found dead with multiple stab and gunshot wounds. Kenneth Noye served seven years of his sentence and was released in 1994, two years later he murdered motorist Stephen Cameron during a road rage incident and received a life sentence. In the same year, fellow money launderers Keith Hedley was shot dead by three men on his yacht anchored off Corfu, and John Marshall was killed in Sydenham, South London. In 1994 Sidney Wink, gun dealer and supplier for the heist, committed suicide. In 1995 Pat Tate, friend of Kenneth Noye was shot dead in east London, and money launderer Donald Urquhart was murdered in West London. In 1997 associate gangster Danny Roff was mown down in Bromley Kent. In 1998 Hatton Garden jeweller Solly Nahome, who was said to be involved in the smelting of the gold bars, was shot outside his home. In the same year gang enforcer Gilbert Wynter disappeared and his body is rumoured to be part of the foundations for the O2 Arena in Southeast London. In 2000 witness Alan Decabral was about to give evidence against Kenneth Noye when he was gunned down in a car park in Ashford, Kent. In 2001, Brian Perry was shot dead outside the Bermondsey, south London-based premises of his taxi business. In 2003 Brinks Mat gang member George Francis was shot dead outside his south-east London courier business by John O'Flynn. In 2007 vice king Joey Wilkins, who grassed on Kenneth Noye, died mysteriously on the Costa del Sol. In 2015 John Palmer was shot dead. One man managed to avoid the curse. He was the close associate of Kenneth Noye and was present at the stabbing of DC Fordham and right now he was standing before a rat-faced skeleton of a man known as Freddie the Fence.

"What can I do for you, Brian?"

Reader lowered himself into the only available chair and tossed a black velvet pouch across the table that divided them. "Yesterday I met someone who was hoping to do a bit of business with me. He left that and said you would know what to do with it. The offer is eight per cent."

"I couldn't possibly do it for any less that twelve."

Reader just sat and looked him in the face.

"Ten."

"Deal."

Freddie opened the pouch and his jaw dropped. He quickly logged onto his laptop and began to search. It took him just ninety seconds to find it.

"Something wrong?" asked Reader.

Freddie swung his laptop around. On the screen were two onyx and leopard diamond bracelets wrapped in a snake gold chain. One of them was currently resting on top of the velvet pouch. "They are worth forty grand as a pair. I know who has the other one so shifting it will be easy."

"Is the diamond special?"

"No, but the gold is. It has been proven to come from the Brinks Mat job."

Reader moved uneasily in his chair. "I thought that lot had been turned into dirty gold, mixed with impurities and stuff."

"Most of it was, but a small batch that was passed from a smelter in Bristol to a clearing house in Hatton was pure. It was put into these bracelets and a well-known local gangster bought them for his wife. Five years ago someone broke into his gaff and shot him. Jewellery was taken to make it look like a robbery but word is the lift was just to cover a sanctioned hit. What name did he give?"

"What?"

"The possible business partner."

"Basil."

"Basil, Basil, Brush, Fawlty, Rathbone. What was on the TV?"

"You what?"

"That's what he used to do, never mind, this guy, did he have any distinguishing marks?"

"He had a three-inch cut on his left arm."

"Did he say how he got it?"

"From a grass."

"He's legit, I've dealt with him several times, and you can trust him."

"Trust a guy I don't know."

"Nobody knows him. Those that have tried have all come off worst. There's a rumour that he used to be a copper."

"Just a rumour?"

"Don't worry, he's not a sleeper or anything. Word is that he's pulled a few strokes over the years and it's all personal. I don't know the details but all I can say is that all my dealings with him have been above board and he has always stood by an agreement."

"So, you have no problems working with him?"

"Look Brian, he's never had a tug from the law. He's respected and he pays on time. The guy is smart and he's thorough. He knew everything there was to know about me before we did business."

"That's good to know."

"Listen mate, I know it's none of my business but if he's onto something it won't cost you anything to listen. And by the way, if you do, always remember."

"Remember what?"

"My door is always open to a good deal."

DIAMONDS

When Kenny Collins knocked at the door of Danny Jones he held his breath and counted to ten. He used those seconds to ask the good Lord to show him the respectable side of his old mate as he had important business to discuss. That hope was shattered when a grey-haired sixty year-old army private answered the door with a plastic radio and a wooden rifle.

"Halt! Who goes there?"

"Danny, it's me, Kenny."

"Dunno anyone by that name."

"Kenny Collins."

"Still don't ring a bell. What's the password?"

Collins rolled his eyes. "Fish and Chips."

"What else?"

"What else? Err, salt and vinegar."

"Right, someone tried mushy peas earlier, had to slot him. You can't be too careful these days. Ok friend, you can pass."

When Collins entered the house and made his way to the living room he found a very young, frightened and puzzled face wrapped in a cheap suit.

"I can come back later?" announced Collins.

Jones jabbed him in the side with the rifle and pointed to a nearby chair. "It's ok, it's just my insurance company. Apparently, the policy I have allows me to have a will done for nothing so Adolf here is kindly helping."

"It's Alan," said the shaken voice.

"Right, anyway Colin, you have the required security clearance so you can stay put."

"Kenny."

"Right, many questions to go, Adolf?"

"Just a couple."

Jones sat down and lifted the radio to his ear. "Station secure, all units' silent routine, on my word." He then began a sweeping motion with the rifle. "Ok Adolf, let's have them."

"Would you like any percentage of your estate to go to any outside interests, organisations or charities?"

"Let's give ninety-nine pence to the Raving Bonkers Party, five Euros to UKIP and sixty-nine pounds to Sex Addicts UK."

"I don't think they exist?"

"Who UKIP? They do. They may only have one MP and he's a bit of a wet flannel but come the revolution he could have the deciding vote."

"He meant the Raving Bonkers Party," added Collins.

"But I read their manifesto just the other day…" began Jones. "Great policies. Lead-free pencils for all schools and heated pavements so that when you fall over when you are pissed you won't get cold."

"That's Raving Looney not Raving Bonkers!" exclaimed Collins, rolling his eyes.

"Steady on old man, that statement is a bit rum of you don't mind me saying," replied Jones. An uneasy moment of silence followed before being broken by a shaken voice.

"I'll get back to you on it. Would you like to be buried or cremated?"

"Well let me see, you know I once knew a man that wanted to be the baby at every christening, the groom at every wedding and the corpse at every funeral. Self-centred twat he was. Cremate me." As he just sat there and nodded his head the shaken voice ended his torture with, "Well that's enough for now. I will sort all the paperwork out and call you sometime next week."

As Collins looked on, Jones grabbed the radio and screamed, "Incoming!" He then lifted one leg and let rip with a very loud fart. "Love the smell of napalm in the morning." The shaken voice left them both with an excuse of having to be somewhere in a hurry and let himself out. As soon as the door closed Jones burst into laughter. "He thinks I'm mad. Won't be a minute pal, just get this stuff off." He went into the bedroom and Collins just shook his head and waited. A few minutes later Jones returned dressed in his mother's dressing gown with a red fez on his head. Collins relaxed, he had seen it many times before and now knew he could get down to business.

"Danny, the governor has a job in mind."

"One last throw of the dice, you mean."

"Never say never."

Jones pulled a face. "You do know he's got a few health issues, don't you?"

"Of course, but he's dealing with them in his usual positive way. Are you interested or not?"

"What is it?"

"Safety deposit boxes."

"Where?"

"Capital."

"How big a slaughter are we looking at?"

"It could be a few million each."

"As much as that. Will we have to hurt anyone?"

"No, out of hours job, no manned security, just alarms and cameras to deal with."

"Why me?"

"There will be some heavy work involved and you always did look after yourself."

"Ok, count me in. When are we doing it?"

"Well a few days ago I would have said six to eight months from now but yesterday we got a jolt in the arm."

"Problem?"

"It could be quite the opposite. I don't know why but the governor has been dragging his heels with this one. It's not the physical setbacks either, it's more like a mental thing."

"He's not the type to bottle."

"Yeah I know, anyway things are on the up so you may have to be ready to go soon."

"No problem, just let me know."

They shook hands and Collins was shown to the door. As Jones opened it two smartly dressed men in suits were standing there with their book of faith.

As Collins passed by, Jones kissed him on the cheek and whispered, "See you later, baby." As he walked away smiling Jones turned his attention to the callers at his door. "And how can I help you gentlemen?"

"Sir, do you have a few moments to listen to a few passages about the appearance of our saviour in the Americas after his resurrection?"

"I know that book."

"Do you, sir?"

"Of course, it's a bit like *Rambo, First Blood: Part Two* isn't it?"

"What?"

"Well, in the bible the main character died, didn't he? But there's no money in that is there? That's why he was brought back to life so that there could be a sequel. A bit like *First Blood*. It was a very good book but in it the main character died. We then had a sequel because by the miracle of word he was brought back to life again. It was called *Rambo First Blood: Part Two*. Main character was John Rambo. What's your main character called?"

"Jesus Christ."

"There is no need to take that tone, young man."

"No, I mean, well, you are not taking this seriously are you?"

"For Rambo's sake, no I'm not." At that Jones slammed his door shut.

The two smartly dressed men looked at each other.

"Is he for real?" said the first.

"No, he's fucking nuts," replied the second.

The units were situated just a stone's throw away from the O2 Arena. They came in rows of three and each of them had a storage capacity of four hundred square feet. They all had power supplies and access to running water. The minimum lease was one year, all of which was payable in advance and cash was the preferred payment. Basil took up an option on the only three adjacent units that faced the river. Once he had possession of the keys he started to make the follow up phone calls he had promised to various suppliers.

The first order placed was for three slabs of concrete that each measured one cubic metre high by one cubic metre wide by twenty inches deep. The second order was placed for six metal joists with a universal size of four inches. The next order was for a single low loading trolley complete with a standard pack of wooden pallets. That was followed by an order for six, one hundred and twenty-litre water drums complete with hoses and clips. After arranging for all of them to be delivered at the same time he took a taxi to a nearby vehicle renting company and took out a fourteen-day hire on a transit van. He then spent the next four hours visiting a variety of DIY stores, purchasing an assortment of portable hand tools. It all went well until it came to the final purchase of the day.

The Hilti DD350 is an 110v diamond drill that has a core range of fifty-two millimetres to five hundred millimetres. Its RPM (Revs Per Minute) go from two nine eight to six seven, and with one and one quarter inch UNC (Unified National Coarse) drive type and ten gears; Basil knew that it would be the ideal tool he needed to get past the vault door. There were a few things that had to be taken into consideration. With a rig weight of thirty-two kilograms and a motor weight of thirty-five kilograms on site, transportation would be a bit of a struggle but nothing that a bit of muscle power couldn't sort. In addition, fitting the anchor bolts would need a bit of preparation but he had time and the lockups for that. As for operating the LED control pad then the only problem would be stopping anyone from fighting over it as it was child's play.

The reputable backstreet outfit that Basil was going to hire one from had two on their books but both of them were out on hire. He never made any fuss about it but he did chat with the sales assistant long enough to find out what construction company had hired them. He then logged onto their website and looked into their bragging folder on what projects they had on the go that were, as all such projects were, on time and within budget. Three of them were within a one hundred-mile radius of his current location, the latter of which had the drills in question. It just took a yellow high visibility jacket, a white hard hat, a fake ID badge, clipboard, a pen and a thirty-minute site walk to confirm their location. Even though the security was lax at the site he was careful not to overstay his welcome. He returned to his van and spent the next twenty minutes locating an elevated location where he could park up and watch the end of shift routines.

Forty minutes later, the entire workforce streamed out of the site leaving a single security guard to carry out one final inspection. He watched him switch on the perimeter lights, align the only security camera that covered the entrance gate before locking up the site. He checked his watch, it was six o'clock. He drove home and returned four hours later. He spent the next two hours watching the site to confirm that no additional security checks would be performed and that gave him the time period he needed. He then drove back to his apartment, opened a bottle of wine and turned to the print on his study wall. Twenty-five names had already been selected. He spent a further ninety minutes marking up another twenty-five before crashing out on the bed.

At around 10.00am on Easter Monday, 4th April 1983 a gang or armed robbers, using fake Irish accents, hit the headquarters of the Security Express Depot at Shoreditch, East London and made off with six million pounds of used untraceable bank notes that weighed in at just over five tons. Upon entering the premises, the gang systematically bound and gagged each staff member as they arrived. They were on site for a total of five hours and eventually gained access to the vault after dousing sixty-year old security guard James Alcock in petrol and rattling a box of matches in his ear. They eventually left with bundles of bank notes in denominations of fifty downwards that ran to a total of five million, nine hundred and sixty-one thousand and ninety-seven pounds. Most of the money came from the Ideal Home Exhibition and was being stored over the weekend. Scotland Yard's Flying Squad were called in and pretty soon some one hundred and fifty officers under the co-ordination of Detective Superintendent Peter Wilton went to work on tracking down the culprits involved.

It soon became apparent that it had been an inside job as the gang had let it be known that they knew all the personal details of the guards. With there being no forensic evidence available the squad put the squeeze on all known contacts and after six months of solid police work information came to light that three known criminals that frequented the Albion Pub in Dalston, Hackney had been organising certain deals that involved large amounts of cash. After a further two months of surveillance one of them, John Horsley, was pulled in for questioning. He first came onto the police radar when he was linked to a van that had been used in the Brinks Mat robbery. After interrogation his bank account details were checked and police found that large deposits had been made over the previous months. With nowhere left to go Horsley began to co-operate and in his testimony he incriminated known associates William Hickson and John Knight. They were put under surveillance and when a property owned by a relative of Hickson was checked, police found money hidden behind a false panel along with a running log of cash sums that had been transferred to different locations. Word soon spread and Horsley was warned of the consequences if he continued to grass. He immediately terminated his co-operation and accepted charges of handling stolen proceeds.

The squad then began to investigate the movement of money and soon enough they traced a white van that had been used. It had been hired by the M&M garage under the control of Alan Opiola. When he and his wife Linda were pulled in for questioning they quickly began to grass on those involved. They implicated James Knight, the brother of John, and after he began to make threatening calls they had to be put under the witness protection scheme. The property of James Knight was searched and when large bundles of money were found he was arrested. As he was in police custody the drug squad passed information over to the flying squad about a warranted search that they had carried out on a scrapyard owned by Knight just three weeks previous. Details were found on Ronald Everett and John Mason and shortly after being questioned and released without charge they both fled to Spain. Further investigation into to James Knight led to Ronnie Knight, Freddie Foreman and Clifford Saxe, all of whom had accounts that went from minimum savings to bursting at the seams with large deposits. They weren't questioned as they had already moved to Spain and were buying local properties there and renting them out. It was 1984 and there was no extradition treaty with Spain so they all thought they had found a safe haven to spend their ill-gotten gains. That all changed in 1986 and after the British authorities began to put pressure on their opposite numbers in Spain the police were left with no option but to act. It began in 1989 when Freddie Foreman was arrested and carried kicking and screaming onto a plane at Malaga Airport and deposited to the authorities waiting for him at Heathrow. It ended in 1994 when Ronnie Knight was all washed up and accepted fifty thousand pounds from Sky News so that they could take the final pictures of him in Spain with his third wife Sue Hancock before boarding a plane to Luton Airport. He was met by DCI Reid McGeorge of the Flying Squad. His attempts to talk away the large amount of money in his account being part of shares in a pornographic business deal collapsed when the name he gave as a partner belonged to someone that had died two years before the actual deals had taken place.

Of the six million pounds stolen, two million was never recovered. For those involved it was a mixture of luck and heartache. Ronald Everett, Clifford Saxe and John Mason remained on the Costa del Sol and avoided all extradition attempts. Alan Opiola was sentenced to just over three years for handling stolen goods and then he and his wife Linda disappeared off the grid. The underworld still has a contract on their lives. For the same offence William Hickson received six years, Ronnie Knight received seven, John Horsley and James Knight both got eight and Freddie Foreman end up with nine. John Knight admitted taking part in the robbery and was sentenced to twenty-two years of imprisonment. The only person that had been traced via the Albion Pub as being involved pleaded not guilty to the robbery but he also ended up with twenty-two years at Her Majesty's pleasure. His name was Terence Perkins and right now he had a headache.

Margaret Mitchell, author of *Gone with the Wind*, once wrote that for childbirth, death and taxes there was never a convenient time for any of them. Perkins was in the middle of sorting the latter and with having a pile of mixed up receipts, bills and invoices to go through that needed to match figures produced for an up and coming return, it was turning into a nightmare. After nearly two hours of truth and thirty minutes of fiction, Perkins thought he had a good enough story that would see him through another year. His only concern with it all was the lack of funds going into his pension. He spent the next hour in between his study and the kitchen with a glass of wine in one hand and a calculator in the other. It was no use, no matter what formula he tried to use the only one that made any sense was 'Vault x Soon = Basil'. He put both items down and picked up the phone.

It was decision time.

Reader was advised by Freddie the Fence that the onyx and leopard diamond bracelet had been sold for fifteen thousand pounds. He then took one thousand five hundred of it and handed the delta over. They chatted for a while before Reader set off for The Castle pub. When he arrived Collins and Perkins were half way down a beer.

"Did you see Danny?" asked Reader.

"Yeah, he's up for it. He's going to call in and see us," replied Collins.

"Is that wise?"

"Why wouldn't it be? Are you thinking of letting Basil take the reins on this one?"

Reader threw an envelope full of money on the table and Perkins picked it up and looked inside. "How much?"

"Just over thirteen."

"What did Freddie say?"

"He rates him and if we can put any business his way then he can accommodate us."

"Did he have any details we can go on?"

"Smoke and mirrors."

"Well I know we've all done time and the last thing we all want to do is go back to the little rooms, the boredom and the slop out but you know my opinion, I reckon we go with it."

Reader looked to Collins.

"I'm in. It's now or never for me. Things are getting tight mate, and besides, what harm is there in listening to the man. Let's see if he's done his homework."

Reader nodded. "I know what you mean; my bloody time share contracts in Cyprus have just collapsed leaving me with a large bill to pay. Why don't we go along with this thing on the proviso we can pull out at any moment if we feel uncomfortable about any aspect of it." The others agreed just as Danny Jones entered the pub.

"Oh no," said Reader.

"He'll be fine," replied Collins.

"I'm not worried about him, it's that nutter Finch."

Billy Finch told everybody he was sixty-seven years old and buckled with cash. In reality he was sixty-five and on the bones of his arse. He let it be known that after leaving university he joined the SAS and was an advisor on the Iranian Embassy siege in London. Truth be told he couldn't even spell university and as for the SAS siege, he once rented the DVD of the associated movie starring Lewis Collins. He regarded himself as a hard man and because everyone knew that he was mentally unstable with a head full of cartoons they just let him get on with it. To most he was a fool, to a few he was a nuisance, to one he was a pain in the arse and that one had just crossed his path.

"Well if it isn't old man Jones."

Danny stopped in his tracks besides an empty table. Finch walked over to it, bent down to grab one of its legs and proceeded to lift it off the floor. He managed to get it to shoulder height before his arm began to shake. He held it there for a few seconds before letting it drop to the floor. "Can you do that?"

Jones looked over to Reader and after receiving a shake of the head he just smiled at Finch and replied, "I don't have to, you just showed us all how to do it." As he walked away Finch was about to follow but thought better of it and retreated to the bar. Jones lowered himself into a seat besides Reader. "One of these days," he whispered. Reader patted him on the thigh. "It can wait, right now we have business to attend to." The four of them talked for fifteen minutes before Basil arrived. The first thing he did was call Danny Jones by name and shake him by the hand. As he sat with his mouth open Basil took a seat and opened his arms.

"Well gents, have you made a decision?"

It was Reader who spoke up on behalf of those present.

"We've gone over the idea and we are prepared to go along with it as long as we reserve the right to withdraw at any time if we feel that any of the risks are unacceptable. If such a case did arise then as per protocol the withdrawal would be carried out so as not to compromise the project in any way."

Basil nodded his head. "Seems fair enough to me. With that in mind I suggest that we then go through the project in set stages and confirm participation as we go. That way we can complete each stage and anyone calling it quits will have no further knowledge of the remaining plans."

Four heads nodded in unison. At that Basil took a piece of paper out of his pocket and unfolded it. Four still heads suddenly moved closer.

"This is the exact layout of the vault. There are nine hundred and ninety-eight safe deposit boxes in there that come in three different sizes. All but sixteen of them are in use."

"That leaves us with nine hundred and eighty-two to go at," said Perkins.

"We are only going to do between fifty and one hundred," replied Basil.

"Bit of a lottery," added Reader.

"Not if you know what's in them," began Basil. "Well let me clarify that. When you have all the details on the box owner and how often he or she goes there then you have a pretty good idea. I will know the exact number closer to the time depending on how long we intend on being in there."

"Makes sense," said Collins.

"So let's start in reverse. To stand in that room we will have to take a few cabinets off the wall. To do that we will need a hydraulic ram to dislodge them." He looked across to Reader. "Can you give one of the lads some of the cash you picked up and go and buy two just in case? They don't have to be high spec as the bolts holding the cabinets in place are just seventy-five millimetres long."

Reader pulled a face. "Why do we have to move any cabinets?"

"Because we are not going through the vault door we are going through the wall."

They all threw him a look and he just continued.

"They knew what they were doing back in the forties when they put that thing in. It's two feet wide, twenty inches thick and made from solid steel. If you had a choice would you go through that or through a concrete wall that was reinforced with steel?"

"Even so, you would have to use a powerful drill to get through that. Have you got one?" asked Jones.

"No, but I know where two are being kept so all you and I have to do is pick them up. Are you free on Sunday night?"

Jones laughed. "No problem." He then got to his feet. "Let me buy you a beer."

Basil rose from the chair. "Better still let me get you one, it saves on the furniture."

Jones thought back to Finch and laughed once more. As Basil headed for the bar, Jones pointed at him and turned to the others. "He's alright by the way. I can feel it in my water. We are all going to get rich."

Two sat in silent agreement, one was having reservations and it wasn't about Basil.

The dream returned. Lance Corporal Gavin Foble of 3 PARA (Third Battalion, the Parachute Regiment) began his remembrance at the Tower of London. As it was exactly one hundred years since the guns had fallen silent he found himself looking at an unusual artistic commemoration by the name of 'The Blood Swept Lands and Seas of Red'. It came from a poem written by an unknown soldier in World War I and took the form of eight hundred and eighty-eight thousand, two hundred and forty-six ceramic poppies, one for each soldier from Britain or its colonies who died in the conflict. Even though it wasn't his war the cascading bloom that ran from one of the tower windows like a waterfall before curving over the towers main entrance, brought tears to his eyes. His war was only thirty-three years old and the medals currently hanging from his breast were testament to the bravery in it. They were also a reminder of absent friends and he had to stop himself thinking of them as now wasn't the time. That moment would come and when it did he would be surrounded by those that lived, and those who were now waiting for him to take his place with them in the parade. They would get him through it just as they did on that mount back in 1982. He stiffened for a moment and gave a salute. Those nearby gave a dignified nod of understanding and watched him march away. It was time for everyone to remember.

As always the silence at the Cenotaph began with the firing of a field gun on Horse Guards Parade. After that the only thing that could be heard were the fluttering of leaves that eased away to a crisp autumn breeze. Two minutes later it ended with the same gun. Buglers from the Royal Marines sounded the *Last Post* and the RAF buglers did *The Rouse*. This was then followed by the laying of wreaths. The Queen laid the first one and she was then followed by other members of the Royal family. Wreaths were then laid by the Prime Minister, leaders from the major political parties, the Foreign Secretary, Commonwealth Commissioners and representatives from the armed forces, fishing fleets and the civilian services. The Bishop of London then followed it all with a short religious service before a parade of veterans marched past the Cenotaph in salute. The commentators looked on and whispered to a listening nation about the togetherness of it all. They mentioned the formal and informal dress that was on parade and how they were all combined by a red poppy that stood proud on the chest of them all. The words 'democracy' and 'freedom' were mentioned several times as was the price paid. For the ten thousand veterans that marched to the rousing soundtrack from the massed bands it was payment enough. When they returned to Horse Guards Parade their final salute was taken by the Duke of York. After the officiating was over he mingled with veterans and old comrades and shared stories about the D-Day landings, Iraq and Afghanistan. The tears appeared when he was reminded about the fall of

Stanley in the Falkland Islands and the images of what happened during his battle of Mount Longdon.

It all began on the 11th June 1982. The Argentinian forces consisted of three hundred men from 'B' Company of the 7th Infantry Regiment backed by two Marine Infantry platoons all of which came under the leadership of Major Carlos Carrizo Salvadores. The British outnumbered them by one hundred and fifty as 3 PARA were supported by 2 PARA and the 29th Commando Regiment Royal Artillery under the overall command of Lieutenant Colonel Hew Pike.

In the run up to it all Foble had endured Indian file marches of soaked terrain with horizontal rain and wind chill factors in excess of minus forty degrees. If that wasn't bad enough he had been overlooked on two occasions to lead snatch squads aimed at penetrating the Argentinian defences to secure a prisoner. He was however, allowed to lead a few night-time patrols and whilst having to avoid sniper fire, spent those hours drenched to the skin and numb to the bone. It eventually resulted in the onset of a fever, which, along with lack of sleep, had seen him lose his cool a few times with soldiers under his command. Although it was just put down to the conditions, Foble felt as if it was more. He did mention it to the medical officer and in doing so he was added to the company observation list.

On the evening of the eleventh Foble got the news he had been waiting for. There was going to be a three-pronged attack on Mount Longdon and his company would be going up the northern and western slopes. No sooner had they moved off, the excitement of it all quickly turned into despair when the sappers came across formations of anti-personnel mines laid across their route. For Foble it meant more waiting. Once a path had been cleared the advance was on and this time there was nothing to stop him. It took four hours of slog to get into the planned attack position and when all final checks had been made the order was given to fix bayonets. Foble looked to his left, standing there was Yorkshireman Barry 'Biff' Randall, a mountain of a man with flaming red hair and massive hands. He had two cars, three girlfriends and was never short of problems. On his right was George 'Geordie' Wright, a compact bundle of muscle that moved with the grace of a cat. He was single, lived at home with his mum, couldn't drive, frequented pubs and whores and never really had room for problems. Both of them were solid soldiers and Foble knew that he was with the best. They shared a knowing nod and were about to step forward when all hell broke loose.

A Corporal lost his footing on some craggy rocks and stumbled onto a mine. As he took off into the air the Argentinian sentries above them on the mount began to lay down fire. After a torrent of screaming and shouting more Argentinian units took up a forward position and began to open up. Foble and the rest of 3 PARA returned fire and after a brief exchange the company stabilised their position before surging forward. The Argentinians made up from their 2nd and 3rd platoons, many of which were untested conscripts, began to panic and scatter across the ridge they had been defending. They never stood a chance. Foble shot three through the chest and impaled a fourth on his bayonet. Just as 3 PARA piled on through what opposition remained and thought the ridge was about to become theirs, Argentinian reinforcements arrived.

Their 1st platoon was led by Lieutenant Hugo Quiroga. He pushed 3 PARA back with hardened troops, heavy weaponry and organised formations. 3 PARA regrouped and then knuckled down for a fight. Under a blanket of mortar fire both armies smashed into each other and the charity of distance was quickly replaced by the unforgiving terror that comes with hand-to-hand combat. As Foble surged on through it all he eventually reached a saddle point on the ridge just as Biff Randall was about to launch a grenade into an enemy bunker. There was a scream after which Foble saw Biff's arm split in half after a bullet from a sniper ripped right through it. As the grenade spun into the air Foble screamed out a warning and ran into Biff, forcing him to tumble backwards. The grenade went off and some of the shrapnel peppered its way into Foble's arm and legs. As he screamed out in agony his whole body began to shake uncontrollably. That's when he saw the raging faces of the Argentinian soldiers as they bore down on him. He reached for his rifle and attempted to take aim but the unbearable pain that now controlled his body forced his limbs into an uncontrollable spasm. After that it was a kaleidoscope of flashing lights accompanied by ear-piercing screams. He felt his finger press down on the trigger and after that he passed out.

"Alreet bonnie lad?"

At that Foble stiffened and he was back on Horse Guards Parade with Geordie Wright standing before him. "Hello mate," he whispered before taking the offered hand.

Geordie looked down to the medals on Foble's chest. "I see you're still not wearing it then."

Foble shook his head.

"Ne bother like, it will happen one day when you are good and ready. Let's gan and have a beer and toast a few friends."

"Aye, let's do that," replied Foble and both men then quietly slipped away from the gathering.

The following morning Foble drove to 88-90 Hatton Garden. Once there he signed in and was shown to his safety deposit box. As soon as he was alone he took a box from his pocket and opened it. The newly polished medals sat side by side. Before placing them inside the safety deposit box he gave them a smile a goodbye that usually lasted for one year. They fitted snugly besides another box that he hadn't opened for over thirty years. He spent a few minutes looking at it and at one point he even attempted to reach for it but something stopped him. The flashing lights returned and the shaking began.

Boom. The dream was over.

Foble opened his eyes in shock and stared into the mirror. Although he could see a solid yet slightly scarred frame, the head on top of it all was ghost-like. Below him a tap was running cold water into a sink. He scooped a handful and poured it over his face and down his neck. He then looked back up to a haunted expression. It hung over a heavy heart and a broken soul. He knew that there was one single cure for it but right now he just didn't possess the courage needed to take it.

EUROS

As Basil brought the van to a halt and checked his watch, Jones put down the manufacturer's instructions on the Hilti DD350 110v diamond drill.

"Problem?" asked Basil.

"Nah, we can sort it in a couple of trips. How close can you get the van?"

Basil reached back and lifted a set of wire cutters out from an open canvas bag. "About ten metres."

Jones nodded. "What are they using the drills for?"

"They are turning the old multi storey car park into a block of flats. The drills are being used to give them inspection access to check for hidden cables and pipes before sections can be brought down in controlled demolition."

Jones looked into the back of the van at the bag and could see what looked like a powered impact driver. He knew that would be for the anchor bolts and nodded his head in approval. He thought about the job they were preparing for and was already impressed by the man sitting next to him. But he also gave thought to the 'Old Master'. This was his job and yet he let it slip through his fingers. It wasn't just his health he was worried about, it was also his state of mind. The questions came. What if he fails to keep up his end? What if he makes a mistake at the job face? What if he leads their pursuers straight to him?

"Are you ok, Danny?" asked Basil.

"What?" muttered a distant Jones.

"Are you alright with this?"

"I'm fine, just a bit of trench fever that's all. I will be alright once I go over the top."

Basil went to turn they key in the ignition and Jones grabbed his arm.

"The guy coming in from the west, black hat and jacket, one pound an hour walk."

Basil looked on to see a slow moving figure approach the entrance to the site.

"That's the security guard. There was no shift today so he's probably doing a spot check."

They both sat in silence as he checked the gate and security camera before doing a single anti-clockwise circuit of the site. One cigarette later and he was gone. Fifteen minutes later Basil reversed the van up against a section of fence via a storage area and Jones grabbed the bag. It took Basil just three minutes to cut a line up the fence as close as he could to an upright post. Jones pulled the fence away and folded up against the next adjoining section. Basil slowly eased the van onto the site and Jones guided him with within ten metres of a single twenty-foot container. He then took a lock cutter from the canvas bag and opened its doors. They found the two drills they were after bolted to a rig frame covered by a tarpaulin. Using the impact driver, Basil had all the anchor bolts loose in just two minutes. When Jones attempted to take the weight of one of the units Basil patted him on the shoulder. He then turned to see two metal bars with rubber grip handles on either end. He laughed and shook his head. Moments later they were both lifting the first drill into the back of the van. Five minutes after that the second drill was alongside it. Basil eased the van back to the perimeter fence and Jones closed the container and snapped an identical replacement lock on it. The fence was rolled back into place and Basil used tie wraps to secure it. As the day came to a close Basil and Jones deposited the two drills into one of the storage units opposite the O2 Arena and went their separate ways.

The following morning local media news bulletins mentioned the theft at the site. When the evening papers hit the streets they all allocated a small column to it. Some of the lines mentioned a puzzled management, no fingerprints, a low-key investigation and a plea for information. No reward was mentioned, and as everyone was more interested in checking out Christmas bargains, the story became instantly forgettable.

The year had started with the Ebola virus becoming an epidemic in West Africa and pro-Russian unrest in the Ukraine leading to the annexation of the Crimea by Putin and his federation. Two hundred and seventy-six women and girls were abducted and held hostage from a school in Nigeria and a Sunni militant group called Islamic State (IS) began to spread its terror. Legendary Portuguese footballer Eusebio left this world and Germany had hammered Brazil in their own backyard in the FIFA World Cup. Malaysian Airlines, flight 370 disappeared over the Gulf of Thailand with two hundred and thirty-nine people on board and Malaysian Airlines flight 17 was shot down over the Ukraine with the loss of two hundred and ninety-eight lives. And as everyone began to distance themselves from Syria, the United States of America rekindled its friendship with Cuba. All that was 2014 and as Basil and Reader spent the first day of 2015 with a raised glass, they had a few people to agree on.

"Do you know a good getaway driver?" asked Basil.

Collins nodded. "We can use Billy the Fish."

"Who?" smiled Basil.

"Billy Lincoln. He lives with Kenny's sister. He's a solid guy, cool under pressure and is one of the best behind the wheel."

"Right, why the fish bit?"

"Oh that, he's always down at Billingsgate Fish Market looking for good deals."

"Has he worked for you before?"

As Reader raised his eyes. Basil continued. "I'm not asking for details. I just need to know that what you have told me isn't filtered recommendation."

"Yes, he has worked with me and I can vouch for him."

"Then he's in. Have you thought about a Quartermaster?"

"Yep, there is a lad we have used before called Carl Wood. He has a canny knack for all that logistics, food, first aid and storage sort of thing."

"You vouch for him then?"

Reader tilted his head. "He's good at his job but at the moment he's in a bit of debt and that may shake him a little. Don't get me wrong, he won't let us down but he will have an edge to sort."

"How much is the debt?"

"Nine grand."

"Give him a sweetener from the bracelet cash. That will take the edge off it and get him into focus for the rest."

"Will do."

"That leaves the slaughter. We are going to need a safe place to count the score and divide it accordingly. It has to be inconspicuous and somewhere that none of us has ever been before and are not likely to ever go again. No cameras anywhere, concrete floor and brick walls, somewhere we can wipe down without much fuss."

Reader sat back and took a mouthful of beer. "There's a lad that gets in here and sits with us now and then. Reasonable sort, very trusting, honest, hardworking. He has a place over in Enfield."

"Will he let us use it?"

"As long as we don't tell him what for. He's not stupid, he knows us and so he will know it's not fully legitimate but if the price is right I'm sure he will turn a blind eye."

"Will he stay quiet?"

"Like I said trust is one of his qualities and it's better to use someone we know as to someone we don't."

"Ok, have a word with him and let me know."

Both men took to their drinks and sat in silence for a while. It was Basil that broke the ice. "Ask away, Brian."

Reader moved forward in his chair. "I thought I knew everyone on the Brinks Mat job."

"Ahh, the bracelet you mean. I was on the European part of that one. I set up all the right communication and travel links as well as all the banks. It worked well to begin with but then they got stupid."

"With the travel mules you mean?"

"Yeah, shipping large amounts of cash in the boots of cars isn't exactly clever, is it? It was out of my control. As soon as it began I took my cut in stones and bailed out."

"I didn't see my bit coming."

"You weren't stupid Brian, you were careless and paid the price."

Reader just nodded, he knew the rules.

"Anyway," began Basil, "I have thought this one through, I have it all under control and if everyone does their job right we will be well sorted."

"The only thing I'm not one hundred and ten percent on is Carl."

"With the debt thing."

"Yeah."

"Pay it all off then."

"That won't leave me with much and we need to discuss getting a few items sorted."

Basil handed Reader a small black velvet pouch.

"Another one."

"Take it to Freddie. It will be a bit of education for you."

Reader put it in his pocket and pulled out a piece of paper.

"Right, tools. Have a butchers at this."

The meeting took place in the office of Michael Holt, the senior partner of Holt and Cram, a reputable solicitor that had been situated on Tottenham Court Road for just over forty years. In that time Michael Holt had chaired a variety of complex meetings littered with all manner of twists and turns and he thought he had seen it all, but that was about to change. Holt looked to the clock on the wall, it was ten minutes to the hour and that gave him just enough time to skip through the only file currently on his desk.

Twenty three-year old male nurse Ralph Wilson from Holborn and twenty-two year old graphic designer Amanda Devlin from Goodge Street had met on holiday in Ibiza in the year 2000. He was tall, blonde, muscular and funny, she was tall, dark, slim and bright. They had a brief romance and when it was time to return home they exchanged phone numbers and promised to keep in touch. The calls began as five minute chats, once a week, and then quickly turned into daily bill-busting lengthy exchanges. That led to weekends away, shared hopes and dreams and in 2002 a marriage. It took them both two years to create a home and six years to try and create a human being. What had begun with love, soon turned into torment and despair and just as they were about to admit failure, Amanda was accepted onto a fertility program it all moved on a step to hope. In 2012, after much heartache, it all became worthwhile when their prayers were finally answered. Amanda gave birth to a seven-pound baby girl and after all they had been through the proud parents agreed on the name 'Faith'. The celebrations followed and after it had all sunk in the two of them went through the usual labours of love that go with bringing up a child. They both talked of it lasting forever but three years of long shifts at St Mary's hospital and sleepless nights at home finally got to Ralph. The arguments were small to begin with but then they grew to raging exchanges of abuse and then one day Amanda fought back so hard Ralph raised his hand and struck her. It was the final straw and there was no going back after that. He moved out of the family home and six months later he moved in with Susan Charde, a temp nurse that had been seconded to St Mary's Hospital for a few months. She was blonde, demanding and high maintenance and he was just tired of fighting. Money became tight and when he found her requirements hard going he began to default on the required payments for his daughter.

Bitter phone calls became official letters and whilst Amanda had turned to her parents for support Ralph had turned to drink and drugs. As his life became a blur and he began to drown in his own pool of hopelessness, he was thrown a barbed lifeline by local moneylenders. Left with no option he took it, went from one disastrous situation to the other, and when Susan eventually threw him out he had to go cap in hand to his parents to help keep the wolves from the door. Just when he thought it couldn't get any worse he sobered up to the fact that during one of his binges he had accused Amanda of having an affair and cast doubt on the paternity of Faith. Before he knew it he had been ordered to take a DNA test along with Amanda and at that point Michael Holt closed the file.

When the secretary showed them into the office they entered in silence and lowered themselves into the two available seats. Holt began the meeting with simple greetings and the usual throwaway chit chat. When he was satisfied that the mood in the room had eased a little he placed both hands on the table and offered a little smile.

"Well, we all know why we are here so let's get to the business at hand." At that he reached back into the file and retrieved a small envelope. He took out two pieces of paper and placed them both on the desk. "There isn't an easy way to say this so I will just go ahead. The tests results show that you Ralph are not the father of Faith." As he just lowered his head, Holt then went on. "And as for you Amanda, you are not the mother." A gasp was followed by a few moments of bewildered silence. Ten minutes of puzzled questions followed before Holt brought the meeting to a close once a way forward had been agreed.

Back on the street Ralph and Amanda offered each other a form of goodbye before turning to go their separate ways. One of them went straight home and with a vacant look on their face and broke the news to confused parents. The other cursed all the way to their safe deposit box in Hatton Garden to look at a birth certificate. As one of them cried, the other began to look for a way out of the mess they had created.

When Reader, Collins and Perkins arrived outside the lockup opposite the O2 Arena they were met by Jones. He stood and chatted with them for a few minutes before he received a call.

"Right, you haven't been followed so let's get to work."

The three of them followed Jones into the end unit where Basil was waiting by the Hilti DD350 drill. Next to that was a slab of concrete, two metal joists, two water drums and four hoses. They shook hands, exchanged pleasantries and then Basil went through what they were about to do.

"This slab represents the wall we have to go through. It's the same concentrate of concrete, same reinforcement and the exact width. Danny and I have checked through the operating documentation on the drill and we've watched a few videos on it courtesy of YouTube so all we have to do now is have a go." Basil waited for questions but when none came he just nodded to Jones. Watches were checked, Reader, Collins and Perkins were handed a set of ear defenders and sat on a nearby bench. Jones picked up the portable hand drill, Basil nodded and the clock began to run.

Jones took up position at the concrete slab and drilled a twenty millimetre hole. He cleaned it with a nylon brush and then flushed it out with clean water. Basil then used a plastic gun to fill the hole with a quick-setting adhesive compound and inserted an anchor rod. One cup of tea later Jones erected the pivot column on the Hilti, tightened the screws and fitted the required hand wheel. He then screwed the clamping spindle over the anchor rod, positioned the drill stand, levelled the column and tightened the clamping nuts with a wrench. Basil then removed the end cap from the column and secured an extension with a locking bolt. He then added a spacer to the carriage of the drill and locked it into position. Jones then lifted the machine into place and secured it. Basil connected the water hoses to the supply drums and screwed the collector into place. Jones took hold of the hand wheel and turned it until the core bit of the drill made contact with the concrete. He then set the depth gauge and secured it with a clamping screw. Basil passed him a diamond core and he engaged it with the gear teeth, tightening the drill chuck.

Both men stood back, gave their work a final inspection and Basil connected the drill to a power supply and switched it on. Jones put on his ear defenders and everyone else did likewise. He then checked the ground fault interrupter and once he was satisfied that everything was ok Basil opened the water flow regulator. Jones then positioned himself over the machine's LED control pad, released the carriage lock, turned the hand wheel and began to apply pressure. As he went up through the ten gears on the machine and the noise and dust levels increased Basil and turned on the building's extractor system. Through the rising clouds the eyes of Reader, Collins and Perkins were all glued to Jones. They sat and watched in silence as he cut through the concrete and never once let the machine's performance indicator stray away from green. Ninety minutes later he broke through the concrete and received a round of applause.

"Child's play, this," beamed Jones.

"We have done the maths and we will need to drill another two so that Danny and I can climb through, unless of course one of you want to do it?"

As Basil looked on Jones patted Reader on the stomach and smirked. "Give over, we don't have a drill bit that big, besides it would take us a week."

Reader laughed. "Ok smart arse, we get the point." He then turned to Basil. "Are you going to drill the other holes now?"

"No, this was just a test to see if the damn thing works. I have another two cubes next door so when we are all here and clued up with what is required we can do a full dummy run on one of them. If anything goes wrong we learn from it and move on to the third cube. Hopefully things should be ok if we stick to procedure."

"Next door?" asked Perkins.

"I have rented three units."

"What's in the third one?" enquired Collins.

"Come on, I'll show you."

When Reader, Perkins and Collins stepped into the unit it was like a DIY Aladdin's cave. On the tool front there was an array of portable drills, angle grinders, hammers, screw-drivers, crow bars, wrenches and torches. On clothing there were coveralls, hard hats, high visibility jackets, facemasks and gloves.

For communication there were four Motorola two wave radios and for storage there were a set of plastic containers and two wheelie bins. Collins picked up what turned out to be a retractable ladder. "Where are we going with this?"

"Towards treasure beyond your imagination?"

"You what?"

"What he's trying to say is you will find out at the next meeting, if you're there?"

Basil smiled. "Did you get the hydraulic rams?"

"I have one on the car, I'll bring it in now. I'm still shopping around for a backup."

As he retreated out of the unit Perkins rested on a portable air extractor near Jones.

"He's very organised, isn't he?"

"Of what I have seen of him so far he's all class. I have a good feeling about this one, Terry."

"Yeah I know what you mean. He's proved that we can get through the wall. It'll be interesting to see how we get through those doors leading to the vault without setting off any alarms."

"I'm sure he has the answer to that."

"Makes for an interesting meeting, doesn't it?"

"Are you two alright?" interrupted Basil.

"Yes boss," beamed Danny. "Terry here can't wait to see how we get to the vault."

Perkins reeled back on his feet "Well I was just wondering how we actually get into the building itself. As Reader approached with a holdall containing the ram Basil took it off him and before walking away whispered, "I have the key to the front door."

When he said that you could have heard a pin drop.

There were four people in the vault with him. Richardson was the master key holder with the company. Taylor was from the records department. Williams was there on behalf of the treasury and Anderson represented the independent authority. He was there to co-ordinate the proceedings. With everyone signed in and ready to go he checked his watch and began on it.

"Gentlemen, it's exactly 9.00am on Wednesday 14th January 2015 and all required laws and regulations have been adhered to, and so if there are no objections we will begin to open the agreed boxes?"

He got four nodding heads.

"Mr Richardson, if you please we will start with box number twenty-seven in the name of Ethel Stewart." Richardson inserted two keys into the box, opened it and took a step back. With gloved hands Taylor stepped forward and retrieved the container within it. He then placed it on a nearby table and, in full view of everybody, opened it. "Gentlemen, the box is empty." It was recorded as such and the appropriate signatures were given.

"Mr Richardson, if you would be so kind as to open box number three hundred and seventy-five in the name of Sean Murphy." Richardson did as requested and Taylor opened the container. "Gentlemen, we have one wrapped bundle of five pound notes. The wrapping is stamped with the Royal Mail logo and carries the number one thousand across its centre." Taylor eased the wrapping off and counted the notes and confirmed that it amounted to one thousand pounds. He was then asked for some of the serial numbers of the notes and he duly called out ten different ones. When he was asked for dates on the notes he gave one single answer, "Nineteen sixty two." Williams asked for a small break in the proceedings before leaving the room with the information. He made a single phone call and then returned.

"Ok Mr Richardson, next up we have box number six nine four in the name of Stuart Greenwood." Moments later a small velvet covered box was placed on the table. Taylor lifted the lid on it and announced, "Gentlemen, we have six cushion cut diamonds that all contain a vivid yellow colouring." It was agreed and signed and noted that the holding company would get two independent evaluations on the diamonds and issue the required notification to the treasury. They then moved on to box eight seven two owned by Miranda Drews. In it there was a typed letter, it read;

Two whom it may concern,

If you have found this then I am already dead. I took out this box in the name of an old school friend of mine in the year 1982, the year she died. She knew of my intentions before she passed and gave me her full blessing. I am not ashamed of what I am about to tell you and I ask for no forgiveness. I am at peace with it all now and I'm quite prepared to meet whatever maker I may come across in the afterlife.

On Friday 3rd February 1978 I murdered Colin Drews.

My friend Miranda Price met Colin in 1972 in a Soho dance hall called 'The Inn Place'. I was there to witness how he fell for her and spent that entire summer by her side. They were inseparable and were married a year later. They spent the following year just being together, laughing, dancing and travelling. In 1974 they decided to start a family. After one year of trying nothing happened. Tests were done and although Miranda's results were above average Colin's were found to be low. They both attended sessions on the matter, paid the required fees and completed the required courses. The treatment didn't work and it broke their hearts. After the tears had dried Miranda proposed adoption but Colin wouldn't hear of it. I felt for her because although she tried everything to assure Colin and cement the bond between them, the lack of a child just tore them apart. Colin slumped in and out of depression and then took to drink. That's when he became abusive. He began to beat her and she did her best to hide it. I lost count of the times she had come to see me just to break down and cry. On numerous occasions I asked her to report it but she would have none of it. She hung on to fragile hope that things would work out in the end but they never did. It all came a head in 1978.

The year was only one month old when Miranda lost the job she had held in the warehouse of a local electrical distributor. She was given four weeks' money and Colin, who by now was incapable of holding any job down, spent it in one. On the evening of the 3rd he came home drunk and beat Miranda within an inch of her life. I had called around to visit on the off chance that she may need something as I knew she was going through a real bad patch. I found her slumped on the bedroom floor and him in a rage on the edge of the bed with a bottle of beer in his hand. I tried to calm him down but he just continued to rant until the bottle in his hand went empty. He threw it against the wall and then made his way out of the room to go and get another one. I have never felt such hatred as I did for another human being as I did at the moment. I followed him to the top of the stairs and screamed at him to stop. That's when he raised his hand to me and I just managed to avoid his lunge before pushing him down the stairs. I watched him fall, I heard the loud crack and that's when the blood appeared. I panicked and fled home.

I waited for the police to arrive but when they did it was just to tell me that a friend of mine was in a coma at the hospital and that her husband had taken a fall from which he had not recovered. His death was recorded as accidental. He had no other family to speak of and so most of the organisation was done by the church. Miranda came out of her coma the day after he had been buried, a blessing in disguise really. She recovered from her wounds and spent the next few years in an abuse-free environment. We remained close until her death from cancer on Wednesday 20th October. She was just twenty-six years old. We used to joke about reaching the age of sixty-four, looks like neither of us has made it.

Anyway, in her final moments I told her what I had done and she just held my hand and admitted that she saw me do it. We both cried, she then died and part of me died with her.

You may be asking as to why I have confessed to this crime and what could I possibly gain from it. The only answer I have is peace of mind. Wherever I go from here I don't want to take this burden with me, I have carried it long enough.

The letter was signed by Angela Shaw.

Williams left the room once more and rang Scotland Yard. A few moments later he returned to the vault. "I'm afraid we are going to have to remain on the premises until the police arrive."

"They want statements on the letter?" asked Anderson.

"Yes, and the money that was part of the Great Train Robbery back in '63."

Richardson and Taylor just stood there in shock.

The co-ordinator smiled.

Reader slid the pouch across to Freddie.

"That was quick."

"It's old stock, to cover the cost of some supplies."

"No cash available then?"

"I'm sure there is but Basil reckons I will learn something from this."

Freddie opened the pouch and gently poured a small ring onto a cushion on his desk. He then grabbed the portable camera linked to his computer and took a few pictures of it. Once the images had been captured on screen he ran his finder software and within a minute he had them.

"According to this you have just brought a 3.11ct Fancy Deep Blue Diamond ring that was worth eighty-five thousand pounds."

"*Was* worth?"

"That's before it was stolen from the premises of Graff Diamonds in New Bond Street."

Reader blew out his cheeks and reeled back in his chair.

On August 6th 2009 around midday, professional make-up artist known as 'Shadow' had two clients in his studio. In reality they were Aman Kassaye and Craig Calderwood but Shadow had been supplied with two names that he surmised as being false. The clues were all there, the job was booked as preparation for a music video by a band name he had never heard of and the full amount had been paid up front in cash. A timeframe of four hours had been agreed and without any questions, Shadow had put every second to good use. When it was over Kassaye and Calderwood had their faces covered in prosthetics with layered skin tones topped off by neatly fitted wigs. The job was so well done, both men were convinced that their own mothers wouldn't recognise them. They would have loved to put it to the test but they had a tight schedule to keep.

Just under one hour later at exactly 4.40pm, dressed in new suits, both men calmly stepped out of a taxi and entered the jewellers. Once inside they held the staff at gunpoint and removed forty-three items from the display cabinets. The carefully selected watches, bracelets, necklaces and earrings that were taken had an insurance value of thirty million pounds. It was all over in two minutes and it was so calmly done that both robbers even took time to smile at the CCTV cameras before leaving the premises. As local security guards were alerted and tried to intervene, Kassaye and Calderwood took a hostage outside and fired warning shots into the air and that gave them enough time to make their escape in a blue BMW. They drove it to nearby Dover Street, and after colliding with a taxicab, they switched over to a silver Mercedes. After moving on and eventually abandoning the Mercedes in Farm Street they did a final changeover to a red Audi in Ross Street. After that they handed their haul over to accomplices on a motorcycle and just disappeared into the city thinking they had pulled off the perfect crime.

Although the Flying Squad had no identification or prints to go on they did get a clue that was to prove vital. During the collision with the taxicab a pay-as-you-go mobile phone fell from the pocket of Aman Kassaye and had wedged itself between the seat and the handbrake. Once the police had traced the numbers on it they began to round up those involved in the robbery. For his part in the robbery Craig Calderwood received a twenty-one year custodial sentence. After being identified as the planner behind it all, Aman Kassaye received twenty-three years. A further three accomplices identified from the phone each received sixteen years for conspiracy to rob. None of the jewellery from the robbery was ever recovered and as it had all been laser inscribed with the Graff logo and carried a Gemological Institute of America (GIA) identification number, it was thought that all the pieces had been broken and recut.

"They never did catch the brains behind that one?" said Freddie.

"Makes you think…" pondered Reader.

"You mean if it's him? How much cash do you really need? Why is he still at it? Questions like that?"

"Yeah, you would think he would have retired by now."

"Like you, you mean?"

"Point taken," smiled Reader.

"It's the buzz, isn't it?" began Freddie. "That rush that keeps you alive. What else are you going to do? Take up golf like all those plus four-wearing twats that can't ever seem to put four decent shots together? You going to go for long walks and marvel at old churches that strangers used to go visit to pray to someone they hope is going to be there at the end? You…"

"All right for Go– fuck's sake, I get the message."

Freddie laughed and held up the ring. "Usual percentage?"

"Why not."

In 1978 legal proceedings had begun against the 'Banco Ambrosiano' in Italy after state banking internal affairs department issued a report on its illegal transfer of over seven billion lira to various unsecure outlets across South America. As two of its main shareholders were the Mafia and the Vatican, the waters of concern rippled throughout the entire country. It soon blew up into a storm and in the June of 1982 after three years of criminal investigations its chairman, Milan born Roberto Calvi, known by many as 'God's Banker' received a four-year suspended sentence and was fined twenty million dollars. Once he was in police custody he began to panic and started to name names.

Afterwards he was informed that two senior family heads and a prominent figure within the 'Holy See' had sanctioned a contract on him. In total despair he attempted to commit suicide by slashing his own wrists. The emergency services got to him in time, and after patching him up, he was allowed to go home in order to aid his recovery. That's when Pope John Paul II sent an envoy to meet him to go over the whereabouts over certain missing funds. His apartment was found to be empty and when the police eventually got involved it soon became clear that he had absconded from the country. During a thorough search of the place the police uncovered a safe hidden beneath floorboards in the bedroom. There was no money in it but there were three passports, all of which were quickly confirmed as false. All ports, airports and border posts were immediately given pictures and details on Calvi and it took the authorities just three hours to trace his steps. He had shaved off his moustache and under the name of Gian Roberto Calvini, boarded a flight from Rome to Venice. From there he had hired a private plane to take him to Zurich before taking a British Airways flight to London. A local informant had advised the police that the move had been facilitated by the 'Propaganda Due' or P2 clandestine Masonic Lodge, of which he was a member.

On Thursday 17th June Calvi was sacked from his position at the Banco Ambrosiano. On that same day his fifty-five year old private secretary Graziella Corrocher committed suicide by throwing herself out of a fifth floor window of the bank.

On Friday 18th June a postal clerk was crossing Blackfriars Bridge over the River Thames between Waterloo Bridge and Blackfriars Railway Bridge and noticed a body hanging from the scaffolding beneath. When the river police arrived they found the dead body of Calvi with pockets full of bricks and wads of money.

There were two inquests carried out on the death of Roberto Calvi. The first was in July 1982 and ended with a recorded verdict of suicide. The second inquest was carried out exactly one year later and ended with an open verdict.

In 1984 the Vatican Bank agreed to pay one hundred and twenty-three disgruntled creditors of the Banco Ambrosiano sums totalling some two hundred and fifty million dollars.

In 1991 a Mafia informant by the name of Francesco Marino Mannoia claimed that Calvi had been killed by facilitator Francesco Di Carlo and the sanction had come from bosses Giuseppe Calo and Licio Gelli as punishment for the loss of funds during the collapse of Banco Ambrosiano. As a result, a private investigation into Calvi's death was commissioned by his family. After two years of thorough investigation backed by additional forensic evidence, the Home Office was handed a report that left no doubt that Calvi had been murdered. Results had proved that Calvi could not have hanged himself from the scaffolding under the bridge and there were no traces of paint or rust on his clothing and shoes.

In 1996 facilitator Francesco Di Carlo turned informant and admitted that although he had been approached by Calo with respect to doing the job he'd refused on the account that he was in prison at the time.

In 1998 after almost six years of lobbying government Calvi's body was exhumed so that further invasive tests could be taken. It was found that, the injuries to his neck were inconsistent with a suicidal hanging and the fingers on his hands had not come into contact with bricks found in his pockets. In addition the tide levels at the time of the reported death were checked and after measurements had been taken it was shown that the rope tied to the scaffolding could not have been reached by someone standing in a boat. After the authorities in both Great Britain and Italy finally accepted and recorded the fact that he had been murdered, the Calvi family were able to cash in the life insurance policy on him and receive a net pay out from the Unione Italiana in excess of five million dollars. After that all outstanding investigations began to falter and in 2007 the five people thought to be responsible for his murder were acquitted.

The crime had remained unsolved for thirty-three years. The closest the police ever got to truth was a case file that had five possible names for co-ordination of the hit and four fabricated names for executing it. Truth be told there was only a single co-ordinator involved running a two-man black operation. One of those operators was Massimo Alessi, a pint-sized bull of a man, and he was currently standing over the grave of Bernardo Cortona, his close friend and the best operator he had ever worked with. Cortona had been given full responsibility on getting rid of Calvi, and when he asked Alessi to be his number two on the project, he immediately accepted. The orders were quite simple. Find him, take care of him and make sure it becomes headline news. A message had to be sent to those thinking of messing with family funds and discrediting the lodge with prominent business partners across Europe.

As soon a single six-figure transfer had been paid into the account requested by Cortona, he began to move quickly. A call was made to an associate he had with the British Home Office, a meeting was arranged, some money changed hands and an address was given. Cortona and Alessi spent thirty-six hours using cross shifts to stake it out. Once they had a confirmed sighting it was all down organising the right moment. That came on the evening of Thursday 17th June when Calvi left the safety of the apartment he was using to rendezvous with a member of the P2 lodge to collect some contact numbers and high denominations of cash in order to pay off those that had assisted him in setting up a temporary home in Great Britain. He had every intention of moving on to South America once the dust had settled on his disappearance and the planned meeting was just the first step in that move. It took place near Waterloo train station, and to any onlooker it just looked like an everyday pick up in a black taxicab. Calvi had memorised the registration supplied and the driver had placed a brown envelope on one of the available seats. He then drove his passenger three miles and then parked up in a secluded street. One minute later a black BMW appeared and flashed its lights. Calvi was advised that the car was a precaution to ensure he got home safely and duly changed vehicles. As soon as he got into the BMW, Alessi nodded to him in the mirror and pulled it away from the kerbside, from the front passenger seat, Cortona turned to him and smiled before pulling out a gun.

Alessi could remember every detail of what followed, and of the many things that stuck in his mind, Calvi's acceptance of it all was most prominent. He never cried out, he never begged for mercy and he never put up a struggle when they transferred him to a boat, filled his pockets with money and bricks and wrapped the rope around his neck. He did have one final request and that was to kiss a family photograph that was in his wallet. There was a further exchange, Alessi obliged and immediately afterwards Cortona eased the boat into gear. Neither of them looked back as it wasn't protocol. The death struggle was left to Calvi alone.

Standing over the grave of his friend, Alessi remembered every detail of the burial he had just witnessed. There wasn't a single lodge member there, no flowers had been sent and according to family members present, no pension had been paid. He just shook his head, for he knew that the days of care had gone. Now it was all about sucking up to new money and when the time was right, controlling those that had it until it became theirs. As he looked around at an empty cemetery he gave thought to where the soldiers were. Were they at some football match in some executive suite, at some charitable dinner making a sizable donation, or were they just at some business contract award party with fine food and free flowing whores. He just shook his head once more and walked away in disgust.

Standing over his safe deposit box at Hatton Garden Alessi remembered what it was like to be part of something special. All that had gone now. Below him was a coded hand-written contact list, a one hundred dollar bill, a fifty pound note, a one thousand cruzeiro note and a family photograph. They all had one thing in common, and that was they all belonged to Roberto Calvi. As he stood in silence Alessi was starting to have thoughts about what the church would do to get their hands on them.

IOLITE

Just across the road from the railway station in Enfield was a two-bar Edwardian House by the name of the Old Wheatsheaf. It was a football-mad pub and as it was the local of Brian Reader, no-one objected to having the next meeting there after it had been proposed by Basil. Perkins and Collins liked the fact that it served Courage Best Bitter and Jones liked the fact that the nutter Billy Finch never frequented it. Reader had reserved a table and ensured that he was there before Perkins, Collins and Jones had arrived. The four of them just had time for a ten-minute chat before Basil appeared. Half a glass later and Basil was introduced to the sixty-year old fat-faced wobbling frame that housed Billy Lincoln.

On first account Basil wasn't too impressed at what he saw. The walk that approached him said seventy-five, the uneasy upper frame said eighty and the hair looked ninety-five. The voice, when it came was a bit bolshie and loud and the handshake had a strange finger over the knuckle movement on it. Basil thought it best to reserve judgement for now as he didn't want to sour the surrounding atmosphere that was upbeat and confident. As a round of drinks arrived, a fifty-year old bearded fidget that looked out through heavy-rimmed glasses approached the table and was introduced as Carl Wood. As he shook hands with Basil, Perkins looked around the room and saw no strangers. Collins then placed a few newspapers on the table so that Jones and he could turn the pages at set intervals to give the impression of an everyday gathering. Basil let the chat run free for a while before pulling out a piece of paper and unfolding between the two newspapers. On it was a detailed map. Everyone went quiet and he then began to speak in a quiet voice.

"We will pay it a visit at Easter."

Some said to themselves '1st April' whilst others smiled 'April Fool's Day'.

"Why then?" asked Reader.

"Crossrail are digging a tunnel from Holborn station, under Hatton Garden and on to Farrington Station. The residents have already received letters apologising for the disruption and noise they are going to endure, even at weekends and across holiday periods."

"So our noise will just be part of it," beamed Reader. "Have you decided on the boxes?"

Basil shook his head. "There are just under one thousand boxes. We will only need to do a selection and once I have all the information in place I will let you know which ones. We must ensure that we do it by time, value and legitimate association. The last thing we need is to hit a box of certain undesirables."

Everyone knew that their lives could depend on it.

"Danny and I will be in the vault. Contents will be passed to Brian, Terry, and Carl. You will sort into plastic containers by type and then stack them in wheelie bins for ease of transport out of the building. That will mean leaving certain pieces of equipment behind so Danny will remove the serial numbers from them so all the rest of you have to do is keep your gloves on. Remember to wear throw away footwear as there will be some dust around after we have drilled through the wall."

Everyone nodded. Danny turned a page in his paper and Reader took a sip from his drink and scanned the room.

"To gain access to the vault area we will have to get through a door strengthened by metal bars. Brian, you and Carl will be shown how to get through them with a grinder. Each bar will take ten minutes tops and you will only need to do four before you gain access to the lock on the other side."

As Basil moved his finger across the map Collins turned a few pages of his paper.

"In the room before that you can see a lift shaft, a cupboard under the stairs and another metal door backed by a solid wooden one. The metal door is a sliding type controlled by a power switch kept in the cupboard under the stairs. The alarm system is also kept in there. I will sort both of them. Once

I have the metal door open Danny will smash through the wooden one. That door leads us to the fire escape where you Brian, Terry and Carl gain access to the building. Brian, we will need you to organise movement of the tools."

"Understood. How are you and Danny getting in, that lift is key code controlled."

"We are not going down in the lift as it doesn't go all the way to the basement, we are going to isolate it on the second floor and then use a ladder to descend the shaft itself from the first floor. We will use signs to show that it's temporarily out of order for maintenance. At the bottom of the shaft we shift a roller switch to open the door and when there we open the shutter door with a crowbar."

"Got that," began Reader. "But for us to be waiting for you at the bottom we need to get in via the fire escape. The only way to that is through a passage from the main door."

At that Basil placed a set of keys on the table.

"Courtesy of the manager. But before I can use them, Kenny you will have to make sure the coast is clear. Opposite the main door is an empty building with space for rent, it's been like that for six months now. You will need to either rent a room or see if you can easily gain access to it without raising suspicion."

"I'm sure I can handle that," beamed Collins.

"Now before you start bombarding me with questions remember that we are going to do the detail as we go on a need to know basis. I take it that those of you that will be working on access to the boxes are ok with what we have in place?"

Four heads nodded.

"What we need to do now is work on getting the boxes open and getting through the door strengthened by metal bars. Brian and Carl, I will let you know when I'm ready for you. Danny, you come with them and we will go through the best methods to get the boxes open. In the meantime, Kenny, work on access to the building, Terry and Willie, we need you to sort transport to and from the job. We need a primary vehicle for carrying the gear but we also need a fast secondary just in case we have to get out of there sharpish."

Perkins and Lincoln nodded.

"Check if any work is being scheduled in that area and confirm what detours will be used, the council will help with that one. Check the bus timetables to see what could get in the way. Pick a variety of times day and night and drive it. You need to know where you are going, and more importantly, how long it's going to take you to get there."

"Speaking of which…" announced Reader, twisting his head.

When Hugh Doyle entered the pub he looked around and then noticed Reader with a glass raised. He smiled, moved over to the bar and exchanged a few words with the girl behind it and then made his way over to the table. Introductions were made and once everyone was settled the drinks arrived and Jones offered a silent toast. It was to the Hatton Garden eight.

Fifty-five year old Detective Constable Michael Dea had been with the Flying Squad of Scotland Yard for ten years. He stood six feet five in height and had a mop of grey hair that topped cold blue eyes over a sharp pointed nose. He never married, he never supported any team other than Chelsea and he never took much shite off anyone. He was a no-nonsense copper that got results and that's why the squad stole him from uniform.

Dea was an early riser and always reached his desk before six o'clock each morning and that why he was usually first to see the new jobs of the day. This early February morning there were three. One was a pimp that had murdered one of his girls and was trying to pass the blame onto one of his drug addict associates. The second was a drive by shooting that had gone wrong ending up with the death of the target and the two-man team contracted to kill him and the third was the find at Hatton Garden. Dea currently had four cases on the go and with one of them about to be closed he was looking for a gap filler of interest. Only one of the new jobs smacked of intrigue and so fifteen minutes later he obtained the authorisation and the file he wanted. Four hours on the computer, two hours on the phone, two hours in the labs, ninety minutes in the archive, two coffees and one cheese sandwich later he had enough to go on. He read through the statements of the depository employees and the representatives from the treasury and independent authority before turning to the contents of deposit box three hundred and seventy-five in the name of Sean Murphy. The serial numbers on the five pound notes had been verified and confirmed and so he knew that he was dealing with money from the Great Train Robbery of 1963.

The application for the box had four fingerprints on it and none of them were in the police database. The personal address given had been demolished four years ago to make way for a new shopping mall and the previous landlords didn't exactly keep full records going by the times they had been investigated by HM Revenue and Customs. Dea knew that he was looking at bogus names and false identification and knew all too well that following it up would be a waste of time. Handwriting specialists had checked the signature on the application against all the statements made by those involved in the crime and all the reports filed by investigating police officers, and no matches were found. The account used to pay for a fifty-year lease on the box only had one single transaction made on it before it was closed. It had been taken out in the name of a person that had died one month before it had been opened. Dea quickly knew that he wasn't chasing someone that made many mistakes. After ticking his way through the points he then came to a history report on the men at the heart of it all.

Jack Slipper retired from the police force in 1979 and went on to work as a security advisor for various companies. He was diagnosed with cancer in 1999. He died in 2005 at the age of eighty-one. Bruce Reynolds spent ten years in prison and was released in 1978. He returned to jail in 1983 for drug related offences and was released in 1985. In 2001 he helped Ronnie Biggs return to Britain. He died in 2013 at the age of eighty-one. Charlie Wilson was released from prison in 1978. In 1990 he was shot dead by drug dealers at his villa in Marbella, Spain. Buster Edwards spent nine years in prison and was released in 1975. He ran a flower stall outside Waterloo Station in London. In 1994 he committed suicide, he was sixty-two years old. Ronnie Biggs returned to Britain in 2001 after spells in Australia and Brazil. He was immediately jailed but because of ill health he was released on compassionate grounds in 2009. He died in 2013 at the age of eighty-four. Roy James tried to resurrect his racing career but failed. In 1993 he shot his father-in-law and was sentenced to six years. He died of a heart attack in 1997. Brian Field was released from prison in 1969 and after ten years of going straight died in 1979 as a result of a motorway accident. Jim Hussie was released in 1975 and opened a restaurant in Soho. He was jailed again for assault and drug smuggling and was sentenced to terms of seven and eight years respectively. He died in 2012 and before he did so he made a deathbed confession claiming that he was the gang member who coshed the train driver. He just managed to outlive Roger Cordrey and Jimmy White, both of whom actually managed to go on and live the quiet life.

That left Dea with the three last men standing. There was Bobby Welch, who was released in 1976 and was left crippled after a botched operation on his leg and became a car dealer. There was Tommy Wiseby who was released in 1976. He dealt in cars and cocaine and got another ten years for it. He had just recently written his life story entitled *Wrong Side of the Tracks*. And last but not least there was Douglas Gordon Goody who was released in 1975. He moved to Spain and ran a bar there. It didn't take Dea long to track them down and when he called them, the two word answer he got from all of them didn't take long either. Dea was about to close the file when he remembered the Ulsterman, the so called informant that gave the gang the idea of robbing the train and backed it up with details on the cargo and the schedule of the train itself. He looked back to the box application form and over to the report on gang member Brian Field, the bent solicitor that acted as the go between. Dea made a single call and put a note in the file before closing it.

He opened the file on box 872 owned by Miranda Drews and checked his watch. Suddenly he felt tired. He knew fine well that if he began to read on, none of it would sink in properly. He closed it again, grabbed his hat and coat and walked out of the building. Thirty minutes later he was tucking into a hot chicken dinner and a cold pint of beer. As he did so his head was full of robbery. He didn't know it but his life was about to be consumed with one that had not even been committed yet and two paths were about to cross.

The four crates arrived separately and Reader used four different names on the delivery notes.

Basil ensured that they were positioned on the required pallets before breaking them all open with a crow bar. Two of the crates contained rod lined frames that housed twenty-five security boxes and the two contained a single gate with a central locking system supported by a frame connected by reinforced bars.

"So you and Danny are going to do the boxes?" asked Reader.

"That's the idea," replied Basil. "And as discussed I…"

"I'll do them, if it's ok, I'll do the trial run on the gates."

"Ok, they are all yours."

"I am up for it you know."

"I never thought otherwise."

"We all know I have a few health issues but I will hold up my end, I'll do my bit."

Basil smiled. "Brian, for us to pull this off I am going to need you right by my side every step of the way. Everyone knows that you are one of the coolest heads in the game. You see things that other people don't, including me. I know you will get stuck in but just remember to take time to watch us all and make sure we are not going off plan. I need you to be our eyes and ears, that's all. Look after us and make sure we get away clean."

Reader gave a thankful nod. "Can I ask you something?"

"Something about Graff diamonds?"

"Yeah, do you know what happened to them?"

"They ended up in the diamond quarter in Belgium."

"I thought they were legitimate."

"Yeah, most people think that. But now there are over four hundred workshops over there servicing two thousand companies. The number of merchants has just recently topped four thousand. The Jews and Indians are losing control to the east Europeans and there is nothing they can do about it. They did put up an initial fight but when the guns came out that soon died."

"How did the diamonds get there undetected?"

"Illegal immigrants."

"What?"

"Well, when I say that I mean couriers with fake documentation. It was simple really. We set up a controller at the other end and he organises a team with the required paperwork that ensures they don't match the required acceptance criteria. They then join the usual herds migrating towards here. We make contact, pass them the goods and they return home with them. To the watching world it just another sad case story. Sometimes the governments even take care of their transports costs."

"Don't they ever get checked?"

"The border controls have enough on their hands without carrying out searches on desperate people. The slightest thing can set a riot away and that's the last thing the do-gooders want when there are cameras everywhere. They just want to get rid of them and when the occasion arises, speed is the key."

"In case a country changes its mind you mean?"

"Yep, no time for checks, it's just a case of passing the problem along the line for someone else to sort out. I just wish the job itself had gone better."

"With the guns you mean?"

"I don't like to use them and that's why I only accepted the offer to co-ordinate the planning and execute the sales side of things on condition that they weren't used. I have no problem with a cool head firing a few warning rounds into the air but Kassaye bottled it. Even when they had the accident there was no need for him to do that as we had all the right blocking vehicles in place."

"There wasn't much reported on that bit."

"It was a simple set up. I had them commit the escape route to memory. I then had four drivers in place so when the time was right they just blocked the road and abandoned the vehicles. A support van picked them all up in sequence. That part went like clockwork."

"And the biker?"

"I had used him before. Cool-headed lad, even when he had problems with the fuel supply he didn't panic. Watching him speed off into the sunset made me smile."

"You were there?"

"I rented a place overlooking the final transfer spot. Call me a fool if you want but seeing it happen keeps me alive."

"I know what you mean. The money is only part of it, isn't it?"

"Yeah but I think this will be that last one for me."

Reader laughed. "I have lost count of the times I have said that. How old are you anyway?"

"I'm fifty-two."

"You're only a pup. There's loads of jobs still waiting for someone like you."

"I don't know. The police keep getting closer, it's only a matter of time before something goes wrong and I won't be able to fix it."

"I don't worry about that anymore. I'm in my winter years so I have nothing to lose really."

"Except your freedom."

Every time little brunette Juliette Roux lifted the letter from her deposit box it made her think of Paris. It had been handed to her by her mother Isabelle just a few days before she had passed away and it came with a simple promise. That was, to keep it safe and only ever use it if the need arose. That was at a time when Juliette lived the quiet life in France before moving to England in search of something new. What she found was a liberating lifestyle, alcohol, drugs, an endless string of lovers, and it ended with her pregnant and alone. Nine months of regret were quickly followed by years of joy and love. She thought it would last a lifetime but that was before she had been dealt a cruel blow. As she thought of her own daughter and the operation she may need and the time she had left, Juliette had just about reached that point of need. She looked down at the letter and her mind went back to the mansion located at 4 Route du Champ d'Entrainement within the Bois de Boulogne. It was a story of love that rocked an establishment, shook a nation and intrigued a world.

He was born in 1894 at White Lodge, Richmond in Surrey. He was the eldest son of King George V and Queen Mary. At the age of sixteen he became the Prince of Wales and then went on to serve in the Grenadier Guards during the First World War. Often found on morale-boosting visits on the front line he was awarded the Military Cross. He was the first royal to gain a pilot's license. He talked battles with soldiers and hardships with civilians and they loved him for it. When the conflict was over he settled into the boredom of pomp and ceremony that came with being a royal and countered it with a celebrity style that upset many a government mandarin.

She was born in 1896 at Blue Ridge Summit in Pennsylvania. Her father Teackle Wallis Warfield was a son of a flour merchant and her mother, Alice Montague, was the daughter of an insurance salesman. She attended Oldfields School, the most expensive in Maryland and through constant hard work and dedication she was often found to be top of her class. In 1916 she married a U.S. Navy aviator by the name of Earl Winfield Spencer and after spending most of the time apart because of duty, they divorced in 1927. The following year she married Anglo-American shipping executive Ernest Aldrich Simpson with whom she had been involved with for some time. The marriage began well but all that changed in 1931 after a chance meeting at Burrough Court near Melton Mowbray. Three years and several house parties later she became the mistress to the man she met and the corridors of power began to rumble.

In 1934 the affair between Edward, Prince of Wales and divorcee Wallis Simpson became such a concern to the government that they were followed by the Metropolitan Police Special Branch in order to see what hold she had on the heir apparent. It turned to dread when on 20th January 1936 when King George V died and Edward immediately broke with protocol and watched his own proclamation of accession from a window at St James Palace with Wallis by his side. As soon as he became King Edward VIII the first thing he did was to have the staff at Sandringham put all the clocks back to GMT. His father had all of them set thirty minutes fast so that he could have extra daylight in which to slaughter more pheasants. The second thing he did was change the protocol with regard to coinage. Incoming monarchs usually had their image facing in the opposite direction to their predecessor marking a change in reign. George V faced left and Edward VIII demanded the same so that his image would show the parting in his hair. Later on George VI would also face left so that his successor would fall back into line with the protocol.

Edward grew increasingly bored with ceremony and tradition and in particular the government's views on his relationship with Wallis, a woman he had become totally besotted with. On 16th November 1936 he invited the Prime Minister, Stanley Baldwin, to Buckingham Palace to see if a compromise could be obtained. Assisted by his friend Winston Churchill, he floated the proposal of a morganatic marriage in that he could be King with Wallis not being queen but having a lesser title and any offspring would not have an entitlement to the throne. Baldwin demanded that Edward either gave up on the marriage idea, went ahead with it against the governments wishes or abdicated. Edward knew that if he went against the wishes of his ministers they would resign and as he wanted to marry Wallis he was left with no option but to give up the throne.

Edwards's younger brother Albert ascended to the throne under the name of George VI. He bestowed the title of 'Duke of Windsor' upon Edward, and in giving him a royal title, that ensured that he could not hold any form of political office. Edward then married Wallis in 1937 and after that both of them were kept away from Britain with roles in the Bahamas. Eventually, they both settled in France at a mansion supplied by the government and were granted a tax free status. 4 Route du Champ d'Entrainement became their home and they were supported by a staff that included the maid Isabelle Roux.

Isabelle spent several years in service at the mansion and was in attendance upon the Duke's death in 1972 and the passing of the Duchess in 1986. In all that time the only break she had was to have Juliette, a present from a father she refused to name. Isabelle was well respected by all at the home and when it was handed back to the city of Paris in 1986 and then purchased by Egyptian businessman Mohamed Al-Fayed, she was asked to co-ordinate the cataloguing of all the items within the property that were part of the deal. All but one item went onto the list. In the Duke's library there was a small red case that carried the words 'The King' in gold lettering. The case itself once carried three documents but when Al-Fayed gave up the property and auctioned everything off in 1998 only two documents went on offer. They were private letters of love and were purchased by the British Royal family and have never been seen since.

Juliette read the third document to herself once more. She studied the four signatures upon it. She looked at one in particular and thought of Paris. She then thought of London. Was it a tale of two cities? Were they the best of times? Were they the worst of times? Was it an age of foolishness or wisdom? Were not kings empowered to give life? She then thought of her daughter. After placing the letter back into the box, she then went home to write one of her own. It was a document that was going to carry far more importance than the one her mother had passed to her. It was time to correct a wrong.

DC Mick Dea returned from an afternoon briefing on European gangs that were forming in the city to find two notes on his desk. The first was from archives to confirm that the files he had requested were on the way and the second was to let him know that he had a guest waiting for him in interrogation room three. The file on his desk had given him a few sleepless nights but in the end they had been worth it. He checked through it one more time just to make sure the additional documents were all in place and then set off. Ten minutes later he had read out the usual rights, switched on the required video equipment, arranged a file on the table and made himself comfortable in the chair opposite a very elegant looking woman that defied her age.

"Miss Shaw, tell me about Miranda Drews."

"Miranda, my god that was a lifetime away, what's happened?"

"Just answer the question please."

"Errr sorry, many years ago Miranda and I used to be close friends."

"Used to be? What stopped it?"

"Her husband Colin. He was fine to begin with then he became aggressive, controlling."

"Abusive," added Dea.

Angela Shaw began to tremble and nodded her head.

"Miss Shaw has acknowledged the point," began Dea, before sliding a piece of paper across the desk. "I have passed Miss Shaw the statement she made in 1978 after the death of Colin Drews." As tears appeared in her eyes he continued. "In your statement you say that the first you learnt of what had happened was when the police called around to see you two days later, is that correct?"

"Yes, that's correct."

"Miss Shaw, be in no doubt about the gravity of what I am about to say. Evidence has come to light that contradicts your statement and places you at the scene of the crime when it happened."

"Crime," muttered Shaw before breaking down.

"I know you were there, Miss Shaw. I know about the drunken rage, I know about the altercation at the top of the stairs. I know Colin didn't fall, he was pushed to his death, Miss Shaw."

The tears flowed for several moments before Angela Shaw managed to compose herself. She was given space and a cup of tea and when Dea could see that she had regained control he asked the next question.

"Why push him to his death?"

"She was angry."

"She?"

"Miranda, we couldn't calm her down. She just went absolutely crazy and lashed out. Colin was trying to protect me when she pushed him."

"Miranda pushed Colin down the stairs?" exclaimed Dea. "Tried to lash out at you, what on earth for?"

That's when Angela looked him in the eyes and whispered, "Because Colin and I were having an affair."

"There is a lot of history here," said the wispy grey-haired old caretaker as he let Collins into the building at 25 Hatton Garden."

"Not one of my subjects," he replied. "I never get the time."

"That's a pity, it's so fascinating. This area was given to Sir Christopher Hatton by Queen Elizabeth I after she admired his moves on the dance floor at some fancy shindig."

"Did she really?"

The old man led him up the staircase to a first floor landing that ran to three doors.

"Did you know that the machine gun was invented here by a local guy? He had a factory not far from where we are now."

Collins nodded as if in appreciation of the lesson. "Clever, but it's the sort of thing you wish we could uninvent."

"You are right there. I have mates underground that are testament to that, god bless 'em."

"This is a nice building," said Collins, hoping to change the subject.

"Not many like this left. This area was full of lovely Georgian structures. During the blitz the Luftwaffe got rid of most of them. Idiot architects did for the rest."

"Yeah, I'm sure a lot of fine buildings have been forgotten but the people that made all of this what it is will be remembered forever."

"Like Dickens you mean?"

"Dickens?

"Charles Dickens, the author. In his novels *Oliver Twist* and *Little Dorrit* he mentions places here. Some of his characters were based on local misfits."

"I never knew that," lied Collins in an attempt to keep the old man off the death and destruction theme."

He rattled one of the keys hanging from an overflowing keyring in one of the doors, and as it opened he turned to Collins and whispered, "They say that a ghost haunts this room. Apparently, she was murdered in here by her cheating husband."

As the old man left the keys hanging in the door and walked into the room he never saw Collins raise both his hands in pretence of wanting to throttle him.

The room was spacious with a mini en-suite kitchen and toilet facility. There were two windows and both could be used to check all the approaches to the depository across the street.

"Not a bad little place, is it?"

"Yeah, I might just be what I am after," replied Collins. At that he pressed the send button on the phone he was holding in his pocket. Lincoln was down on the street when he received the text. He then rang the number Collins had supplied and then began to knock on the door to the building.

The old man suddenly went into mild panic. As he answered the phone he made his way back down the stairs. As soon as he was out of sight Collins took a small tin from his pocket and flipped the lid open. All he had to do now was follows Basil's instructions. He took the key out of the door and made an impression in the plaster mix. He then turned it over and did the same again. From the ring he then picked out the key the old man had used to open the front door and took two impressions from that too. He then took a wet wipe from his pocket and wiped both keys. By the time the old man had reappeared cursing wrong numbers and bloody kids, Collins was ready to leave and mull over his decision on taking up a lease on the room. He gave his thanks and left the building. The old man lingered in the room for a while but when the curtains began to flutter he headed for the door. When the voice called out to him for help he just about shit himself before scarpering down the stairs.

Collins and Lincoln left the area in the same car. They binned their respective disguises on the way to a recommended key cutter in Wimbledon.

JADE

"I'm afraid it's no longer confined to your prostate."

At that a balding and fragile-looking ninety-two year old Karl Brant just nodded his head in acceptance. "How much longer do I have left?"

"Six months to a year. I can prescribe the required drugs to keep you comfortable in what time remains."

Karl shook his head once more. "There won't be any need for that."

The doctor put his hand on Karl's shoulder. "Don't do anything silly now."

The old man smiled. "On the contrary doctor, I am going to do something I should have done years ago." He then got dressed and took a two-mile bus trip to 88-90 Hatton Garden. He signed in at the reception desk and was shown into the vault. The official that accompanied him put a key into safety deposit box eighteen and turned it. Karl did exactly the same and that's when the official retreated out of the room. Once alone the old man retrieved his box and placed it on the available table. It contained a book, a photograph and a starburst diamond brooch. He lifted the book first and slowly turned a few pages. They were just names along with all that they owned. He never really knew any of them. Only one ever came close. He found her name and picked up the brooch. When he pictured her sweet little smiling face in his mind his hands began to shake. He placed the brooch on top of the book for fear of dropping it. He then picked up the photograph and held it up. It was a fine picture. The eyes were clear and bright. The jaw was firm and the smile was that of a proud young man. He was dressed in a field grey uniform with the button pip insignia clearly visible on a collar patch opposite his unit collar badge. He was proud of himself back then but that was before he went to work in that camp. It was before he'd learnt the truth and paid the price for it. Before he became Karl Brant and left SS Unterscharfuehrer, Otto Faber and Bergen Belsen behind.

Otto was born in Dresden, Germany to a lawyer father and dressmaker mother. He attended local schools, obtained average grades, joined the Hitler youth and after the good fortune to once shaking hands with the Fuhrer himself, allowed himself to be programmed as required to meet the demands of the cause. He eventually joined the SS and was given a position in their Wirtschafts-Verwaltungshauptamt *WHVA* logistics department. His organisation skills were quickly recognised by his superiors and in 1942 he was given the position on the administration staff at a prisoner of war camp known as Bergen Belsen. Within a year Otto went from organising the transfer of German prisoners of war from overseas with Jewish hostages, to logging inmates that were either worked to death or had perished due to disease or starvation. He began a register of names and possessions and some of his earlier entries included the scholar Kalmi Baruh (thesis), artist Josef Capek (sketches), journalist Georges Valois (short stories) and politician Augustin Malroux (speeches). They all had small amounts of jewellery but as such valuables were posted to Berlin they quickly left his mind. The items of talent always remained.

Otto used to keep an all-male register but in the summer of 1944 that all changed. An extension to the camp was built to house women and small girls who were in transition to slave labour camps or laboratories for medical experiments. That's when the register had female additions such as the diarist Anne Frank and her sister Margot as well as Helene Berr, who would go down in history as the French equivalent of Anne. There were two more names that Otto remembered, purely and simply because they could have had him lined up before a firing squad and shot.

In the winter of 1944 the camp was visited by Heinrich Himmler, and after he had taken fancy to a certain gold necklace that he thought would look good around the neck of his wife Margarete, Otto was tasked with getting it to her. The necklace was boxed and wrapped and Otto was given a staff car so that he could take it to regional headquarters for immediate postage to Berlin. As he drove there a constant noise coming from the boot of the car began to drive him mad. Pulling over at the side of the road he went to find the cause and was shocked to find a Jewish woman holding onto a small girl. They both had the same eyes and nose and hair and whilst the woman had a small bitter smile, the little girl had one of those smiles that could melt any heart. Otto thought for a moment and then beckoned for them to get out. He then reached into his pocket and pulled out a bundle of money. He handed it over to the woman and pointed. She nodded, grabbed hold of her daughter and thanked him. The words shook him and he didn't know why he asked for her name, he just did. She told him it was Marie and when he looked to the little girl she let him know that her name was Rachel. When he smiled at her she held out her hand. He took it and as it slipped away from his gentle grasp a small brooch appeared in his palm. It was a while before he looked up again and when he did they were nowhere to be seen.

After sending the necklace to Berlin and the brooch to Dresden, Otto returned to the camp and went back to registering the names of people who were about to perish. In the months that followed he submitted three transfer requests to camp commandant Josef Kramer, all of which were refused and destroyed. It all came to an end on 15th April 1945 when the camp was liberated by the British and Canadian troops. Otto was standing by the commandant on the afternoon in question having refused the agreed offer that had been made on the previous day allowing certain officers to leave. He did however ensure that one of his registers went with them.

Otto Faber was arrested along with Kramer and a further forty-eight members of staff. They went on trial five months later in Luneburg, Germany. Eleven of the defendants were sentenced to death, and Kramer was one of them. Otto was found guilty of war crimes and was sentenced to ten years imprisonment at Spandau prison. He spent five years amongst the likes of Karl Donitz, Albert Speer and Rudolf Hess before being released in the December of 1950. He returned home and quietly worked as an administrator for a local construction firm. He never married and when both of his parents were killed in a car crash in 1973 he gave up his name and chose a new one. He made his way across Europe and took jobs in various cities before arriving in London in 1980.

Karl Brant placed all the items back into the box and locked it. The official re-joined him and did likewise. Pleasantries were exchanged, Karl signed himself out and went home. Once there he picked up the phone and dialled a number he knew off by heart. When he heard the voice on the other end of the line he began to tremble.

Angela Shaw shuffled uneasily in her chair. "It all started when he was alone and couldn't get work. I used to sit and talk with him so that he wouldn't go to the pub and get drunk. I considered it a favour to Miranda but then it became comfortable. He would pour his heart out to me and give me a depth of trust that no-one had ever done before. I found myself wanting to heal him and that's when I fell for him. We knew it was wrong but we couldn't stop ourselves. After a while the passion was replaced by guilt and that's when the arguments started. I tried to stop it on several occasions but he was just too strong. I was so confused. You see it was a Jekyll and Hyde sort of relationship really. He was nice at first but then he became overpowering, erratic, domineering. I was just trapped."

"How did Miranda find out?"

"On that night back in '78 she was supposed to be stopping over at a friend's that was sick but then some family members took over. When she arrived home she found Colin and myself in bed. She went absolutely crazy. She tried to attack me, and as Colin had been drinking he began to beat her. I tried to stop him. I did manage to pull him away and when we reached the stairs she lunged at him. He swung for her and the next thing I know I'm picking myself up off the floor to find her lying motionless at my feet and Colin at the bottom of the stairs. I could hear voices so I just panicked and fled."

"Have you ever owned a deposit box?"

"What?" replied a startled Shaw.

"Have you ever owned a safety deposit box to store items in?"

"No never, why?"

Dea ignored the question and pushed an application form across the table.

"I am now showing Miss Shaw an application form for the depository at 88-90 Hatton Garden. Is that your signature on the form, Miss Shaw?"

Angela checked it. "Well it does look like mine but…"

"After what had happened did you and Miranda keep in touch?"

"No she hated me with a vengeance."

"How do you know that?"

"She told me so when I went to visit her in hospital. She said that she never wanted to see me again and that one day she would pay me back for what I had done to her."

"How old are you, Miss Shaw?"

"I am sixty-three."

Dea pulled a single piece of paper out of the file and slid it across the desk. "Would you like more tea?"

"No thank you," she replied, not looking up from the desk.

"I will get myself one." At that he got up from the chair and made his way out of the room. In the time it took him to get a drink and walk into the technician's room Angela Shaw had become a shuddering wreck. Dea sipped at the tea and watched her crumble on screen. After a few moments one of the technicians turned to him and said, "That's real."

"I know it is," replied Dea before leaving the room. He wandered the corridor for a while before returning to his seat in the interrogation room. Shaw had the crumpled piece of paper in her clenched fist. She was still shaking. She attempted to speak but no words came. She then clasped her hands together and took so deep breaths. She looked up to Dea and opened her mouth.

"She…"

"She was lying," interrupted Dea. He reached into the folder and pulled out several sheets of paper and spread them across the desk. "The records show the box at the depository in Hatton Garden was taken out on a long term lease just before she died. She probably used some of the money she got from selling up her possessions. The dates on the lease coincide with your sixty-third year. It looks like she never wanted to reach sixty-four after all. Her prints are on the application and on the letter and I'm sure when I get yours, they won't be. The signature is a copy and it was the letter 'a' that gave it away. There are two in yours and in that document they both have different characteristics. I had it checked against samples of her writing and it was confirmed that she had attempted to forge your signature. Then there are the phone records. On the night in question your number was called on three occasions over a thirty-minute period from the friend's house. You never answered, you could have been anywhere but you have already confirmed where you were. Then there are the calls between your residence and her residence. Several were made during times when she was working so obviously the exchanges were between Colin and yourself and now we know why. Not much use in a court of law I know but these aren't the numbers that interest me."

Dea placed two pieces of paper together. On each a single number was highlighted. "You see something just didn't seem right in all this. An affair, hell hath no fury and all that but what would make a woman go to such extremes? Why would she attempt to try and frame you for a murder you did not commit? Ok, you took her man away from her so how could vengeance be best served? Could she take someone away from you? But you didn't have anyone did you? Or did you?"

Dea pointed to one of the numbers. "Abortion clinic." He then pointed to the other number. "Adoption clinic."

"What did you do with it, Angela?"

On the right bank of the River Mole in Surrey there is a town called Leatherhead. In 2002 it became notable for an area of constant traffic jams and accidents and its high street was voted one of the worst in the United Kingdom. After that the Mole Valley District Council was prompted into doing something about it and although its roads are still a nightmare, the town itself has reinvented itself and its modernisation has attracted a variety of businesses. Leatherhead is home to research centres, engineering consultancies and the headquarters of the Police Federation of England and Wales.

Five minutes after getting off the train at Leatherhead, Perkins and Lincoln smiled their way past the federation on their way to a garage that Lincoln had used several times in the past. It was owned by professional ex-boxer Lenny 'Lightning' Bolt, whose claim to fame had been that he had knocked Frank Bruno on his arse twice and still went on to lose the fight on a split decision.

As they entered the garage Lincoln took an incoming call on his mobile and Perkins headed for a white panelled transit van. As he stood before it a large shadow was cast on the van and a voice boomed out from it, "Two point four litre, diesel, six months MOT, excellent bodywork, black cloth interior, electric windows, central locking and it has medium wheel base, one careful owner."

Perkins turned to see a mountain of a man with the biggest hands he had ever seen. He never offered his hand just in case he never got it back.

"How fast does it go?"

"It can do nought to sixty in three weeks."

"Top speed."

"It will do one twenty if you drive it off a cliff."

"What's the mileage?"

"What do you want it to be?"

"What's the registration?"

"What do you want it to be?" interrupted Lincoln, slapping Bolt on the back. As they shook hands Lincoln nodded. "How much?"

"Six grand."

Lincoln just stared at him.

"I can let you have it for four."

"That's with the loading ramps thrown in, right?"

"Right."

"Now Lenny, we are also going to need two nippy cars as insurance. We may use them, we may not, so factor that into your offer." Bolt lumbered over to the back of his lot, Perkins and Lincoln strolled in his wake. As they began to look around he suddenly stopped and pointed. "Black VW Golf Sv hatchback, it's one point four, five door, petrol, and can do nought to sixty in nine seconds. It has a top speed of one twenty-five. Next to it is a Black Audi A7 sport. It's two point eight, five door, petrol, and it can do nought to sixty in eight seconds. It has a top speed of one forty. To buy they would be fifteen grand, to lease you can have each one for three hundred a month."

Lincoln nodded. "We'll lease them and if you don't get them back I'll send the additional fifteen grand in the usual manner."

"When do you want them?"

"Can we collect them in a few weeks?"

"No problem, what about traceability?"

"There can't be any."

"The van has already been through the routine so no cost there but the cars, well, they will be a grand."

"A bit expensive."

"Once we do them there is no going back and so if you do return them I will have to move them down the line quite quickly."

Lincoln offered his hand and Bolt took it and nodded to the office. Once inside the pair chatted as Lincoln paid up in cash and Perkins just kept to the background. He spent the whole time looking at the photographs on the walls. Most were of Bolt holding up trophies and belts. There was a picture of him leaning over a set of ropes with Mike Tyson, one of him sparring with Lennox

Lewis and there was a signed picture of Frank Bruno. Perkins noticed that it was the only picture that Bolt wasn't in. He stepped forward and tried to read the words above a strange signature but couldn't make any of them out.

"It says 'I got up both times, The Widow Twankey'," boomed the figure, now by his side.

Perkins turned and pulled a face. "The owner of the laundry in Aladdin?"

"Yep, I called him that every time I met him as he spent most of his time doing pantomime. It used to wind him up a little and so one Christmas he sent me that."

"What did you send him in return?" asked Perkins.

"The glove I floored him with."

As Perkins laughed Lincoln rang Jones.

Just as Jones ended the call, Reader and Woods were crouched by the first set of gates and Basil was looking down at his watch. After Jones updated them on the cars Reader and Woods donned safety glasses and Basil set the stopwatch function away. Woods connected the power supply and Reader turned the angle grinder on. The sparks began to fly and seven minutes later he was through the first reinforced bar. As he backed away Woods put on a pair of gauntlet gloves and pulled at the bar. It moved with ease and he was able to bend it through ninety degrees with little effort. Reader was keen to get the job done and went straight at the second bar. It took eight minutes to cut and the two that followed took a further ten minutes each. Reader and Woods then climbed through the opening and Basil stopped the timer on thirty-five minutes and forty seconds. Satisfied with how well it went both of them retreated to a seat and Basil handed them both a cool drink.

Jones was raring to go and was already standing over the first frame housing twenty-five deposit boxes. On the bench nearby he had the tools he needed to test three possible methods of breaking into them. The first was a small claw hammer and chisel, the second was a large hammer and the third was a power drill. Basil approached and Jones picked up the first item. The clock was set away once more and Jones fought with the first box. After two minutes of hammering he had made enough of a dent to ram the chisel into the frame of the box and force it open. Basil stopped the clock thirty seconds later. Jones just shook his head and threw the tools onto the bench. He then picked up the large hammer and steadied his feet. Basil set the timer away once more. Six swings and thirty-eight seconds later it was all over. Jones held up the hammer and gave an approving nod. He then reached for the power drill and Basil passed him a pair of safety specs. Jones begrudgingly put them on and positioned himself before one of the boxes. He pressed the trigger and the drill tore through the lock in fifteen seconds. That brought a smile to his face and an appreciative pat on the back from Basil.

Reader and Woods had the bit between their teeth now and went to the second gate. It took them just twenty-nine minutes to get through it. Jones returned to the boxes and managed a best time of eleven seconds. When he had finished they all looked at each other and burst out laughing. When they eventually stopped it was Jones that spoke first.

"Three hours."

"What?" asked Woods.

"It would take me just three hours to open every box in that place."

"Superman couldn't even do it in that time and you are no superman."

"I don't look good in tights, that's why. But then again if you had said Batman I would consider wearing a pair."

"Perish the thought," interrupted Basil. "Besides, we won't be opening nowhere near that number."

"How many are we doing?" asked Reader.

Everyone went quiet and then, after a brief uneasy pause, Basil spoke.

"It will be less than one hundred."

"What specific criteria are you using?"

"Known local dealers and savers are in, gangs are out. We don't hit anything American or Russian. We go for jewellery, art and cash and we leave any other items of sentimentality alone."

"How can you tell? Have you got some fool proof method?" asked Jones.

"Not really," replied Basil. "There are several certainties but there are a few unknowns."

"So if we open an unknown and it has trouble written all over it we leave it alone?" said Woods.

"Exactly."

"But why take the risk? We could still annoy someone by doing that."

"And we could also show them respect," added Reader. "Messages like that get around the world and they are the sort of messages some dreamers get off on."

"Nineteen minutes," announced Jones. At that they all cast him a glance. With a burst of the drill he said, "One hundred boxes can be done in nineteen minutes."

Woods looked to the sky. "Meanwhile, back in Gotham City..."

Jones tapped Basil on the arm. "Let's do the full run on that other concrete slab now. I'm dying to know long it's going to take us to get the three holes done."

"If you're sure."

"I'm sure."

Reader and Woods were asked if they wanted to witness it and were already making their way to the other unit before Basil had finished the sentence. Three hours later, an elated Jones was climbing through the holes in the concrete. Basil was then put on the spot and he did exactly the same. Both men shook hands and Reader patted Woods on the back. They were so close they could feel it.

It was the third Saturday in February and as Mick Dea had a signed overtime request, he was working it. It was a day all about research and records and it was only broken once when he had been summoned before his boss. Detective Inspector Mark Rearden was heading for retirement and rumour had it that he wanted Dea to replace him. It was a rumour both men had heard but never shared. Both of them were always too busy focusing on the job at hand and today was no different.

"Well done Mick, that was a nice piece or work on the Colin Drews thing."

"Sir."

"Is Miss Shaw going to get in touch with the child?"

"I think she will, it's the right thing to do."

Rearden signed the file and put it in the appropriate tray. He then opened the second file and scanned the pages. He stopped at the hand-written notes from the man seated before him and began to read out loud.

"Brian Field, solicitor's clerk that worked for John Wheater & Co. He was the known link to the so called 'Ulsterman' and arranged for the purchase of Leatherslade Farm that was used as a hideout for the gang that carried out the train robbery in 1963. He was responsible for cleaning the farm but when the gang had to leave earlier than expected, he panicked and failed to ensure that it had been carried out. Brian Field was then implicated after associate Lenny Field, no relationship and conveyor of the farm, John Wheater gave evidence. He was sentenced in April 1964 and got twenty-five years for conspiracy to rob and five years for perverting the course of justice. Upon appeal the whole sentence was reduced to five years. He was released in 1967, changed his identity and went into the book trade. He died in 1979 after being involved in a car crash on the M4 motorway. He was forty-four years old." Rearden placed the file on the desk and raised his fingers to his lips. After a moment in silent thought he looked up. "Where is this all leading to, Mick?"

Dea took out a notebook and thumbed through a few pages before he reached the one he needed. "In February 1961 a bookie's courier got on a train at York with a carryon bag that contained five thousand pounds in cash. When he got off the train at Kings Cross the money was missing. There was an investigation during which various passengers and crew were cautioned and questioned but in the end no-one was charged and the money was never found. Six months later a sizable deposit was put down on a place in Covent Garden. Six months after the train robbery another place in Covent Garden was secured in the same manner."

"Connection?"

"One of the train crew that was questioned when the bookie's money went missing was one Sean Murphy. His legal representation contained a certain Brian Field. The first property purchased in Covent Garden was by Sean Murphy, the conveyance was taken care of by John Wheater & Co."

Rearden began to nod.

"As for the second property, that was purchased by Trevor and Angela Davis."

"And?"

"Angela Davis nee Angela Murphy."

"His daughter."

"Yes."

Rearden signed the file. "Ok, go with it and see where it leads."

When Dea left the office Rearden picked up the next file on his desk. It was a weekly report from archives and it listed all the files had that had been signed out along with a timeline. At the top of the list was the man that had just left his office. Rearden knew that Dea only ever took a file when he wanted to check on the finer points of something and it was that attention to detail that had closed seven unsolved crimes in the last twelve months. That said, Rearden had noted that some of the files he had booked out were to do with some of the biggest crimes the country had seen. He stared at them for a while before signing them. If Dea was onto something he would find out soon enough. He then checked his watch. He was going to have to get a move on.

Sixty-year old Boston-born Dwight Shunter wasn't having a nice day and there were three good reasons for it. The first was down to the unpredictable British weather. According to the arm-waving woman on morning television the map behind her was going to be baked in sunshine. According to the app on his phone it was going to be a cool morning backed by a slight breeze. As the rain hammered down and soaked him he cursed them both. The reason for walking was down to the second thing that was playing havoc with his day. For the three years he had owned a 3 series BMW it had never let him down once, until today. According to the on-board audit system his brakes were illegal due to a leak and the call out team couldn't get to him until lunchtime. He cursed once more and headed off towards the third thing that had initiated the mood. According to the message left on his phone, records had shown that the lease on his security box had expired and they would be grateful if he could call in to discuss it. 'No rush', the voice had said. 'My ass' had been his response and so with paperwork in pocket he was on his way to do battle. The last thing he needed right now was to have hassle with the contents of his box as it had been his life insurance for the past twenty-five years. The box had many secrets and one of them held the reason a young Walter Stewart became Dwight Shunter.

It happened on 18th March 1990 and Shunter could remember it as if it were yesterday. Just before midnight Shunter had stolen a red Dodge Daytona that had been parked outside a bar in the heart of the city. Just after midnight he had eased it to a halt on Palace Road, just opposite the side entrance of the Isabella Stewart Gardner Museum. His two passengers were forty two-year old

Carl Benner and forty-year old Rick Mason. Both were first class thieves. They were slim in build, had dyed black hair and fake moustaches and were dressed in police uniforms. Upon leaving the vehicle the first thing they both did was chat with drunken partygoers that had just broken away from a St Patrick's Day party that was being held nearby. At exactly 1.20am museum security guard Richard Abath checked the Palace Road door by opening and closing it as was required in his log. He had followed this procedure for years and never had any issues with it until now. On this occasion, as soon as he closed the door the access buzzer on it sounded off. Abath opened the door to find two police officers standing there. According to one of them a disturbance had been reported and Abath went on the radio in attempt to get in touch with his colleague that was currently walking the floors inside the building. No contact could be made and the trusting Abath allowed the two police officers to enter the museum. He then led them back to the main security desk where he was able to meet up with his returning colleague. As soon as they were together Benner and Mason pulled out their revolvers and cuffed both guards. They then took them down to the basement of the museum and secured their hands and feet with tape.

In accordance with the shopping list they had agreed on, Benner and Mason spent the next eighty minutes collecting the thirteen items they had come for. From the Dutch Room they took a Chinese bronze GU dated from the 12th century Shang dynasty. They also cut five paintings from their frames, *Landscape with an Obelisk* by Govaert Flinck, *The Concert* by Jan Vermeer and from Rembrandt, *A Lady and Gentleman in Black*, *Portrait of the Artist as a Young Man* and the *Storm on the Sea of Galilee*. From the Blue Room they cut the oil on canvas *Chez Tortoni* by Edouard Manet, out of its frame. From the Short Gallery they took a bronze finial eagle that once sat proud on top of a Napoleonic flag and five drawings by Edgar Degas. With the help of Shunter it took three journeys to transfer the collection into the Dodge Daytona. Five hours after they had got clean away the day shift security had the unenviable task of informing the museum's director Anne Hawley, that the place had been robbed. The police, FBI and the US Attorney's Office set up a special taskforce to investigate the theft and after three years came up with nothing. Even to this day the museum still has the empty frames hanging on the walls in homage, tribute, and hope to the artwork that had been taken. The case remains open to this day and at last count the reward for information had reached some six million dollars.

As Shunter pushed on through the rain he thought about the six files that had been safely stored in his box. Three of them contained completed invoices. One was for the GU and eagle that had been sold to a cattle baron based in Texas. One was for the five drawings by Degas that had gone to the head of a law firm in Philadelphia and third was for the Vermeer that had gone to a local banker. For his part in the transfer, Shunter collected one point three million dollars. The good start was soon brought to a sudden end when Benner and Mason fell afoul of a local organisation that was going to look after the remaining three acquisitions. The buyers were in place but just as the coordinator-come-enforcer Bobby Donati was concluding the deal, he was murdered. Benner and Mason went on the run but they both ended up floating in nearby rivers. Shunter fled for his life. They tracked him to New York and would have killed him had it not been for the whore he was about to take into his apartment. She took the bullet and he took the nearest exit. That's when he changed his identity from Stewart to Shunter and spent two years in Canada and a further two in Paris before moving on to London. He would have moved again but thought better of it after depositing the files he had kept at Hatton Garden.

Shunter spent just fifteen minutes in the depository. It was all the time the receptionist needed to confirm that his account was in order and the phone used to make the call to him was from a courtesy phone down at the vault. He laughed it off as a prank from a friend and she apologised for the time wasted. Shunter took two taxis on a detoured route towards home and checked his car. A brake fluid line had been cut by a knife. He made a single phone call, emptied the contents of his safe and packed a bag, checked the streets outside of his apartment, noted a certain car and quickly planned his move.

The two men parked in a red Audi opposite his apartment had just received the green light on their contract when they were suddenly showered in glass. The one in the driver's seat got most of it. The one in the passenger seat ended up with the end of a gun pressed against the back of his neck. From the back seat of the car, Shunter fired out a series of demands and the Audi pulled away from the kerbside.

All seven of them were standing around a bench in the middle unit. There was a map in the centre of it and Basil had just gone over the vault section and access doors to ensure everyone knew it inside out. There were no questions so he pointed to the lift.

"You can't access the vault via the lift as it stops on the floor above. So what we are going to do is enter the building, send the lift up to the second floor. Once it's there we isolate it. We then wedge the doors open and climb down to the basement using the retractable ladders. At the bottom we ease the doors apart and then force the sliding shutter open."

"How do we isolate it?" asked Perkins.

Basil placed a small tubular angle bar on the table. "When you are at the lift door just look up and you will see a small recessed plug. You insert that and turn it through ninety degrees. That breaks the contact and you can slide the doors open. Just inside on the top of the doorframe there is a small isolator. You slide that in the direction of the arrow shown on it until it locks into place. Once you have done that the lift will not move.

"You keep saying *you*," puzzled Perkins.

"Well," began Basil. "I thought that you could try it out on one of the lifts where you have one of your apartments."

Jones slapped him on the back. "You walked right into that one, old son."

"How do we make sure no one tries to investigate what is going on with the lift?" asked Collins.

"Brian has obtained an 'out of order' sign than can be placed on it. We already have a safety barrier and two joists that can be placed across the door frame."

Wood turned to Reader. "Where did you get the sign from?"

"I had a spare one at the showroom. Good job as I didn't want to order one in case it left a trail."

Basil looked around the bench. "Everyone happy?" Everyone nodded and when all the heads went still, Lincoln spoke up. "We are going to test the van and the cars over the next few days so we will let you know when we have it sorted."

"And Hughie is ok with us using a unit at his place to divide the slaughter," added Reader. Just as the heads began to nod again Basil brought them all to an abrupt halt.

"Good, because we are not going to split it all there."

As everyone went silent he reached under the bench and pulled out a box of canvas bags. "After the job we are coming back here. We will do an eighty-twenty split with the haul. The eighty goes in these bags and then we use an independent to sort it and ensure the money is kept in a safe place until we need it. If you want to go through the twenty in more detail then you can use Hughie's place."

"When you say 'an independent' I take it you mean Freddie the Fence?" announced Reader.

"Unless anyone has any objections?"

Wood tapped the bench and got everyone's attention. He looked up surprised and shook his head. "Sorry, no objection, I was just wondering why we get twenty per cent straight away."

"Two reasons," began Basil. "The first is to stop anyone spending stupid and attracting unwanted attention. I don't just mean the police. You all know that there are networks out there that would like to see us fail and there are certain individuals that would willingly trade information on us to get a deal for themselves against financial reward or reduced sentencing, etc. The second reason is if we get caught." Everyone stiffened at that. "Now you all know that if we leave any evidence and the police latch onto it and get a breakthrough they could connect every one of us. If we all get a tug from the law then obviously the searches will begin and whatever you have will be lost forever. This way you give up the twenty and plead ignorance on the rest. If you get time then it will be waiting for you when you get out. I have dealt with Freddie on several occasions and he's solid. He doesn't make mistakes and can be trusted and that's why he's been in the game for thirty years. He has the network required for this and if you are ok with it I will set it up."

Within two hours of them all leaving the unit Freddie began to set up eight accounts.

DC Mick Dea landed at Almeria airport amongst lager louts, coffin dodgers and the ugly people in between. He picked up a hire car and drove seventy miles south to an elevated mountain village in Mojacar situated in the south-eastern section of the Province of Almeria. He checked into a four star hotel that had a three star bed, a two star swimming pool and was full of people with one star haircuts. After a quick shower and change of clothing he had a light lunch with a cold beer and then wandered around like a lost tourist. It took just one hour to find the man he had come to see and a further hour to approach him. He was wearing a straw hat over solid-framed glasses that hung on a pointed nose over a grey bushy beard. He was sitting alone, reading an English newspaper and his glass was almost empty. Dea went over to the bar, bought two beers and went and sat at his table.

Gordon Goody, the mastermind behind the great train robbery, looked across the table and smiled. "If you are press I'll drink the beer and tell you nothing you haven't already heard before. If you are police you can stick the beer up your arse as there is nothing we need to talk about."

Dea took a few photographs out of his pocket and turned one to face Goody. "The money is from the robbery and the safe deposit box it was in belonged to a certain postal manager that just happened to come from Belfast."

Goody picked up the photo in one hand and lifted his own beer with the other. He emptied the glass and then spoke. "You have a name?"

"Yep, but it's not the one you think it is."

"And who might that be?"

"Patrick McKenna."

Goody placed the empty glass on the table and lifted the full one. He took a few mouthfuls from it.

"I thought so," offered Dea.

"Now hang on," began Goody. "I never said a word."

"You won't want to just yet as it will ruin your book sales. You are writing a book, right?"

Goody shook his head. "I didn't get your name."

"DC Mick Dea."

"Sweeney."

"Who else?"

"You have done your homework on me alright but what about McKenna, he wasn't a manager."

"I never said he was. At the time of the robbery McKenna was a forty-three year old postal worker. He earned a modest wage and lived in moderate accommodation in Islington, North London. He was the one that gave you the information on the train and he even persuaded you to change the date of the robbery from the 7th of August to the 8th as the train would be carrying more cash. Well that's what you thought."

"You mean it wasn't him?"

"He was part of it but someone else was pulling his strings."

"How come?"

"I've checked him out and he never had access to the information that you received. After it was over and you gave him a share he must have took his cut and passed the rest on. He obviously had second thoughts about it all because there is no record of him taking early retirement and spending big, and when he died he only had three thousand pounds in his bank account. Mind you, not long after the robbery his local catholic church did get its roof sorted and had several of its windows repaired thanks to an anonymous donation."

"Well I never." Goody took more of the drink and stared at Dea. "Well, are you going to give me a name?"

Dea turned another photograph. "Recognise this guy?"

Goody nodded. "That's McKenna."

Dea turned another photograph. "Recognise they guy with McKenna?"

Goody stared at it for some time. "Yeah I have him now, I met him once when I went to see McKenna. I don't recall his name though. Is that the real Ulsterman?"

Dea picked up his glass and emptied the contents in one go. He then got to his feet. "Say hello to Maria for me, look after those dogs and good luck with the book." Goody jumped to his feet and touched his arm. He then nodded to the barman and turned back to Dea. "At least let me buy you a drink."

For the next few hours both men chatted about the chosen careers. During his, Goody made it known that he had no time for Ronnie Biggs and regarded him as a small time crook that got lucky with the big boys. One of those boys was Bruce Reynolds and Goody classed him as a first class thief and an even better person. He then became a little bitter when he mentioned how he had been fitted up with false evidence when the police had taken a clean pair of shoes from his house and when they reappeared in court they had paint on them that had been found at the hideout. Goody assured Dea that he never used them and wore a pair of desert boots during the raid. Dea knew he wasn't lying on that one as he had read the file notes and was aware of the doubts raised by the judge during questioning. When the inevitable question arose with regard to the violence used Goody also dismissed the notion that it was James

Hussey that coshed the train driver even though it was claimed that he admitted it in a deathbed confession. Goody knew who did it but he never let on.

Dea spoke of the time he spent chasing murderers, gangsters and thieves and made it known that he never had much time for certain parts of the justice system. Sentencing was top of his shit list. He never could work out how some animals got away with lenient sentences while everyday thieves were banged up for years. He got a knowing nod on that one from the man across the table.

As time started to get the better of them both, Goody admitted that he was going to mention McKenna in his book and Dea assured him that he wouldn't be making his findings public any time soon. At the end of it all both men shook hands with a firm grip of mutual respect and parted on good terms.

LAPIS LAZULI

Wearing coveralls, boots, hard hat, safety glasses and a high visibility jacket with a fake company name on it, Perkins approached the lift door. He paused for a moment and looked over both shoulders. The twelve-storey apartment block he had chosen contained an empty apartment from his portfolio as the last thing he needed was to come into contact with one of his tenants. As for any other resident then he had practiced a few routines to get by with as he had no intention of staying long. He looked down to the floor. There was a toolbox, a portable barrier, a sign and two joists. He had one last look around and then pressed the button to the right of the door. He then looked up and stood in silence as the digital display ran up the numbers. When it got to twelve he stiffened a little before reaching into the toolbox for the key that Basil had given him. He was just about to insert it into the recess when he got the fright of his life. Standing in the lift was a small bald-headed barrel-shaped fidget in one of the most shocking orange coloured suits he had ever seen. Before Perkins could speak a small card was thrust into his hand. He looked down at it and read out loud, "Billy Bog." He then looked at the smiling face in the lift. "You must be joking." The card in his hand was flipped over for him and Perkins looked down once more. "World class comedian, available for children's parties, adult parties, and anywhere else where the drinks are free." As he looked up, Bog, with one finger on the panel in the lift, stepped forward.

"I bumped into a midget running out of the PC World the other day. The little twat had a forty-two inch plasma screen in his arms. He almost sent me flying. I said hang on, what the bloody hell is that? He said fuck off, it's my Kindle."

Perkins burst out laughing and Bog retreated to the lift. With the finger still on the button he came forward once more.

"I went to the doctors the other day. He said what wrong? I said there's something not right with my speech, I can't pronounce my F's, my T's and my H's. He said well you can't say fucking fairer than that then, can you?"

Perkins laughed out loud and shook his head. "I dread to see what act you do for the kids."

"That is the act I do for the kids," he replied before telling a few more gags and disappearing behind the lift doors. Perkins waited for it to reach the ground floor before summoning it back. When it reached the eleventh floor it stopped and the lights began to flash. Perkins poked the button a few times but it never moved. After cursing under his breath he set off down the stairs. When he got to the corridor he was met by a vision in a pink flowered lingerie set. She stood six feet from the ground, had flowing blonde hair, the most kissable red lips he had ever seen along with breasts and legs any man would die for. She was standing with her finger on the panel for the lift and when she saw Perkins she just looked to the heavens. That's when a large monkey in a suit came rushing out from her apartment. He was trying to put his jacket on and assure his wife via mobile phone that he was on his way. As he reached the lift he straightened the jacket, handed the vision a fist full of sterling and gave a wave goodbye. When the lift fell once more she walked over to Perkins and handed him a small card. According to it, her name was 'Infinity' and if you wanted she could 'Take you there and beyond.' When he looked up she pulled away at a few laces and Perkins was treated to a glimpse of one of the finest bodies he had ever seen. As his mind raced she blew him a kiss and swept back into her apartment. He stood in the afterglow for a while and it only came to a sudden end when the phone in his pocket began to vibrate. He waited until he was making his way back up the stairs before answering it.

"Hello?"

"What are you doing?" asked Reader.

"Getting told filthy jokes off a madcap comedian and getting propositioned by a high class whore."

"Where the hell are you?"

"Approaching the lift."

"In the apartment block?"

"Yep."

Reader laughed. "Is that place of yours still empty?"

"No, I'm going to move into it. Now fuck off I'm busy."

Reader was still laughing when the call ended.

Perkins pressed the button once more. When the digital display on the panel above him said twelve he checked his watch. The doors opened and het let them close once more and then he went to work. The door was locked open, the joists were put in place, the sign was stuck on the panel and the barrier was put in place before the door. He the strolled down to the tenth floor and looked above the lift door. The digital display was flashing on twelve. He pressed the button on the panel and nothing happened. He checked his watch. It had taken him less than three minutes, and that was at an easy pace. He smiled and returned to the twelfth floor. After clearing up he rang Reader.

"How was it?"

"Easy peasy lemon squeezy."

"Let's hope it works on the real one."

"I'm not leaving it to hope."

"What?"

"I'm going there now to test it."

"Is that wise?"

"Do you want to know or not?"

"It could bring the whole thing down if you get caught?"

Perkins shook his head. "Is something up, Brian, you never used to question things like this before?"

A brief silence was followed by, "Sorry mate, I'm just having an off day."

"I'll catch up with you later."

"Ok. Right then, let me have it."

"Have what?"

"The comedian for fuck's sake. They can't help themselves."

"Aw God, right. I bumped into a midget running out of the PC World the other day…"

Just as Reader burst out laughing Billy Lincoln finished his coffee and nodded. He then left the café and made his way to the Audi A7. Once inside he picked up the map on the passenger seat and scribbled the time down. It was exactly 9.30am. He then set the stopwatch on his phone and drove away from the kerb. Five minutes later he passed through Hatton Garden, fourteen minutes after that he pulled up behind the pre-parked VW Golf Sv hatchback. He updated the map and returned to the café. Reader was still chuckling to himself but he did have a selection of timetables in his hand and another hot coffee waiting.

"How did it go?"

"Nineteen minutes. So that means whatever we use on an early morning we are looking at times between nineteen and twenty-six minutes."

"Ok, so lunchtime was between twenty-two and twenty-nine and late evening it was fourteen to seventeen. That's not bad going for this area."

"Yeah, it would be a little quicker if there wasn't the detour at Holborn but it wouldn't make much of a difference."

Reader waved the timetables. "Did you pass five buses?"

"Yep."

"Wonders never cease."

Reader's phone rang to life and Lincoln lifted his coffee.

"What? Now? Right." Reader put the phone down and nodded. "Come on, duty calls." Twenty minutes later they were back at the hatchback and Perkins was waiting for them in the white van.

"Any problems?" asked Reader.

"With the lift? None at all."

"Was there something you wanted to share?" added Lincoln.

"It was nothing, just some woman wanting to use it, that's all."

"Another whore?" blurted Reader.

"Steady on, Brian!" exclaimed Lincoln.

"No, she wasn't, and before you ask she didn't tell me any jokes either."

"Is there something I should know?" puzzled Lincoln.

"Terry keeps bumping into all kinds these days," began Reader before turning back to Perkins. "How did you get rid of her?"

"She never had much option really as I had the toolkit in the lift with me. Besides that I had the usual sign up so she just had a little whinge before disappearing."

"Well that's ok isn't it?"

"It's just the thought of being recognised, that's all. On top of that if someone gets that pissed by it and they go and make a call to someone, what do we do then?"

"You're starting to sound like me," said Reader.

Perkins just looked at him and smiled. "Two monkeys got into a bath. The first one goes, 'ooh ooh eeh ooh eeh ooh ooh argh'. The second one goes 'well put some fucking cold water in'. I was in my local take away the other night and my order was taking ages. I said to the guy behind the counter, 'Hey Chop Stick, where is my foo young?' He said, 'You can't call me that, that's racist'. I said, 'Naff off, you do it to us. For example, if I was to call you slit eyes what would you call me?' He looked at me and replied, 'Prince Phillip'."

Although laughter filled the air it still left a little space for tension.

Basil poured himself a glass of wine and looked over to the study wall. On the spreadsheet fifty names had been circled in red pen, a further fifty had a pencilled question mark against them. According to the research on his desk ten of those had confirmed links to the local mafia. Basil knew that all ten boxes had rich pickings to be had, and if it were down to him alone he would open them. But the job at hand was going to be done by local thieves that didn't really need to spend the rest of their lives looking over a shoulder. After one final look at the paperwork he walked to the wall and erased the question marks from the spreadsheet.

Five of the boxes belonged to celebrities. One was a well-known comedy actress that he liked and another was a game show host, and although within the inner circle he was a known pervert, he did do a lot of charity work. There was a premier league footballer who had to keep two wives and Basil was a supporter of the team he played for. One of the boxes was owned by a clapped out pop star who had a string of great hits in the eighties and Basil remembered dancing along to many of his tunes with something delightful in his arms. The fifth box was owned by one of the best stand-up comedians he had ever seen on the circuit and he had been left in stitches by him on several occasions. Another five question marks were removed from the spreadsheet.

Back at the desk he picked up another five files. The first belonged to a British politician and cabinet minister and the second was a high-ranking police officer who was obviously on the take. The third was for a local low life money lender, but because of his own stupidity, was contracted to the hard case that currently ran most of the drug trafficking on the manner as well as a lot of its informers. It wasn't big league but it had a mess written all over it. The fourth file was in the enigma category. It was owned by someone who worked for a company that he couldn't find any detailed information on. They had no fixed abode and didn't seem to own a phone or a car. The fifth file was owned by secretary of a property tycoon who was making his money off the back of immigrants. It was obvious what she was doing and as he had it coming to him, Basil had no intention of in getting in the way of it. Back at the spreadsheet another five question marks were removed.

With the help of a few glasses of wine he made quick decisions on another twenty-three files and all of them soon became a red circle on the spreadsheet. That left just seven files. After thumbing through each of them one final time he walked over to the spreadsheet and put a black square around them all. Something wasn't quite right about them so they were going to get checked to see if they had anything worthwhile. He then focused on the one name that was going to cause total and utter confusion. The one name that was going to be his trademark detour. It was the name a certain DC in the Flying Squad was also looking at.

From the comfort of a bench in Hyde Park, Yuri Tavlenko watched the world go rushing by for a while before returning to his eBook reader. He opened a recent purchase on poetry and swiped to a page that contained a piece by Konstantin Simonov that he once sent to Valentina Serova during the Great Patriotic War in 1941.

> *Wait for me, and I'll come back!*
> *Wait with all you've got!*
> *Wait, when dreary yellow rains*
> *Tell you, you should not.*
> *Wait when snow is falling fast,*
> *Wait when summer's hot,*
> *Wait when yesterdays are past,*

> *Others are forgot.*
> *Wait, when from that far-off place,*
> *Letters don't arrive.*
> *Wait, when those with whom you wait*
> *Doubt if I'm alive.*

The contact kept a discreet distance and checked the description he had been given. In his early thirties, blonde hair, blue eyes and a small bitter mouth. It topped a muscular frame that would be wearing all black. If it was clear to approach then a red scarf would be visible. Freelance Reporter Victor Ramere could just about see it beneath the eBook. He took a single photograph, set the portable tape recorder in his inside jacket pocket to record, walked over to the bench and lowered himself down.

> *Wait for me, and I'll come back!*
> *Wait in patience yet*
> *When they tell you off by heart*
> *That you should forget.*
> *Even when my dearest ones*
> *Say that I am lost,*
> *Even when my friends give up,*
> *Sit and count the cost,*
> *Drink a glass of bitter wine*
> *To the fallen friend –*
> *Wait! And do not drink with them!*
> *Wait until the end!*

Yuri looked up to see a balding middle-aged man with clear brown eyes and an easy smile. The clothing was formal and right as was the correct selection of newspaper in his hand, folded at the crossword page. Victor then handed over a piece of paper with a phone number on it. Yuri nodded. "What do you know about Grigory Rodchenkov?"

"He ran the laboratory that tested the Olympians during the winter games at Sochi last year. It was rumoured that he was involved in a doping program but nothing was ever proven."

"In the previous games in Vancouver, British Columbia, we finished sixth in the medal table. It was a disaster and many people at the top were going to lose face and ultimately their jobs if the same thing repeated itself at Sochi. Anyway, that didn't happen as it was a great success as we won thirty-three medals, ten of which were gold. And all of it was down to a top secret program run by Rodchenkov."

"Run by your Olympic committee."

"Run by the state."

"You mean…"

"You don't think Putin and his cronies were going to spend so much time and effort on that place to have it all thrown back into their faces as a waste of time and money? Russia had to be shown as a strong global power on the world stage."

"What was used?"

"A mixture of metenolone, trenbolone and oxandrolone."

"How did they avoid detection? I mean the samples themselves and the sealed bottles that get used have to go through such a rigorous process the powers that be believe it's fool proof."

Yuri handed over an envelope. "I have given you enough for now. My requirements are on there. If you can meet them then you get the whole story."

"But…"

"Goodbye, Victor."

The reporter nodded and got to his feet. He then hurried away. Yuri smiled and turned back to the poem.

Wait for me and I'll come back,
Dodging every fate!
"What a bit of luck!" they'll say,
Those that would not wait.
They will never understand,
How amidst the strife,
By your waiting for me, dear,
You had saved my life.
Only you and I will know,
How you got me through.
Simply - you knew how to wait -
No one else but you.

As he closed the book he was photographed. He learnt of it just a few moments later via text on his phone. He smiled once more.

On the last Friday in March all eight of them met up for last time in The Castle pub in Islington. They had a few beers, shared a little general chat and when Hugh Doyle made his excuse and left, Basil went through everything in reverse just to make sure everyone knew their place. He asked each member of the team one question and it was answered immediately. He then folded the layout drawing he had been using and put it in his pocket.

"Right, let's cover the most important thing of all and that is leaving any clue that can lead the law to any one of us. Make sure you wear your gloves at all times and that will keep forensics at bay. As for identification then make sure that your features are covered in some way. Wear a hat, put on some glasses or some other type of disguise. Only use what you feel comfortable with as there will be ten security cameras on us."

"Ten? I only ever counted five," said Collins.

Basil began to tap away on his fingers. "Five cameras are communal and are controlled by the building owners, the other five are specific and are run by the depository. On the communal side, two cover the ground floor area, two cover the Greville Street access and there is one on the first floor roofing area. Because it's flat they are taking no chances with it. On the specific side there are two in the vault, two just outside the vault and one on the front door. They are backed up on two separate drives, one is in the office used by the security guards and the other is kept in a cupboard between the reinforced gates. I will collect them before we leave."

As Collins nodded, Perkins piped up, "What about the other buildings in the area?"

"Some of them do have motorised units so that's why it's important for us all to stay covered up."

Everyone nodded and Basil went on. "Once we get clear and get to the units we can do the split and go our separate ways until the heat dies down. Initially, you will all have a part share and I don't have to tell you how to deal with it. Tread carefully, take light steps and keep below the radar. Freddie will have your details and he will get in touch. Under no circumstances must any of you contact him."

"How long will we have to wait?" asked Lincoln.

"It depends on two things," began Basil. "The first is down to how close the Old Bill are to you. If there is no trace then he will get in touch soon enough. If it goes tits up for any of you then rest assured your share will remain safe until it's ok for you to use it."

"About the share," said Perkins, "we are looking at stones, metals and cash. Are we letting Freddie take all three?"

"No, that's why we need a little common sense when we are at the vault. We have bags for the bins and we will have time. Keep the cash isolated from the rest and keep the rest by association. There will be no need to rush it. You have all been in such situations before and I'm sure you have your own particular way of sorting it so stick to what you know."

"You know something," said Wood, "last night I had this horrible dream in that as soon as we started to collate it all the police walked in and got us all bang to rights."

"I dreamt that I could still get a hard on," blurted Reader. "I thought it was a wet dream until I suddenly woke up. Luckily I was lying in the shallow end."

As everyone burst out laughing Reader gave Wood a reassuring tap on the arm and from across the table Basil gave an appreciative nod. When the noise subsided Jones got all serious in looks. "I have a question and it's an important one, you could say life-changing."

Everyone gave him their full attention and he paused before going on. "Who is going to play me in the movie about this as there is sure as hell going to be one." A few curses were exchanged before each of them gave it some thought. That's when the answers came.

"My role would be a good one for Michael Caine," offered Reader.

"Michael Gambon for me," said Collins.

"Ray Winstone," announced Basil.

"Christopher Plummer would probably do a good me," beamed Lincoln.

"Well that leaves Bill Nighy for me," said Perkins.

"Simon Pegg is my choice," decided Wood.

Everyone turned back to Jones. He looked around the table and shrugged his shoulders. "Mine's easy, it would have to be Roger Lloyd-Pack."

"But he's dead," said Collins.

"Idris Elba then."

"He's black," said Lincoln.

"Look, it's a Hollywood movie, right? A bit like *The Eleven Commandments, Snow Black and the Seven Vertically Challenged People, Titanic Two*, and my favourite, *The Magnificent Eight*. Hey, hang on a minute that could be our title."

"Who is going to play Hugh then?" asked Wood.

"That little girl's blouse that does those chat shows."

"Graham Norton?"

"Yeah him, eyes too close together, he fits the bill."

"Diamond Geezers," announced Reader as everyone turned to face him. "That's the title of our movie. As the titles got dafter Basil emptied his glass and got to his feet. "Time for me to go. Take it easy and I will see you all next Thursday." Within an hour Jones was the only one left at the table.

Basil went to see Freddie the Fence to go over an additional requirement. It was something the other seven didn't need to know about as he knew it would be of little consequence to them in the end. Brian Reader went home and poured himself a drink whilst he went through a photo album that was full of pictures of him with his late wife, Lyn. He didn't remember going to sleep but when he woke up a few hours later he was soaked in sweat. Moments later his hands began to shake. That's when the demons arrived. Kenny Collins and Terry Perkins called in to their local Indian restaurant, The Royal Bengal. Over king prawns and tikka masala they discussed the shopping lists they were going to do in once they had received their share of the spoils. Billy Lincoln took a taxi home and went straight to bed. His new hips were beginning to play up and he knew that the only way to deal with the pain was tablets and sleep. The tablets were in alcoholic form and the sleep was in deep snoring form. Carl Wood went home and opened a file that contained all the debt in his life. He just sat there with a smile on his face and stared at it.

Danny Jones finished off his pint and just as he was about to make a move, Billy Finch walked in. He looked a bit worse for wear and after scanning the room a few times he just about managed to focus on Jones. As he staggered across the floor the whole pub went silent. Finch got to the table and grabbed two stools by a single leg. He lifted them above his head and held them there for twenty seconds. After dropping them on the floor he screamed at Jones, "Can you do that?" Jones got to his feet and looked him in the eye. "No," he said before reaching into his pocket and taking out a bundle of twenty pound notes. As everyone looked on he tore the bundle in half and threw it on the table. He then looked across to Finch and whispered, "Can you do that." The roar of laughter could be heard streets away.

Retired Nurse Mary Randall poured another cup of tea and passed it over Gavin Foble. He never noticed it for he was still looking through the photographs of her son.

"Don't let it get cold," she offered.

"Sorry Mary, I just can't get over the fact that Biff isn't here anymore."

"Don't be silly, he's everywhere. He's in me and he's still in you. That's what keeps you coming back."

"I could have saved him. If only I could have tried harder I could have saved him."

"You did save him in the Falklands. It was the drink that killed him here. The army let him down not you. Nobody came to see him. It was all phone calls and official letters. He just needed the more of the human touch but he only ever got that from you."

"It didn't save him."

"It kept him alive, it kept me alive."

"And now?"

"His case is still keeping me alive. It's my turn to fight now. I won't stop until I get justice, not just for him but for the other lads that have been allowed to go the same way."

Foble smiled. "I could have done with you over there, Mary."

"It doesn't work like that, love. You men do all the fighting and we women are left to pick up the pieces. The only problem with that is the fact that neither of us is very good at it."

"Can't give you argument there."

"There is somewhere else you can't give me an argument on either. That medal doesn't belong in a box. It belongs on your chest. You owe it to Barry and to yourself so stop buggering about and wear it."

Foble look at her in surprise.

"Hey, listen to me," continued Mary. "I sound just like him, don't I?"

At that Gavin Foble lowered his head and quietly began to fall apart. That's when Mary Randall picked up the pieces and held them in her arms.

He had five missed calls on his mobile phone but right now Ralph Wilson just couldn't be arsed to answer any of them. Two were from Amanda, three were from Susan and one was from a money lender. Ralph took another swig from a bottle of vodka he had just stolen from a local newsagent and cursed. As he sat on a bed in a spare room of his parents' home he began to mull over just how he had got in such a mess. Why did it get to this? If Amanda only knew the risk he had taken to keep her happy.

It was he that got the money for the fertility program. It was he that had arrange to be on shift at the right time. It was he that found the lifeless body of his daughter. It was he that had found the closest match and replaced the tags and changed the documentation. It was he that took out the box at Hatton Garden so the little secret could be kept safe.

Ralph had another go with the bottle. It wasn't helping but it was. The pain had gone but the problem remained. He had lost a life but helped to shape another. He had escaped prison but right now it could be the safest place for him to be. He wanted to live but he had so much to die for. Just as a germ of an idea flashed across his mind he tried to catch it with the help of more vodka but it slipped away. Laying back on the bed he stared at the ceiling and tried to search his scrambled mind for the flicker of hope he knew he had just seen. He could see both babies. Images of life and stillness came and went. Then there were the tags, the empty room and busy corridor. The blinds that closed and then opened to what he had just done. The walk along the corridor and the open door to the administrator's office, the filing cabinet with the key hanging from it, the files and the photocopier, the exchange of documents. And then there was the half-empty bottle of gin in the bottom drawer. That's when Ralph began to see more clearly. That's when he remembered he wasn't the only one with a bottle habit.

Back then someone had one long before him and he could be the way out of this. He took another mouthful of vodka and smiled. All he had to do was pick the right moment. He knew that they would come for him so all he had to do was play the blame card into the right hand and then he would come up trumps. He began to talk to himself and map out what he was going to do. The words came quick and so did the vodka. When he had reached the bottom of the bottle he attempted to stand but his legs just buckled and he toppled back onto the bed. Moments later the bottle fell to the floor and it all went dark.

After leaving Hatton Garden, Massimo Alessi headed south and after a fifteen-minute walk arrived at the steps of St. Michael's church. The congregation from a recently completed mass were pouring out onto the street and Alessi watched them pass with the odd respectful nod and smile. A few moments later he mounted the steps and crossed himself as he entered the house of his God. The man he was looking for was draped in green and white vestments topped by a black biretta and was kneeling in prayer. Alessi looked around the church. Solid timbers topped historical stained glass windows divided by white marbled statues depicting the twelve Stations of the Cross. Dark oaked pews ran to a majestic alter and that's where Alessi eased to his knees.

"Bless me, Father for I have sinned," he whispered.

"Then you are amongst friends," replied Father John, eyes still closed.

"Father, I need to get an urgent message to the almighty."

"And how may I be of help, my son?"

"Many years ago one of his sheep went astray and I was sent to help the shepherd."

"And did you manage to reunite it with the flock?"

"Sadly not, but there was a legacy entrusted to me and so I seek guidance."

"Then you will need to take the path of truth. Its route is never an easy one but if you start on the right foot the journey can be an uplifting one."

"So how do I know the correct path to take?"

"Each journey has a beginning and an end. Before I can enlighten you with the end I will need to know where you began."

"With the death of Roberto Calvi."

Father John opened his eyes and turned in shock.

"I know where the legacy is, Father. I also know that all roads don't always lead to Rome. I will be in touch soon, so until then say a few Hail Marys for me and don't forget to speak to Our Father." Alessi made the sign of the cross and quietly made his way back out onto the street. The church he left wasn't shaking just yet but that was just a phone call away.

Mohamed Al-Fayed eased the envelope open with a knife. He then removed a single piece of paper from it and began to read.

Dear Sir,
My name is Juliette Roux, I am the daughter of Isabelle Roux. You may remember that she spent most of her working life in service for the Duke and Duchess of Windsor at their home in France.

Al-Fayed nodded to himself. He remembered the pleasant little woman who itemised everything in neat catalogues when the building and its contents were put up for sale.

I regret to say that during a moment of weakness she kept one item away from the auction. She did so in the thought that one day I may be able to use it if my life ever became unbearable. All I can tell you is that like everyone else I have problems but I am not prepared to sell my soul in order to pay for them. I have never felt so lost and confused and as I have nowhere else to turn, please forgive me for such an approach. Could you please find it in your heart to share a moment of your time for which I shall be eternally thankful.

Respectfully yours,

Juliette Roux.

Al-Fayed had two choices. The first was to call the police, the second was to call his private secretary. Ten seconds later the latter entered his office.

Within five minutes of entering the jewellers Karl Brant found himself sitting opposite a grey-haired, craggy faced slim figure of a man who had dark eyes full of pain. His name was Emil Wiener and he was notable for two reasons. The first was that he was one of the most trusted dealers in Hatton Garden. The second was that he survived the holocaust.

"How can I be of help, Mr Brant?"

Karl passed the starburst brooch over the desk. "Can you tell me anything about this?"

The old jeweller took it in his hands as if it was worth a fortune. "I can tell you that many years ago it was common to see items like this on the lapels of your Jewish girls. They were signs of love from a mother to a daughter. Although you don't see these anymore I'm afraid they are of little value."

"That one is worth a life," said Karl.

Wiener's eyes seemed to glaze over. Karl passed a single sheet of paper across the desk. On it were a list of names, one of them had been highlighted in blue.

"Find her, Emil. I know that your organisation can find her. Find her and check on the others. Do it right and more will follow." At that Karl got to his feet and headed for the door.

"Who are you?" asked Emil.

Karl paused for a moment. "I was someone that believed in a cause and then I found the truth." As he disappeared Emil picked up the piece of paper and ran his fingers down it. The screams ran through his mind. The tears then ran down his face. It took him a while before he managed to pick up the phone.

The car was parked on the edge of an embankment overlooking the River Thames. Shunter was in the back seat with a gun pointed at the back of the driver. He had both hands on the steering wheel. His associate in the front passenger seat had both hands on the dashboard.

"I need a name," whispered Shunter.

The head in the driver's seat moved from side to side before Shunter put a bullet through it.

"Jesus Christ!" cried a voice from the passenger seat.

"I'm afraid not even he can help you now. I need a name."

"I have a family to think of."

"So did I, once," replied Shunter before pulling the trigger. The bullet tore through a cage of bone before reaching a heart. As it suddenly stopped, the frame it came in, slowly folded forward. Shunter then waited for a moment before relieving both corpses of their wallets. He then took the handbrake off, stepped out of the car and walked away. He never looked back. He never saw it topple over the embankment and plunge into the water below. His mind was already fixed on what he had to do next. It was something he should have done years ago.

OPAL

Victor Ramere was in the office of weasel-faced Dave Pinter, the chief sports writer for *The Times* newspaper, and although Pinter nodded all the way through the tape recording Ramere had brought, the initial discussion had not begun well.

"He wants one hundred grand, do me a favour."

"Listen to me," began Victor. "I have checked Yuri out. He used to work for RSK, and they are currently the biggest healthcare company in Russia at the moment. They were at Sochi and so was he."

Pinter looked down at the photograph that had been supplied. "So what's he doing here?"

"He's starting up his own company, same line of work."

"And he wants me to pay for it."

Victor handed over the contents of the envelope he had been handed by Yuri.

"What's this?"

"The first ten pages are the results of urine samples taken six months prior to the games. The next ten pages are the official results of the same samples taken during the Olympics. Before the event they were all dirty and contained the drugs that Yuri named. After the event, all ten are shown as clean."

"And…"

"And all ten of the names won a medal."

All of a sudden Pinter stiffened and moved forward in his seat. "If this can be proved?"

"He can prove it. Or should I say *you* can prove it. Just think of the shit storm you can create with this one."

Pinter nodded. "Offer him fifty."

Victor shook his head and reached for the paperwork. "He can get better than that and you know it."

Pinter kept a tight grip on the paperwork. "Tell him I will go to seventy-five but I must have more."

"I'll ask but I already know what the answer will be."

"Ok, I will go to one hundred but I want to meet him."

"Oh I don't know about that."

"There's a bonus in for you," said Pinter releasing his grip.

At that Victor retrieved the photograph and the paperwork and made his own way out. As soon as he was gone Pinter picked up the phone and stabbed at one of the buttons.

"Hello?" said the voice.

"Is the old man in?"

"Yes, and he's alone for the next ten minutes."

"Not anymore."

Basil placed the flowers upon the grave and took a step back. He stayed like that for a while before slowly retreating from the plot and moving away. He never took much notice of the taxi parked just fifty metres away. The wall between them hid most of it. Had Basil bothered to look he would have seen the driver of the taxi with a camera in his hand. Once he was clear of the area that same driver entered the cemetery and took a picture of the headstone with the new floral arrangement upon it. He then made a phone call.

"It's me."

"Alright John."

"You are never going to believe this."

For Brian Reader the greatest job he would ever be involved in was almost over before it had begun. Wednesday 1st April was supposed to be a night of relaxation before the big event but that all stopped when he switched on the

TV to catch up on the news. Iran was complaining about Israeli jets invading its air space, the investigation into the crash of a German airliner had confirmed that it was a deliberate act carried out by co-pilot Andreas Lubitz, and a certain dancing celebrity was caught leaving a hotel with someone he shouldn't have been with. Reader just shrugged at that but the item that followed it had him sitting bolt upright. According to the report, electrical cables under a pavement in Kingsway near the Holborn underground station had caught fire after a gas main burst and blew open a manhole cover. Several thousand residents had been evacuated, offices were closed and all the telecoms in the area had been disrupted. As it was close to Hatton Garden, Reader rang Perkins and Collins. The former was too busy with a bottle of wine so the latter got the ear-bending. It got that bad he even climbed into his Mercedes and drove down to the site of the job. He spent an hour in the area before making an assuring call to Reader and returning home. He then rang Perkins, concerns were exchanged and they both agreed to keep an eye on the situation. They also agreed that there would be no need to mention it to Basil. In reality they didn't have to as he already knew. He had been to check on things for himself after he had received a call from a contact at Scotland Yard.

At exactly 18.00hrs the following day security guard Kelvin Stockwell locked the vault at 88-90 Hatton Garden and set off for home. As he stepped onto the street, building Superintendent Carlos Cruise made one final sweep of the area before activating the alarm system and leaving the premises by the front door. At the same time Brian Reader paid for and collected a stolen oyster card from a local misfit before boarding the number seventy-six bus to Waterloo East station. As he then transferred to the number fifty-five, which would offload him at St John Street, just a few minutes' walk from Hatton Garden, Basil stepped out of a minivan. He kissed the driver goodbye before grabbing a bag of tools and starting the mile he had to cover. Using the Audi, Billy Lincoln picked up Terry Perkins and took him to the Golf. Perkins then drove it to the prearranged spot and transferred back in the Audi. Half an hour later they were walking through Hatton Garden. At exactly 20.20hrs Kenny Collins drove the white van along Leather Lane before parking up on Greville Street. Danny Jones and Carl Wood spent the next ten minutes looking out of it before stepping onto the street. Dressed in hoodies and high visibility jackets they both donned baseball caps and gloves before grabbing a holdall each and setting off to check that the area was clear. At exactly 21.20hrs all the required checks had been made, Lincoln and Perkins had reached the van and Basil joined them. Everyone gave him the thumbs up and he then broke off, raised his bag to one shoulder and headed for the front door to 88-90 Hatton Garden.

Jones followed him most of the way and positioned himself in a doorway that gave him a clear view of everyone. He looked on as Basil took a set of keys from his pocket, opened the front door of the depository and quickly disappeared from view. Jones raised his hand and made his way to Greville Street. As soon as he reached the fire escape the door opened from the inside. Basil nodded and made his way to the second floor and summoned the lift. Jones waved his arm and seconds later the white van pulled up opposite the entrance. Dressed in construction protective gear, the gang poured out and offloaded four drums of water, four joists and two wheelie bins full of tools. As they entered the building Perkins joined Basil at the lift. Jones arrived a few moments later with two of the joists. Using a special key Perkins then opened the lift doors and disabled its metal contacts, allowing them to remain open. Perkins placed an 'out of order' sign on the wall. Shortly afterwards, Reader and Woods appeared with a portable barrier, two retractable ladders, a rope and a bag of tools. As soon as he retreated Perkins erected the barrier, Jones placed the joists between the doors and Basil unclipped the ladders and unfurled them down the lift shaft. Jones attached the rope to one of the bags, clipped a torch to it, switched it on and lowered it to the floor. It landed with a thump and then it all went quiet. Basil descended his ladder first and once clear at the bottom tapped the rungs so that Jones could safely follow him down.

Up on the street Collins drove the white van to nearby St. Cross Street and then made his way to the building opposite the depository. Once inside he made his way the room window that was going to be his lookout post and reached for a radio. Two clicks were followed by a brief 'ok'. When he got four clicks in return he eased himself onto a chair at the window and settled down to a slight panic.

Basil and Jones quietly mouthed 'one, two, three' to each other and then in unison rammed a crow bar beneath the bottom rung of a shutter collapsing metal gate. It buckled and then lifted itself free from the housing on the floor. They lifted it thirty inches from the floor and then crawled into the room situated beneath the staircase. As Jones armed himself with a hammer Basil opened the cupboard door beneath the stairs and then picked up a screwdriver and a pair of wire cutters. Four screws later and the panel cover on the intruder alarm was placed on the floor. Basil quickly found the fibre communications cable he needed and cut through it. He then snapped the aerial off the transmitter situated on top of the panel. Below the panel was a rack of cables, one of which supplied power to the magnetic lock on the nearby iron gate that Jones was perched by. Basil pulled a schematic from his pocket and double-checked the rack. He then cut through the required cable. The door near Jones clicked and that's when he battered it open. The wooden door that now faced him took just two blows before it caved in. He was met by four smiling figures leaning against two wheelie bins. Moments later all six of them were standing before the second metal gate, the last obstacle between them and the vault. Basil checked his watch and noted they were running a little behind schedule. It was 22.34 hrs.

It took Reader just under thirty minutes to grind his way through three of the reinforced bars on the metal gate and Woods had them bent double in a matter of seconds. Lincoln and Basil tipped the wheelie bin carrying the Hilti drill over the gate and Jones pulled it across to the vault door. Perkins strained his way there on two occasions with the joists. Jones lifted the Hilti up against the wall and Basil marked the location where the anchor rod would sit and then drilled the twenty millimetre hole and filled it with adhesive. Ten minutes later Jones erected the Hilti, aligned the columns, secured the clamps and locked the unit into position. Perkins and Reader placed a drum of water nearby and Basil connected the hoses. Lincoln connected the power supply and Jones rubbed his hands before bringing the drill to life. The rest then held their breath and stood in silence as he eased the drill forward. The moment it broke the surface of the fifty centimetre-thick reinforced concrete wall, cheeks were blown and smiles appeared.

Mick Dea lowered himself onto the sofa and placed a glass of wine onto the table. Next to it was a pile of files that he had booked out from the police archives. He checked the clock and noted that the day only had thirty minutes left, and as he never went to bed before midnight, he had time for some light reading. He flipped through the files and stopped at the one marked 'Brinks Mat

Robbery'. Dea picked it up and weighed it in his hand. Although it was a crime that had ended in many deaths and millions in unfound gold and diamonds, the whole thing just never added up in Dea's books. He opened the file to a sheet he had written. It contained nine questions, eight of which had been crossed out. Two of those had resulted in arrests and Dea had received commendation for them both. He tapped the page at the unanswered question, took a sip of wine and began to turn the pages. As he scanned reports, statements and interviews, he noted that the words *luck* and *fortunate* kept jumping out at him. Dea looked for and found the delivery note for the gold and the receipt register for the vault. The shipment had been booked in on the day before the robbery just a few minutes before the day shift was coming to a close. The shift supervisor had made the decision to store it in the vault room and not in the actual safe as it was due for onward shipment early the next morning. The schedule for the following day was a tight one and so it was a simple planning and storage decision, and as such decisions had often been used in the past, no-one thought to question it. Dea could see the sense in that but had a niggling doubt around the timing of it all. Why would such a delivery be sent so late? That was the unanswered question on his page. He looked back through previous delivery notes and log entries and ran the permutations through his mind. There was a gap somewhere but he just couldn't see it. As midnight passed he took another sip of wine, eased his head back and closed his eyes. The images flashed for a while and then darkness crept over them all.

At 00.30hrs Reader and Perkins were shifting equipment across the iron gate when a secondary sensor under the carpet tripped as a toolbox was dropped near it. The vibration triggered a single pulse along the interconnecting fibre and when that reached the circuit board under the stairs, noted a local fault. That relayed a signal to the transmitter and there was just enough signal left in it to send an alert to the Southern Monitoring Alarm company situated thirty miles away. The operator that received it noted the caution and warning but as there wasn't a priority code evident he selected a default classification of three and a text was sent to the two names on file. One was a family member that co-owned the premises and the other was the regional co-ordinator for the security team responsible for the building. Twenty minutes later security guard Kelvin Stockwell got a call and set off to the depository. He arrived on site at 01.10hrs. As soon as he got out of his car Collins sent three clicks on the radio and followed it with the single word 'stop'. As all worked outside the vault ceased, Stockwell checked the main door and walked around to Greville Street and looked through the letterbox. All he could see was a metal box on the floor and a bicycle up against a wall. Procedure dictated that if he wanted to enter the building then he could only do it with police back-up. He called Alok Bavishi, a member of the family that owned the vault. He was just five minutes away in the car. He asked Stockwell to do another quick check, and after a brief chat decided that no further action should be taken. He turned his car towards home and Stockwell called it in as a false alarm. Two minutes later he left the scene and one minute after that work recommenced at the vault.

At 01.30hrs twenty-one year old Hatton Garden resident and would-be mechanical engineering student Gary Holt woke up with twenty thousand pounds per square inch of pressure at the end of his knob. At least that's how he would describe it to his mates the next morning. In reality the gallon of lager he had supped during the evening had now gathered in his bladder and he was forced to take a leak. Although the journey to and from the bathroom would be a hazy one the annoying whining sound reverberating around his building would annoy him for a while. The alcohol that remained in his system would eventually take care of that.

At 01.50hrs a very jet-lagged Susan Taghelo paid for her taxi and then fought her way up to stairs of her apartment. As she collapsed onto her bed she looked over to the case she had just stood up against a nearby wall. In it were a few reasons why she would never have to be an air hostess anymore. She was just inches away from the biggest pile of money she had ever touched along with the deeds to a property that would keep her in comfort for the rest of her life. In a few days she would put it in the box she held in the depository just a few streets away. Four thousand miles away was a broken-hearted man. He was just inches away from a loaded revolver. In a few days the police would find his lifeless body.

At 02.30hrs jeweller Patrick Sterman had the phone in his hand. Looking out from his window he thought he saw somebody lurking around the depository down the road. As he began to press the buttons his mind began to race. There was a figure but it looked like it was in working clothes. There wasn't any vehicle movement. The call connected and then a voice came on the line. At that exact moment Sterman remembered the visit he'd had recently from the police and the warning that he had received about nuisance calls. He also thought of the diamonds he had in the depository. When the voice repeated its message Sterman ended the call. He stood at his window for a further fifteen minutes before returning to his bed. After a further fifteen minutes of staring at the ceiling he slipped into a deep sleep.

At 03.15hrs the gang inside the depository were looking at three overlapping holes that had a height of twenty-five centimetres and a combined width of forty-five centimetres. It had taken a little longer than expected but the clean up during drill runs had been a must to keep the debris contained and the dust to an absolute minimum. When complete Basil had called for a time out to allow Jones to get a cup of tea and relax a little. Perkins had used the time to take an insulin jab along with a few tablets. It was the first time he had been open about his diabetes. Woods spent the time walking around the building muttering to himself much to the dismay of Lincoln who was trying to get a power nap. Reader was far from needing sleep. Something was eating away at him. He was running the schedule and the list of equipment through his mind as he couldn't help but think that he had missed something. He had, and he was going to find out what within the next few hours.

When Mick Dea opened his eyes the file on his lap was closed and the glass on the table was empty. He looked at the clock to see that the day was just over five hours old. After climbing to his feet, he wandered over to the bathroom and took a steaming hot shower. That was followed by a steaming hot cup of tea and a few rounds of toast. Dea had a weekend off and so he wasn't in a rush to do anything. He did have family to visit and a few friends to call in on but apart from that his diary was quite empty. In an attempt to get enthusiasm for the day he poured more tea, returned to the sofa and switched the TV on. It was a system that usually worked as he would channel-hop across thirty minutes of rubbish before forcing himself to make a move towards something more rewarding.

It started with skinny English newsreaders, went on to fat American car mechanics, crossed over to Japanese buffoons on assault courses and ended with a bunch of Australians that couldn't go three sentences without saying 'Fair Dinkum'. Dea just rolled his eyes, downed his tea and pressed the remote control. Instead of switching off, the TV flipped over to an old drama channel. Dea was about to aim the remote control and press the correct button when the commercial break ended and he heard 'de nar nar, de nar nar, da dada da, da da da da'. The musical reminder made him smile as he never knew that they still aired old reruns of the seventies cop show called *The Sweeney*. Dea eased back into his chair as the characters Regan and Carter played by John Thaw and Dennis Waterman appeared on screen.

The scene began with them dressed in security outfits whispering to each other behind a concrete post. Moments later they stepped clear and that's when a large transit van fronted by a reinforced bumper came crashing through a nearby door. Radios went berserk and as four tooled up members of a local gang poured into the warehouse two back-up squad cars came screeching into view. Regan soon found himself standing before a large masked club-wielding mountain of a man. The club swung, Regan ducked and rammed his forearm into the chest of his attacker. As he reeled backwards two uniformed policemen grabbed his arms. Regan slammed a fist into his jaw, and as the writhing mass toppled to the floor, he winced in pain and cupped his fist into his chest. When Carter approached the van the driver's door flew open and knocked him to the floor. He scrambled to his feet just in time to take the oncoming tackle from a long-haired bull-shaped mass of muscle. After rolling across concrete they both got to their knees and that's when Carter threw the first punch. The frame before him moved and Carter's clenched fist whipped across an ear, and in doing so a wig lifted into the air to reveal a bald head. As Carter looked up at it a fist connected with his nose sending blood across his face. As all hell broke loose Dea paused the action and reached for the folder he had been looking at the night before. He went straight to the records on the gold delivery. He checked the times, the distance and the name.

Ten minutes later he made a phone call and set off for the office.

"It's all your fucking fault!" Jones screamed with his face just millimetres away from that of Reader. Two hours earlier he had set up the hydraulic ram in the hole that had been made in the concrete wall. After securing it against the backing plate of the security boxes he set it away but within five minutes the seals on the shaft connections had leaked. After Basil had had several failed attempts on correcting it with shifters, sealant, adhesive and tape he asked Reader to go and get the back-up. That was when Reader was suddenly filled with dread. He did go and check both of the bins and the van but he knew that he was wasting his time. Not being able to put off the inevitable any longer, he came clean. He did remember being asked by Basil to get a back-up but then it just got lost somewhere in his mind. It was Woods that exploded first and he was quickly followed by Perkins and Lincoln but as Basil began to calm the situation it was Jones that grabbed the crowbars and hammers and crawled back into the hole. He spent a solid hour in there during which all requests for a change were vehemently refused. Exhausted and soaked in sweat he eventually retreated away from a scratched and dented backing plate to emerge next to Reader.

"It's all your fucking fault! How could you have missed something like that? Are you fucking losing it or what? Is this caper too fucking big for you or what, Brian?"

"Naff off you moron," bawled Reader.

"Brilliant, just bloody brilliant!" added Woods, throwing his arms into the air.

"Who the fuck are you?" blasted Perkins with his finger raised. "What did you ever bring to this?"

"Jesus H!" cried Lincoln. "Where does this leave us now?"

"Up shit creak without a paddle, that's where!" screamed Jones.

"Alright that's enough!" ordered Basil as tempers soared. "We haven't lost anything. We haven't come this far to fall at the final hurdle. There is always a way so calm down." At that he paused and looked at each of their faces. There was anger and frustration but it was being contained. "Right, everyone is tired and the place is secure so we retreat, get a replacement ram and come back again tomorrow."

"Come back tomorrow, are you kidding or what?" replied Woods.

"No, I'm deadly serious. It's not the first time that I have had to return to a job. All we have to do is get the ram and then we can do a recon of the area tomorrow. If it's still secure we continue."

"The old bill could be waiting for us," added Lincoln.

"Listen, if this place is rumbled by anyone then there will be no way they will be able to keep it under wraps. Box holders will be called and they will come running no matter how much assurance they are given. This place will be mayhem."

Everyone remained silent for a moment and Jones spoke up. "I know a place where I can get the replacement. After a kip I'll go and get one."

"Take someone with you," said Basil.

Jones looked over to Reader. "I'll get Kenny to come, I can trust him."

Reader was going to respond but thought better of it. Basil patted him on the back in acknowledgement. A radio signal was sent to Collins and at exactly 08.00hrs he had a van full of quiet people. He did ask the obvious question but all he got from a dejected Jones was,

"Just drive."

Mick Dea spent two hours in the police archives going through files and making phone calls and a further three at the offices of Secure XL, the company that supplied the bullion drivers at Heathrow Airport. The skeleton staff at both premises were not best pleased to see him. Good Friday was supposed to be an easy payday but Dea had put pay to that with his questions and demands. Those on the receiving end had quickly realised that he wasn't going to go away until he had what he wanted so phone calls were made, schedules were ruined and meals went cold. Several people were glad to see the back of him but one man living in Wimbledon was surprised as hell to see the other side.

On 25th November 1983 Peter Rawling was in charge of security at Unit 7 of Heathrow International Airport Trading Estate. According to the paperwork currently in the hands of Dea it was he that had signed for receipt of the shipment. As both men sat in Rawling's kitchen and discussed the raid, Dea slowly steered the conversation towards the reason for his visit.

"Did they use the same drivers?"

"On most occasions, yes."

"What about on this occasion?"

"As far as I can recall he was new."

Dea handed over a faded photograph. It was from an old I.D badge. The lined face was friendly, the bright eyes were brown and the shabby hair was red.

"Was that him?"

Rawling nodded. "Yep that was him. Very chatty as I remember."

"He joined the firm just eight months before the robbery. He handed his notice in just six weeks after. He had a medical note to say that he was suffering from anxiety attacks and was on permanent medication."

"Because of the robbery? Poor sod."

"I went in search of him. He doesn't exist. The passport, national insurance information and address he gave the firm were all fake. The bank account his salary was paid into was set up with fake information and is now closed. The only transactions going in were the salary payments and they were taken out with a single withdrawal on the day the account was closed. The doctor on the medical note does exist but he never treated the patient in question. The signature on the note is a close copy."

"Bloody hell."

"Do not repeat anything I have just told you to anyone. I am chasing a ghost and the last thing I need is for him to know. The reason I have told you is that I want you to keep thinking about it just in case you remember something new. If you do then contact me direct."

"Yes, of course."

At that Dea made his excuses and got up to leave. Rawling showed him to the door.

"You know something," began Rawling, "They checked the van and it had the same mileage as all the other journeys, it set off at the same time and there were no traffic hot spots so no-one could really figure out why it was late. The driver just said slow moving traffic."

"He must have timed it to perfection," replied Dea.

"Clever, very clever. He's involved but he's not there when things begin to fold and the police come calling. Oh, he's probably on some tropical island now, probably owns part of it." Dea never answered the remark. He just said his farewell and left.

For Lincoln, Perkins, and Wood, Good Friday was just a blur. As they all spent most of the day in bed Collins and Jones had just five hours sleep before heading off to Twickenham. There was a Machine Mart shop there that Jones had used on several occasions and always paid cash. This time when he was presented with the ram he specified he had no option but to hand over his credit card. He knew he was taking a risk and cursed under his breath at Billy Finch. He could see those torn notes in his mind and could kick himself for how stupid he had been. He knew that he should have just knocked him out and as he left the shop he promised himself that he would do just that the next time he crossed his path.

Brian Reader never slept much at all. He spent a few restless hours in bed before going for a walk. He tried to eat something but he just never had much of an appetite. He picked up a book but just lost interest after a few pages. He switched on the TV but as soon as he saw that the euro lottery hadn't been won and so the eleven million euros would go on for a rollover, he switched it straight off. He then turned to music and although a few tunes from old blue eyes Frank Sinatra did relax him a little he still couldn't rid his mind of the mistake he had made. Maybe Jones was right, maybe he was losing it, maybe it was just a step too far for him. He poured himself a gin and tonic and before he could lift the glass to his lips his hand began to tremble. He tried to steady the glass with his other hand but it just got worse. Moments later his whole body began to shake and as the glass dropped to the floor he collapsed into a nearby chair. He tried to cry out but no sound could be heard. That's when he slid down the chair and collapsed into a heap on the floor. He wouldn't come around for four hours and when he did he would be soaked in sweat.

Basil spent a few hours surfing the Internet when he noticed that the moved *Furious 7*, the seventh instalment of the car crazy *Fast and Furious* franchise had just been released. Basil remembered reading about the death of the actor Paul Walker and how they were going to use body doubles and CGI to complete his scenes in the movie. After downloading it he saved it to his hard drive and then went for a drive to Hatton Garden. Unnoticed, he slipped into the depository and found that everything was still in place. Satisfied that the job was still on, he drove home, grabbed a beer from the fridge and set the movie away on his laptop. As he eased himself onto the sofa the movie's theatrical tag line 'Vengeance Hits Home' shot across the screen. Basil afforded himself a wry smile.

Catherine Simpson looked down at the photograph in her hand and then back through the window of the café. The woman she had come to meet was sitting alone at a table in the corner of a crowded room. She had shoulder length grey hair with a band of pink in it. Her eyes were blue, her nose was small and they all sat above full red lips that seemed to carry a constant smile. She looked down at the photograph once more and then lifted the letter that came with it from her pocket, and although she could remember the warm words within it, that didn't stop her hands from shaking. In her mind the words came. You don't know her. It's been thirty-seven years. You have a family that love you. What could you possibly gain from getting to know her? Why now, after so long, why? Catherine closed her eyes, shook her fists and then slid both hands into her pockets. She then turned to walk away. She never knew what made her look through the window but she did. The woman was standing with her hands clasped together as if in prayer. The eyes were moist and the lips were trembling. Catherine took another few steps and then opened the door to the café. A few moments later she was standing before Angela Shaw. After an uneasy silence she plucked up the courage to speak. It was just one word but it was enough to set them both crying before hugging each other. Angela Shaw had waited a lifetime for this. A lifetime of anguish and hope that had just ended with the word 'Mum'.

As mother and daughter were joined together once more not too far away a certain little gang was about to lose two of its members. Even though Basil had carried out a further inspection of the depository and passed the information down the line, Collins and Perkins could not raise Reader. Collins was calling his number and Perkins was at the gates of his house. After a full hour of trying they both gave up. They didn't know it but Reader was sitting in his bathroom being sick and was in no position to move.

Forty-five minutes later Kenny Collins drove his own white Mercedes to Hatton Garden and that's where he parked up next to the white van that had to be driven by Billy Lincoln. The streets were very quiet for a Saturday evening and when Danny Jones went for a fifteen-minute stroll he never met a single person. Back at the van he met Basil and they were met by Terry Perkins and Carl Wood. As soon as the latter discovered that Brian Reader was a no show he went into immediate panic mode. After he had a fifteen-minute shit fit, Basil gave him an ultimatum. It was clear that Wood had lost the bottle to continue and when he let everybody know that he was pulling out it was Jones that reminded him about staying silent. As soon as he left the scene Basil went around the gang and they all confirmed it was business as usual. At that Collins set off towards his lookout post, Jones grabbed the replacement ram and Basil made his way back to 88-90 Hatton Garden.

This time around the atmosphere in the vault room was more relaxed. They laughed and joked about possible songs for what they were about to do. Lincoln opted for *'Take The Money And Run'* by the Steve Miller Band. Perkins chose *'Crime Of The Century'* by Supertramp, and Basil chose *'Smooth Criminal'* by Michael Jackson. Jones thought the apt song would be *'You Can Leave Your Hatton'* but wasn't sure if Joe Cocker spelt it that way. When the banter stopped Jones got down to business. It took him just fifteen minutes to set the ram up and twenty minutes after that the backing plate on the visible cabinet broke away from its retraining bolts. Two minutes after that it fell forward and thumped the floor. Everyone remained silent for a moment and then they all got together to look through the hole. The site of the security boxes brought a smile to all of their faces. Basil tapped Jones on the shoulder and as he moved away Basil climbed through the hole and stood up inside the vault itself. Jones was by his side in less than a minute. Both men shook hands and then Basil asked for the tools they were going to need. As drills, hammers and crow bars were passed through he let Jones sort them out. He was more interested in getting the boxes right. As he took a piece of paper from his pocket and began to double check the numbers on it while Lincoln and Perkins began to arrange the bins. The bags they pulled from them were all clearly labelled with what had to go inside.

Jones fired up the drill and Basil held his arm. "Remember what I said, we do this by the numbers. When we have enough to fill the bags we call it a day, ok?"

Jones nodded and Basil tapped the first box from his list. It took just thirty seconds to drill through the locks. The box inside contained five black velvet bags of sparkling diamonds. Basil poured the contents of one into the hand of Jones. He just stood there and looked at the glistening, shimmering and sparkling reasons as to why it had all been worth the effort. The diamonds were passed through the hole, another box was tapped and drilled and so it went on. Twenty-five boxes later Perkins and Lincoln had bags of diamonds, watches, rings, necklaces, earrings, bracelets, brooches, pendants, lockets, medallions, sovereigns, and wads of bank notes. At that they took a break for tea so that Perkins could celebrate his sixty-eighth birthday with an insulin jab and a few tablets and Lincoln could give his aching back a rub. Collins was given a few clicks on the radio and when the all-clear came back, Basil picked up the drill. Number twenty-six on his list was opened a short while after. It soon became a production line once more with Jones passing the boxes whilst Lincoln and Perkins did the sorting. After opening box fifty, Basil and Jones climbed out of the vault. The bags were checked and once everyone was satisfied, they told everyone to take a break. More tea was poured and Lincoln produced a container of sandwiches. They all settled down with their backs against the wall and their feet resting on the biggest payday they were ever going to see. It was Perkins who broke the silence.

"I'm going to buy a nice place somewhere quiet. I'm going to have a wine cellar full of French classics. My car will be a Bentley Continental GT V8 S. I'm going to visit Australia, New Zealand and China. After that I think I will buy a few properties to rent out to the high flyers and then live the easy life."

Lincoln nodded. "I'm going to pick somewhere nice and warm and move there. Somewhere with orchards or vineyards would be nice. Employ a few people, have some standing in a local community, be respected. I like the idea of South America but to be honest it will probably be France."

Everyone turned to Basil. "I have the place I always wanted, and the car, and the people. I have had them for some time now. I'm not complaining but after a while it really does lose its sparkle. That's why I'm back here. This makes me more alive than anything I know."

Everyone was now looking at Jones. "I'm going to see God and exchange all my money with him for some special powers. I'm going to cure cancer and AIDS. I'm going to turn everything that is black into white and vice versa, just for a while, mind. Just so that people can understand how other people feel. I'm going to send water to Africa and Robert Mugabe to hell. All types of war will be outlawed as will Branston pickle. How anyone can like that stuff is beyond me. Last but not least I would ask for Elvis back, he died way before his time anyway. I know you may think that I am nuts and what I have just said is impossible but right now I believe it can happen and I choose not to be corrected."

Everyone smiled and then Jones got to his feet and climbed back through the hole. Basil followed him and by the time he had the list to hand Jones was waving the drill in the air.

"Keen aren't we?" asked Basil.

"Yeah," replied Jones. "I want to meet Elvis again."

"And I thought it was the pickle thing." At that Basil tapped the next box and Jones cut into it. For the next seventy-five minutes they worked their way through another twenty boxes. It was Lincoln and Perkins that called for a time out. All the bags were just about full. Basil gave Jones the nod and asked him to check on the haul. Once he climbed back through the hold Basil picked up the drill and carried on. Just three boxes on and Jones gave him a shout. There was no room left in any of the bags and so Basil conceded that it was time to call it quits. As Jones continued to help Lincoln and Perkins shift the bags he could hear a right old racket coming from the vault. "Is everything ok in there?" he shouted.

"Yeah, just making sure we haven't missed anything," replied Basil.

Jones shook his head at the attention to detail before getting on the radio. Collins checked his watch. It was 05.30hrs, it was Sunday and it was time to thank the Lord. After a small outburst of faith he acknowledged the signal, left the premises and made his way to the van.

As Jones, Lincoln and Perkins carried the bags up to the fire escape Basil took the CDs from the central consoles that linked the CCTV cameras. At exactly 05.40hrs Collins received the final signal and drove into position. Five minutes later the gang left Hatton garden for the final time. Twenty minutes later Lincoln departed the van and got into the Audi he had parked earlier. Twenty-five minutes after that Perkins was dropped off by the VW Golf. One hour later all three vehicles pulled up outside the units that overlooked the O2 Arena. As they all approached the riverside one the doors opened for them. When they stepped inside they were met by Freddie the Fence and the biggest Oompa Loompas they had ever seen. There were six of them and they were dressed in white coveralls, white gloves, green netted hats and their faces were all bright red from the preparatory work they had been doing. Before them were eight tables covered in weighing scales, magnifying glasses, inspection tools, cleaners, collection pouches and boxes. When Freddie clapped his hands the gang jolted out of their initial shock and when he pointed to the table on the end they automatically deposited the bags there.

As the production line began Freddie pulled Basil to one side for a chat and Jones made some tea. That's when Perkins brought up the subject no-one else wanted to mention.

"What about Brian and Carl's share?"

"They don't deserve anything," replied Lincoln. "Anyone who bails out knows the score."

"Is that right?" questioned Jones. "Even when they put more into this than you did?"

Lincoln stood there in silence and went a bright shade of red.

"They should get something," added Collins. "Even if it's a reduced percentage."

"They get a full share," announced the approaching Basil. "We are a team and the last thing we need is for the business to think that we aren't. Remember it's not just about the money it's about the prestige. Do you want to be regarded as the best or not?"

"Everyone nodded."

A few moments later Freddie called them all over to one of the tables. There were eight small bags positioned in a line.

"In each of the bags is twenty thousand pounds in cash. In addition there is around twenty thousand pounds in jewellery. It's mid-range watches, necklaces and bracelets, the kind of stuff that you can move on easily without arousing suspicion. Let the heat die down before you start and when you do keep away from any of the big dealers on your manor as one of them is bound to be on the police payroll. As for the rest of it, as agreed, I will move it all, take my agreed fee and then park it for you."

"How do we let you know when we are ready for it?" asked Lincoln.

"You don't," interrupted Basil. "Freddie here will keep tabs on you all and you will only get it when it's safe to do so. The last thing we need is for anyone of you to rush into something stupid and bring the rest of us down with you. We do this right. Believe me I have done it this way before and it does work. That's why I'm still here. "

No-one gave him an argument on that one.

POUNDS STERLING

Mick Dea began his Sunday morning at church. It's not something people often said or wrote about him. Although he had been brought up by two church-going Catholics and frog-marched there every weekend, it all ended as soon as he left home. Mick had always struggled with his faith. For him there were far more questions than answers, and as he was a man that dealt in fact, he tended to lean towards the scientific teachings as to the spiritual ones. Mick was in St. Mary's church for two reasons. The first was that it was less than a one-hour drive from his home; the second was going to have to wait.

Although the opening hymn was one he remembered from school, he never joined in with the congregation.

Christ the Lord is risen today, Alleluia!
Earth and heaven in chorus say, Alleluia!
Raise your joys and triumphs high, Alleluia!
Sing, ye heavens, and earth reply, Alleluia!

The first reading came from Matthew:27 and described the moment when Jesus had cried out in a loud voice and the curtain of the temple was torn in two from top to bottom. There was a Psalm giving thanks to the Lord for he is good and that was followed by a second reading from Peter that spoke of a new birth. The Gospel acclamation dealt with belief from those that had not seen. The modern input came from a song by Chris Tomlin that included the lines;

And I will rise when He calls my name.
No more sorrow, no more pain.
I will rise on eagles' wings.
Before my God fall on my knees.
And rise, I will rise.

The remainder of the mass was instantly forgettable apart from a little story about ancient justice that Father Thomas had shared with his flock. It concerned two known thieves that had been arrested for stealing money from a member of the regional senate. Although the thief that committed the crime had taken on a lawyer known for his integrity he still wanted to make sure he got away with it. That's when he told him that he intended on sending two pigs and six chickens to the senator in question as proof of his wealth and respect. The lawyer made it abundantly clear that it was the last thing he should do as it would be seen as a bribe and he would surely be found guilty. He asked the thief to let the system of justice take care of it all. When the case came before the magistrate the innocent thief was found guilty and the guilty thief walked free. When the lawyer mentioned how justice had prevailed the thief then informed him that he had indeed sent the pigs and chickens but added that he had put the other thief's name on them.

Dea's mind wandered through most of the service and continued until after everyone had gone. It was only when Father Thomas asked if he could help with anything did Dea introduce himself and then approached the second reason for him being in the church. Moments later they were both in the vestry and Father Thomas was going through the latest church register.

"Ahh, here we are, Sean Murphy. The only known contact is his daughter, Angela."

"She lives in Bristol and has never visited the grave for years," replied Dea.

"And the flowers are recent?"

Dea flipped through the photographs on his phone and then showed Father Thomas the grave of Sean Murphy. "According to the card they were left by someone known as 'B'."

The priest looked up to the heavens before announcing, "Walter and Percy."

"Who?" replied Dea.

Father Thomas led the DC to a tool shed at the rear of the church and that's where they found them both leaning on shovels, drinking tea. Walter couldn't recall seeing anyone at the plot in question but Percy did mention something. It was red hair.

Lincoln and Perkins went straight to the Old Wheatsheaf pub in Enfield where they met up with Hugh Doyle. He handed them a key to the office in his workshop and they handed him a bag of money. As he left for home and a safe place to store it, they entered the office and poured the contents of their bags onto the desk so that they give it a close inspection. Freddie had been right, the stuff would but easy to shift around without arousing too much suspicion. Happy with the result they both went to the pub for lunch.

Collins went straight home and ran the money through a counting machine; it was all there. After that he divided the rest of the stash into smaller groups and then took a walk to the nearest public phone. He made a few calls and arranged some meetings for later on in the day. He then walked home and climbed into bed. He fell asleep in minutes.

Jones called in on his brother in law and asked him to place on of the bags in his loft. He gave him one thousand pounds for doing so. He then went to Edmonton Cemetery in Enfield to check on two graves that contained relatives of his former partner, Valerie. One carried the name of her father Sidney James Hart and the other was her uncle Sidney John Hart. Jones stopped long enough to lay flowers and check the security arrangements, they were non-existent. He now had the two places he was going to stash his part of the haul. All he needed now was nightfall and a shovel.

Reader made two phone calls but neither was answered. He then went for a walk to buy some newspapers. He then flipped through all the twenty-four hour news channels that the TV had to offer. After that he went for a drive that included various radio channels and a trip through Hatton Garden. Deep down he knew it was all useless but he had to do it anyway. He eventually went home, poured himself a drink and dreamt of what should have been.

Wood spent the day with family and then during a quiet moment hid himself away in his bedroom. Strewn across the bed were envelopes that contained all the debt he owned. That's when a little voice in his head reminded him that he had been just twelve hours away from throwing them all in the bin. That's when the headache came. The pain that followed seemed to have no end.

Basil returned to his apartment and pulled the spreadsheet down from his study wall. After shredding and burning it he had a power nap, showered, had a late lunch and then surfed the Internet for a holiday. After several searches around the globe he settled on Spain and then Cuba. But he wasn't going to book anything just yet.

As the day came to an end Freddie the Fence received four text messages. The first was from Holland, the second was from France, the third was from Belgium and the fourth was from Switzerland. All four couriers that had sent them had made deposits without any drama and meetings had been arranged with contacts for the following day. It was the calm before the storm.

It was Tuesday 7th April and the world woke up to the continued investigation into the Airbus A320-211 that had crashed into the French Alps killing all one hundred and fifty passengers on board. That was followed by more tragedy when a mass shooting at the Garissa University College in Kenya perpetrated by the terrorist organisation known as Al-Shabaab had resulted in one hundred and forty-eight deaths. Those watching were used to such stories and often wondered where all the uplifting stories had gone; the lifesaving ones, the cure-finding ones, even the ones that weren't politically or morally correct but put a smile on your face. Security guard Kelvin Stockwell was about to put that right.

At exactly 8.00am Stockwell let himself into 88-90 Hatton Garden. The first thing that hit him was the dusty atmosphere. That was followed by a floor full of discarded tools. Then there were the broken doors and a wall with a bloody great hole in it. That's when he screamed for his colleague Keefer Kamara. At exactly 8.10am all fucking hell broke loose.

The Bavishi family got the first three calls and the Flying Squad got the fourth. Within twenty minutes of getting the call Detective Superintendent Craig Turner, head of the squad and Detective Chief Inspector Paul Johnson were on scene. As they walked through the depository and listened to input from all the staff, nineteen boroughs of police units were alerted and went straight to work. Records were checked, informants got squeezed and certain criminals received rude awakenings.

When DC Jamie Day arrived on scene he was put in charge of locking it down so that a tight lid could be put on it all for now. Within ten minutes the *Daily Mirro*r newspaper knew about it. Within twenty minutes Sky News had it as a breaking story. Within thirty minutes former robbers and criminologists were being lined up to give their professional take on what had happened. Within the hour every member of the gang got the nod.

According to the initial reports an organised gang from Eastern Europe had stolen fourteen million pounds in jewellery and cash. Three hundred local retailers were reported to be already helping police with their enquirers. As insurance firms braced themselves for the backlash and the stock market went into a slight frenzy, editors across the globe fell over themselves at the prospect of getting the story that everyone wanted. TV screens were filled with black and white footage of the actual vault being shown to the world in the 1948. The word 'safe' was used in every clever headline that could be thought of and local residents lined up to be interviewed about the robbery. Noticeable by their absence were various known members of the local underworld. Two local families that shared control of the manor were said to be seething. Both firms even went as far as having a hastily arranged meeting to ensure that neither of them had any part in it. The discussions were cordial but warnings were exchanged in such a way as they could not be construed as threats. It was a fine line that was being walked as the last thing they both needed right now was a turf war.

Each member of the gang turned on their respective TVs and watched the drama unfold. The stories before them jumped from the size of the haul, to the possible responsible parties, onto how it was done and back again. Most journalists reported that the gang would be miles away; some even went as far as saying it was the perfect crime. A few of the seasoned ones kept their feet on the ground and gave measured offerings. They were the ones that knew one mistake, one piece of luck, one thread of a clue would have the police crawling all over it so that arrests could be made.

Some of the public were convinced they were watching the crime of the century. Some of the gang were sure not even Sherlock Holmes could work it out. Some of the Flying Squad officers that were watching recently obtained CCTV footage were convinced they had the answers to it all.

When Mick Dea returned to his office he was surprised to see no copy file for Hatton Garden in his in tray. That went to mild shock when he went to the tactical room that had been set up and his name wasn't amongst the officers listed on the door. Back at his desk he spent two hours updating case notes and pacing the floor. In that time a secretary handed him two envelopes. The first contained a copy invoice from the treasury for the six cushion cut diamonds that were left in the box of Stuart Greenwood. Their account had just gone up by twenty thousand pounds. The second envelope contained a handwritten letter from Angela Shaw. The contents were heartfelt and well-received. No sooner had they been filed, Dea got the piece of paper he had wanted. Five minutes later he was sitting in the office of DI Mark Rearden.

"Mick, I am leaving you off the main investigation on this one as I have a special duty for you."

"You don't want me to find them?"

"Detective Superintendent Craig Turner has already got a handpicked team in place and as we already have CCTV footage and a few leads from informants, the lads will be able to cope without you on this one."

"Right."

Rearden retrieved a stack of files from his top drawer and placed them on his desk.

"We have a bit of a puzzle here, the sort that you are good at. So I had a chat with Turner and he's given the green light for you to run with it."

"Sounds intriguing?"

"The gang we are after are local. They knew how things worked and what they needed to pull it off."

"Inside job."

"From the looks of things I would say yes. You see, from a total of nine hundred and ninety-eight boxes they only opened seventy-three."

"So they knew what was in them?"

"Yep, I don't believe for one minute it was a random hit."

"So what's the puzzle?"

Rearden tapped the files on his desk. "Although they only opened seventy-three boxes they did have a go at a further eight."

"Have a go?"

"Hammered them but never got as far as reaching the contents."

"Strange."

"It gets stranger," began Rearden as he picked up the files and began to fan them over the desk. "Box 971 in the name of Yuri Tavlenko, box 801 Ralph Wilson, box 767 Gavin Foble, box 492 Massimo Alessi, box 286 Juliette Roux, box 113 Dwight Shunter and box 18 Karl Brandt." At that Rearden held up the last file. "This one is box 375."

Dea stiffened. "Sean Murphy."

"Got it in one. All of the box owners in question have been notified but as of yet none of them have come forward. Now maybe it's just coincidence or just maybe this lot are linked in some way. Maybe someone is playing a game with us. Whatever it is I want you to find out, Mick. You will need to gets your skates on. If I'm right, that depository is heading out of business as no-one is going to trust them after this."

"So the owners will wait until the dust settles and the quickly empty their boxes."

"Exactly, and then they could disappear forever. Keep that in mind as you may have to get to them all before you get to Murphy. Whatever you do, keep me up to date and if there is anything you need, just shout."

"I may need access to other parts of the investigation."

"I will add you to the list and advise the lads that this is a one-way service. I don't want any of them knowing what you are doing. I don't want you being compromised on this. I don't know what it is but I have a feeling about this one."

Dea nodded in agreement.

"With a bit of luck you might just crack it before I hang up my boots."

"When are you going?"

"I plan on leaving at the end of the next tax year."

"Anything planned?"

"I have that place in Spain so I might just base myself there and take the odd trip."

"You've earned it."

"Well I'll be able to relax in the thought that I left this place in good hands."

There was no need for any words. Both men exchanged a respected nod and parted company.

As forensic teams continued to work through the crime scene, the team at Scotland Yard were frantically working through every standard operation, lead and clue. Forty-eight hours in and Manish Bavishi, the manager of the depository, still couldn't be located. As family, friends and officers attempted to make contact with him, his name shot up the involvement list. Two names that were removed from it were the two leaders of the family gangs that controlled the manor. The police were given direct assurance on both accounts, and in addition advised that if any names came to light then the information would be negotiated.

All ferries and airports were checked for sudden departures and the police units of thirty-two countries were web linked on need to know files just in case anything came to light. Seventy-two box owners were given the grim news about their loss. Fifty-three made arrangements for co-operative interviews and catalogue checks on what had been removed. Nineteen refused and in doing so were added to a watch list.

The Crimestoppers number that had been issued received over two hundred calls. Forty-six were prank, a further hundred were useless and the remainder were given task numbers and were being checked out. Fourteen top informants were met for polite chats, money and contact numbers were exchanged and the information circle began to widen. The CCTV footage gave up two vital clues and they weren't people, they were vehicles. When the white van in the footage had its registration checked by Automatic Number Plate Recognition (ANPR) it was found to be using a bogus number. Rather than move away from it officers checked the timing of the van and noted the registrations of the ten vehicles that came before it and the ten that followed. The van appeared on screen eight times and on every occasion one vehicle fell with the timing check. It was a white Mercedes, plate number CP13 BGY that belonged to a naughty boy by the name of Kenny Collins. The squad had their first piece of good news and then immediately received the worst.

When Dea had an initial look into the files he took from Rearden the first thing he did was put in a written request for access to six plain clothed officers and three researchers. Two hours after that the six officers were being given new orders and on the researcher front there was a Foot Tapper, a Pen Twirler and a Face Puller in his office.

Each of them was given two box numbers along with the records that went with them. Dea kept one file for himself. He had no intention of just overseeing anything, for him it was all about the detail. As he began to read the opening report the three men that were at the heart of it all were sharing a coffee in a quiet café not far from the Houses of Parliament. With the polite introductions over it was Yuri Tavlenko that spoke first. After shaking his head at Viktor Ramere he turned to Dave Pinter and announced, "I will give you exactly ten seconds to get rid of your photographer or this meeting is over."

Pinter looked on in surprise.

"He was there in the park and right now he is across the street trying to act like a tourist. It must be said that he really is terrible at it."

Pinter pulled a face and opened his arms.

Yuri looked down to his watch "Seven, six, five..."

"Ok," admitted the editor before raising his hand and waving. Once the photographer left the scene Yuri looked across to Victor. "I thought you were someone I could trust."

"It wasn't my doing," he blurted. "I had..."

"Nothing to do with it," continued Pinter. "I was just trying to make sure as there is a lot of money at stake here not to mention the good name of the paper. I can only apologise and assure you that from here on in you will deal with me and me alone and I will stand by any agreement we make."

Victor patted Yuri on the knee.

Yuri nodded. "You have questions to ask so you may as well begin."

Pinter took out a note pad and pen. "What was in the cocktail they used?"

"It was a liquored mixture of metenolone, trenbolone and oxandrolone and it worked by reducing the recovery times after gruelling training sessions."

"Liquored."

"From men, the drugs were dissolved in Chivas Whiskey and for women, they used Martini Vermouth."

"And it really worked?"

"You saw the results," interrupted Victor. "Look at the success of the cross country ski team and then there's the two veteran bobsledders that won two golds. None of them had the pedigree for that."

Pinter nodded and moved on. "How many samples were expunged?"

"One hundred and eighteen," replied Yuri.

"And you have proof?"

"Of course."

"It must have been a well-run exercise if no-one got caught."

"Yes, they did. Eight months after the operation was in full swing there was a report by the World Anti-Doping that touched on the edges of it. After that all Russian athletes at the 2012 London Games came in for closer scrutiny. There was a race walker by the name of Elena Lashmanova."

"I remember her," said Victor. "She won gold and then tested positive."

"Didn't that give the game away?" asked Pinter.

"No, you see she had also been taking additional substances for stamina. It did raise a few eyebrows though and further investigations did take place. They did find a few minor infringements."

"But nothing concrete."

"The Russians have someone on the inside."

"Who?"

"You are not paying me for that, Mr. Pinter. And even if you offered I would not accept. I value my life too much."

"So this individual is well-connected."

"Let's just say they have a nasty habit that needs a lot of funding."

Pinter noted that Yuri had not used the words he or she. He flipped back through his note pad to a section he had scribbled before the meeting. "This Dr. Grigory Rodchenkov, the one that had been running it all since 2005, how did he swap the samples?"

Yuri pulled a piece of paper from his pocket and opened it up to reveal a graphic of the anti-doping laboratory in Sochi, and pointed. "This is the secured area and right here you can see the official sample room. On the opposite side of the east wall, outside of the secured area is a storage facility, or that is what people thought. It was in fact a secret laboratory with designated technicians." Yuri tapped the east wall. "There was a hold in the wall covered by caps on either end. The samples were passed from one lab to the other as required, and before you ask I do have photographs of both walls showing the detail."

Pinter nodded. "Tell me about the bottles used to keep the samples in, I thought they were supposed to be tamper-proof."

"In late 2013 Rodchenkov and his team received a visit from the intelligence service. Apparently the F.S.B. had set up a team under instruction from

Putin. They were tasked with ensuring the whole process worked and from the start they quickly established that the key to it all was the bottles. They come with toothed metal rings that are self-locking and the world leader is a Swiss company called Berlinger."

"And they had the contract for Sochi?" asked Pinter.

"Yes," replied Victor. "According to reports it took the F.S.B. just six months to work out how to beat the system."

"How did they do it?"

Victor produced two small bottles and placed them on the table. He poured coffee into both of them and sealed the lids. He then passed one over to Pinter. "Open it."

Pinter did just that and the metal ring around the lip of the bottle broke open. He tried to seal it again but gave up after a few attempts as he could see that it was impossible. Yuri then handed him the second bottle. When Pinter opened it the metal ring remained intact. He sealed it and then went through the same process a few times. As Pinter sat stunned Yuri continued with the explanation. "Every athlete has to give two samples. The first one is tested at the games and the second one is put into storage for a period of ten years just in case something is discovered some time down the line. Technology never sleeps. At Sochi targeted athletes were given the duplicate bottles to give samples. When the technician checked the first one he would note the result and pass it and both bottles through the wall. It would be rechecked by Rodchenkov's team. You see they had to keep an eye on every sample given to see if different athletes gave off different signals. That way they could monitor dosage for that athlete. If clear both samples would simply get transferred to the Berlinger supplied bottles and passed back. If the samples showed any sign of the cocktail, then they would be kept by Rodchenkov's team and the clean samples they had on ice would be put into Berlinger bottles and passed back."

"So according to the authorities the exact number of supplied Berlinger bottles were being recorded and used and so no-one could query the numbers," said Pinter.

"Exactly."

Pinter picked up both bottles and checked them against each other. He couldn't find a single difference. "Who makes the duplicate bottles?"

"A company I know," replied Yuri.

"I need to hit the right spot with this," mused Pinter.

"You will know that when sports minister Vitaly Mutko releases a statement of surprise and denial through TASS and follows it up with a press conference. Shortly after that Dr. Rodchenkov will resign."

"By design," smirked Pinter.

"By his own choosing," beamed Yuri. "Mind you he may have to give his 'Order of Friendship' medal back."

"And when this is over that will probably be the only medal that gets returned."

Pinter wrote 'Medal campaign, public support' on his pad.

Yuri tapped the table and when Pinter looked up he whispered, "Russia could be banned from future Olympic Games over this. Just think of the shockwave that will reverberate around the world when that happens. Think of the prestige for the people that fought for justice and managed to win against a superpower. Think of the knock-on effect and what might happen to the football world cup that Russia is due to host in 2018. You are looking at a first class set up that would make Lance Armstrong's team look like a bunch of amateurs. The only question left is mine. Do you want it or not?"

Victor clasped his hands together and held his breath.

Pinter closed his note pad, collected his pen and put them both away. "Let's discuss the price."

"Let's not," replied Yuri getting to his feet.

"Easy now," replied Pinter holding up both hands. "I will give you one hundred for the story but I want the bottles and the name of the company that supplied them."

Yuri picked up the bottles and slid them both into his pocket. "One hundred for the story and the company but the bottles are out of the question. Take it or leave it, Mr. Pinter, it's not negotiable and my patience is beginning to wear thin."

Pinter stood up and offered his hand.

Yuri took it.

Victor gasped for air and then offered his hand.

Yuri gave it a slight squeeze.

As the Pen Twirler received a call from the unit that had been following Juliette Roux, she sat outside the office of Mohamed Al-Fayed, and from the available selection of newspapers she chose the *Daily Mirror*. The front page was all about CCTV footage that had been obtained on what they were calling a real life Reservoir Dog-style heist at Hatton Garden. According to the timelined report it had been carried out by a gang of at least six members and for the benefit of their readers the paper had given each one a nickname. The was a Mr, Ginger, Mr. Strong, Mr. Montana, The Gent, The Tall Man and The Old Man. Juliette began to read the story and look at the pictures that had been obtained from the CCTV camera. There was a picture of a red-haired man carrying a bin bag into the building. Next to that was a bulk of a man in workmen's clothing hauling what looked like a heavy wheelie bin down to the vault. Further down the piece was a picture of a white van besides a grainy shot of someone in a sports hoodie emblazoned with the words 'Montana 93', carrying boxes of tools.

A few columns later came a picture of a dapper man in smart city shoes wearing a dust mask. In the picture he was looking up to man wearing a balaclava, a hard hat and a high-vis jacket. The so-called mature raider was shown in the final section of the piece leaving the building with what looked like part of the haul. Just as Juliette smiled at the sheer audacity a polite cough from the secretary now standing over her was a signal that the man she had come to see was ready to receive her. After collecting her things, she was shown into a large lavishly decorated office that surrounded the small frame of a pleasant-faced man who approached her with an outstretched hand. Juliette accepted the welcome, turned down the offer of refreshment and was guided to a place on a nearby couch. Al-Fayed sat beside her as a sign of informality and as an attempt to ease any fears the visitor may have. It worked, Juliette felt comfortable in the surroundings and Al-Fayed shared a few easy exchanges with her before getting down to business.

"Well my dear, in your letter you mentioned an item that Isabelle kept from the auction."

"Yes, it was document the King kept in a small red case in his study."

"I remember that case, it contained two letters that were eventually purchased by the Royal family."

"According to my mother there was a third document kept in there." At that Juliette reached for an envelope she had brought and retrieved a document from it. "It is believed by most that there was only one such document but the King demanded that two should be made. One of them was handed over to the government of the day and the other was kept by himself." At that she passed a single piece of paper over to Al-Fayed. As soon as he saw the insignia at the top of the page his hand began to shake. Juliette took hold of it and whispered, "It has the same effect on me." Al-Fayed smiled and then began to read;

INSTRUMENT OF ABDICATION

I, Edward the Eighth, of Great Britain, Ireland and the British Dominions beyond the Seas, King, Emperor of India, do hereby declare My irrevocable determination to denounce the Throne for Myself and for My descendants, and My desire that effect should be given to this Instrument of Abdication immediately.

In token whereof I have hereunto set My hand this tenth day of December, nineteen hundred and thirty six, in the presence of the witnesses whose signatures are subscribed.

SIGNED AT
FORT BELVEDERE
IN THE PRESENCE OF

Al-Fayed looked down to the signature of King Edward VIII that sat over those of his younger brothers Prince Albert, Duke of York, next in line for the throne, Prince Henry, Duke of Gloucester and Prince George, Duke of Kent.

"Oh my!" he gasped. "This is incredible. Many a document has passed through my hand but none of them have ever held the importance of this. What were you going to do with it?"

Juliette shrugged her shoulders. "There was a time when I thought it could be sold or auctioned but at the same time I thought about what laws have or could been broken. Then there would be the reaction from the government, the Royal Family, and more importantly, the people of the nation. Mr. Al-Fayed, I have come to you for help and advice. My only intention is to protect the good name of my mother. I am here because of a moment of weakness and it would be a shame if all the dedication and service she gave was to be lost to something like this."

Al-Fayed thought before he spoke. "Does anybody else know about this?"

"Nobody."

"And you are prepared to leave it in my care?"

"Sir, I am giving back to you in the hope that you will do what is right."

Al-Fayed gripped her hand. "I am honoured that you have placed such trust in me and you have my word that we shall bring this to a conclusion that will be satisfactory to all those concerned."

A few moments later Juliette left the office with what seemed like a weight off her shoulders. As soon as she entered the lift Al-Fayed picked up the phone and pushed a single button.

"Yes Sir."

"The girl in the lift. She has a secret. Follow her, find it and let me know."

"It shall be done."

The Flying Squad were furious about the lack of appreciation and co-operation shown by the *Daily Mirror*. It is well known that detectives share certain pieces of information with the press so that they can use it correctly and in return expect the same. The editor of the *Daily Mirror* couldn't see any wrong in what he had done until he was told in confidence that the squad had identified one of the gang and he had just put an on-going surveillance operation in jeopardy. Unbeknown to the paper the squad had just recently obtained permission to put a tap on the white Mercedes of Kenny Collins. The researching Foot Tapper knew about it but he was busily checking on the bank details of Gavin Foble, a soldier that was currently with a nurse at Company HQ. They were both sitting outside the office of the Senior Medical Officer (SMO) going through the final section of a questionnaire.

Q. Have you experienced or witnessed a life-threatening event that caused intense fear, helplessness or horror?

A. Yes.

Q. Do you have repeated, distressing memories or dreams?

A. Yes.

Q. Do you suffer from flashbacks and struggle to focus with what is happening?

A. Yes.

Q. Do you have bouts of intense physical and or emotional distress when exposed to things that remind you of certain events?

A. Yes.

Q. Do you suffer from bouts of anger that make you want to lash out?

A. Yes.

Q. Do you feel detached from certain people you once thought close?

A. Yes.

Q. Do you ever feel worthless or guilty?

A. Yes.

Q. Have you ever discussed any or all the above in detail with a family member, friend or professional?

A. No.

Once complete the nurse left Foble to run back over his answers whilst she went in search of the SMO. He was just about half-way through it when a shabby-looking figure plonked himself down in the next seat. The first thing Noble got a whiff of was stale alcohol, after that it was an accent from the north east.

"Alreet bonnie lad?"

"What?" replied Noble, taking his first glance at what was trying to communicate with him.

"Are ye alreet?"

"I'm fine," guessed Noble. "How are you?"

"Shite," came the reply. "It's a waste of time this like. I see you've done the daft questions so it just the interrogation to go."

"Is it that bad?"

"Load of bollocks. All they do is search for some hidden secret you may or may not have. If you don't have one, then they will create one for you, make you believe you had a sheltered upbringing or you had it so good you never knew the real world until it was all too late."

"Did it lead anywhere?"

"What with me like?"

Noble nodded.

The shabby figure rolled his shoulders. "I had a bad time in Afghanistan, bonnie lad. First tour went ok. Usual skirmishes, etc. Second tour was ending the same way until we got a last minute shout on a flare up in a town on the river Helmand. As soon as we arrived we had immediate contact with the Taliban. A prayer meeting had just turned into a war zone. Chaos ruled as civi's were screaming and running everywhere. Usual drama, plenty of incoming. As we took up position a group of locals appeared from nowhere, saw us and then headed for cover. They knew they had to get well out of it as the Taliban were homing in on us now. As they ran one young kid, must have been six or seven years old, got trampled to the ground. The rest of the group didn't look back, they never did. Anyway, as he tried to get to his feet the incoming rounds started to find their range. They wanted us but it was clear that as we took on the engagement a loose one was sure to come from somewhere. I hesitated for a moment and then took off. I raced towards him. I could see a few cover spots so all I needed to do was grab the kid and get to one. As the drama intensified I was screaming at him, hoping he could pick up my voice in between the volleys of fire. He eventually saw me. He was trembling and crying but instinct helped him to reach out for me. I got to within a few feet, our eyes locked, he smiled and that's when it happened. The ground erupted around us. I remember the pain, the clear sky, the blurred images of the lads, angry voices and then nothing. I lived, got patched up and sent home. They talked, I didn't, and eventually I just went on the drink. I thought it would help with the flashbacks and the shakes but it just made them worse. It doesn't make for good reading. And do you know something? If just one of them had said the words I needed it would have helped me along the way."

"What words?"

The shabby figure just shook his head. "It doesn't matter, so what's your story?"

Foble spent the next ten minutes talking about the Falklands. The shabby figure hung on every word. When it was over he asked, "How many people have you told that story to?"

"Just a couple of people I suppose, and you of course."

"Not nice eh! Did anyone them say anything to you?"
"Just the usual, keep the chin up old boy and all that."
"They should have said what I wanted to hear."
"Which is?"

The shabby figure pulled on his arm, leant over and whispered, "It's alright to cry."

Foble turned and looked him in the eye.

"It's alright to cry," repeated the shabby figure.

Foble began to well up and his eyes glazed over.

"It's ok Gavin, let it go. It's alright to cry."

At that moment Foble burst into tears. As he bubbled away the nurse returned. "Ah Doctor McKeown this is Mr. Foble. The shabby figure got to his feet and smiled. "We have already met."

As the sky darkened on the outside of The Castle pub the mood on the inside began to match it as Brian Reader learnt how the job had gone. Terry Perkins was there to gloat. Kenny Collins was there to add the detail. The two officers from the Flying Squad were there thanks to the tap they had put on his car. As it was their first venture into the pub, they took a lip reader to see if anything of worth would be discussed. As they took in a torrent of information on the heist a certain Face Puller back at base was just closing the file on box 113. As he made a note to contact various authorities in America the owner of the box slipped unnoticed into a discrete internet café just off The Strand.

It took Dwight Shunter six hours and eight phone calls to get the email address he needed and now it was time to put it to use. Across the pond, Detective John Towler had just finished a sandwich at his desk when the surprise arrived on screen. The game began.

Is the FBI file on the Isabella Stewart Gardner Museum robbery still open?

Who wants to know?

Someone who was involved in it?

Towler moved forward in his chair, picked up the phone and asked the Information Technology (I.T.) to carry out an immediate PC trace. With the available hand, he punched away at the keyboard.

Can you prove it?
Not even Columbo could prove it. Mind you, you could employ Banacek.

Although Towler had the files on the robbery nearby he didn't need to refer to them to check on the references to the characters played by Peter Falk and George Peppard. There were six calling cards left behind by the robbers and each of them contained a famous crime-solving expert. At the time, the police took the decision not to make the information public knowledge just in case it could be used as a communication link with the people involved. After twenty-five years of waiting it had just done exactly that.

Do you have a name?
Fred is a name, let's just go with that.
Ok Fred, what are you after?
I want a payment and immunity from prosecution.
We can discuss that when I know what you have.

The I.T. got the required fix on the UK location and advised that if an interception was required then a local asset could be on scene in forty-five minutes. Towler put it on hold.

It's not up for discussion, bye.
Wait, give me something, something I can use to prove who you are. If it's good, then we can speak again in twenty-four hours.

An attachment arrived with no words. It contained a picture showing how the painting of The Concert by Jan Vermeer used to look when it hung on the wall of the museum. With it was a name, an address and a map. Towler recognised the painting immediately and in addition knew of the banker that had been identified with it. In a moment of doubt, he began to type.

How sure are you of this?
Positive. You had better get a warrant.
Can we speak again at the same time tomorrow?
You get one chance.
Until then.

Towler waited for a minute and then rang I.T. They then passed the link details to a safe unit in London along with explicit instructions of when they could carry out an initial surveillance of the target area along with the time they would be needed for a live run. As agents mobilised, Towler met with his boss, secured the resources he needed, obtained a search warrant and set up a briefing room.

RUBIES

Emil Wiener picked up the phone to hear his secretary say, "MK Elazar Stern from The Foundation for the Benefit of Holocaust Victims is on line three." Wiener pressed the button.

"Shalom Aleichem, old friend."

"Shalom Aleichem, Emil."

"How are things in Israel?"

"Much the same, we even get blamed for tsunamis now."

"And the foundation?"

"We are still struggling to make people care. As you know, the survivors should be getting the respect they deserve whilst they are still with us. We don't have a lot of time left."

"What are the numbers now?"

"At last count we had some one hundred and ninety-seven thousand of them living in Israel. We lose thirty-five of them every day."

The number hit Emil hard.

"What about NGOs and volunteers?"

"They are just about filling the gaps left by government but as you know without the funding. We are fighting a losing battle."

"I will do what I can."

"You always have, old friend. We need more people like you. Anyway, the reason for the call is that I have some news for you."

"I am listening."

"Marie Elon died of cancer in 1997. Her daughter Rachel married a doctor by the name of Ari Rivlin. They have a daughter called Nadia."

Emil could not contain himself.

"She is alive?"

"Yes, she is here in Tel Aviv. Can you tell me what this is about?"

"A man came into my office with page from a ledger. All the names on it were from Bergen-Belsen."

Stern stiffened. "Did he give a name?"

"No, but I believe he must have been on the staff there."

"We have the full list of faces and names. I can send a team over."

"Send me the faces and names but there is no need to send anyone. The man is dying."

"He told you that?"

"He didn't have to. I have seen enough of it in my time."

"Yes you have. What do you want me to do?"

"Just send the file. I just need to know who I am dealing with."

"What do you mean?"

"There was a pain in his eyes when he asked me to find the girl. In addition to that he gave me a brooch and I'm sure it belongs to her."

"And you don't believe that he stole it?"

"They got away, Elazar. How many people can you name that got away from that damn place. No, he must have done something to help them."

"I take your point. You said he gave you a page from a ledger. Does that mean you have more names?"

"Yes I have, and I will send them to you in time, you may even get the whole ledger. I just need to make sure that I get to the bottom of this first."

"You trust him?"

"Not all of them were evil, Elazar. Some of them had a heart. Let's just say I want to trust him and right now I am prepared to give him the benefit of the doubt."

"And what about Rachel?"

"What about her?"

"Do you want me to tell her?"

"One step at a time. Let me ask him. Until then take care, my friend."

"And you too."

When the connection ended, Emil made another call. Thirty minutes later copies of both were handed to the Face Puller. Ten minutes after that he played them back to Mick Dea.

Boston banker P.J. Tate Jnr could not believe what he was hearing or seeing. The introduction from Towler had been cordial but direct and it did have Tate on the edge of his seat. He was going to protest but when one of the other three officers that were currently checking his office, moved over to his bookcase he started to tremble. When that same officer slid his hand across the carved edging and pressed a button that was hidden there, Tate fought to keep his emotions under control. As the bookcase slid to one side revealing an archway to a hidden room Tate's mind began to race. Towler watched Tate like a hawk whilst his officers entered the room. After one of them located the light switch, the room's walls lit up with five pieces of art, all of which were protected by alarmed glass frames linked to a keypad. When one of the officers called out to Towler, he raised a finger and beckoned Tate to join him. As soon as Towler entered the room, he saw the Vermeer. He then noticed the keypads and turned to Tate.

"You are in deep shit right now so the best thing you can do is co-operate. Am I making myself clear?"

"Yes of course," muttered Tate.

"I want you to enter the required combinations to each painting with slow key strokes and as you do so call them out loud. We will be watching."

Tate approached the east wall containing two portraits by Lucian Freud. They were early works, and although they were valued at one hundred thousand dollars each, Tate had secured them for twenty. He punched the keypads below each one and the officers took note of the numbers. When the glass partitions slid open, the paintings were lifted from the walls and photographed. Tate then wandered over to the north wall and the work of Jan Van Eyck. Two paintings of saints and sinners hung there. The current market value was three hundred and fifty thousand dollars. Tate had obtained the pair for thirty. As required, he punched in the numbers and they were duly recorded. As the paintings were inspected, he retreated to the east wall and the work by Vermeer. Towler stood by his side.

"The reward for the return of this is currently sitting at four million."

"Is it?" said Tate. "I only know that on today's white market it's worth one hundred and twenty million dollars. Seventy million on the black market."

"If you don't mind me asking, how much did you pay for it?"

"Two million dollars. It's such a waste."

"And you keep it here?"

"Specially designed room. Temperature and light in accordance with the protection of the work."

"And the security?"

"Expensive. It is not easy to get people to meet your specific requirements. It took me a while to find the experts I needed and they didn't come cheap."

"Never mind," offered Towler, nodding to the keypad.

"Oh yes, sorry," began Tate. "It's such a waste." he repeated. Towler registered it just as Tate touched the keypad. He raised a hand and began to move forward but the explosion and Tate's body sent him flying back across the room.

Mick Dea shook hands with the senior medical officer from the military and thanked him for his assistance on current enquiries. After escorting him out of the building he made his way to the room where four detectives were looking at a new piece of evidence that had been pinned to a strategy board. As he began to flip through a nearby file full of progress reports, he was all ears.

"Two of them were stolen from the site?"

"Any news on the second one?"

"Not yet."

"Apparently, the same drill was used on that job in Germany."

"What job?"

"In 2013 a gang broke into the vault of the Volksbank in Steglitz, southwest Berlin. They drilled four holes on that one."

"I remember that. They rented a lock-up garage nearby and tunnelled one hundred feet underground before drilling through a three-foot thick concrete wall."

"Did they ever get caught?"

"No, they set the tunnel alight, destroying all the DNA evidence and fingerprints."

"How many boxes were done?"

"Less than one hundred, a bit like this one really."

That's when Mick dropped the file, and when they all turned he just smiled. "What was the take?" he asked.

"Nine million pounds sterling," replied one before turning to the rest. "I wonder where they hid it all." When no-one spoke, he turned back just in time to see Dea at the door. "Hey Mick, if you were on the job where would you have stashed your share?"

Dea stopped. "I would have gone to the bank a good while before the actual job. I would have rented a large box. I would have worked out how to get a copy of the second key for it. Then on the night of the robbery I would have selected the most expensive items in the haul and simply transferred them to my box. If I ever got caught or had my share compromised, then I would have the contents of the box to fall back on. Remember what they say, the best place to hide something is right under the nose of the searcher."

When he left they all just stood looking at each other with their mouths open.

As the Foot Tapper logged the hospital report he had just received on casualty patient Ralph Wilson, the latter's solicitor Michael Holt had just received the historical data he had ordered from a local research firm. It made for some eye-opening reading and of the eighteen cases detailed there were four that Holt made notes against.

In 2011 it was discovered that in the Ural Mountains, two Russian girls had been switched at birth after the ex-husband of one of the mothers refused to pay alimony on the grounds that she looked nothing like him. A DNA test proved that neither of them were the biological parents. The real daughter, now twelve years old, was eventually traced to a family living on the other side of town. Although the legal battles were still going on, both of the girls involved put it on record that they wished to remain with their adopted parents.

In 2006 two Czech girls were switched at birth at a hospital in the town of Trebic. It was discovered the following year with a DNA test after doubts from both sets of parents. After it was proven that the babies had been swapped they were gradually introduced to their biological parents and returned to their rightful homes.

In 1998 in Charlottesville Virginia it was discovered that Callie Johnson and Rebecca Chittum had been switched at birth in 1995. The discovery came about after Callie took a DNA test over paternity support. It was found that she wasn't related to her purported parents and what made matters worse her biological parents were killed in a car crash just three days after the tests had been completed. A lengthy legal battled followed as Paula Johnson the purported mother of Callie wanted custody and visitation rights to Rebecca. In the end it was left to the grown children to decide and they preferred just to have limited contact with their respective relatives.

In 1995 at the high court in Johannesburg, South Africa, mothers Margaret Clinton-Parker and Sandra Dawkins sued the province over the switch of their sons in 1989. They won medical costs and visitation costs as each family kept the child they brought up. It remained like that for a few years until one of the boys, Robin, decided to leave his foster mother Sandra Dawkins and live with his biological mother Margaret Clinton-Parker. The two boys grew up as brothers.

Holt looked at the file. His options were; child returned to rightful parent, child remains with current parent and child voices opinion on where to stay. There was a possible stay as is and then change later option, and as the child in question was at an impressionable age, the implications were too confusing to contemplate. Holt knew that his first course of action was the find the biological parents and he knew a good investigator that could take care of that. He was just about to pick up the phone when his secretary crept in with a guidance directive he had requested from the child law department at the high court. According to them some form of crime had been committed and the relevant authorities should be made aware of the findings. There was a paragraph on what could happen if the findings were ignored but as Holt had seen that so many times in the past, he never bothered to read it. With his hand still on the phone he was about to press a few buttons when it rang.

Michael Holt was about to have his first conversation with DC Mick Dea.

The Flying Squad were having a good day. A team working in Enfield had managed to attach a navigational micro device to the outside of a blue Citroen

Saxo owned by Terry Perkins. Little did he know it but from then on, everywhere he went and every conversation he had in the car were going to be recorded as evidence. All contacts met and all locations visited were getting checked and it had already paid dividends as the squad got their first break early on. Because Perkins had called in the Old Wheatsheaf Pub in Enfield on various occasions the squad obtained the CCTV footage from its motorised unit. Technicians checking it soon identified associate criminals William Lincoln and Kenny Collins transferring bags into the latter's white Mercedes. Both men were using the services and vehicle of a taxi driver identified as John Harbinson of Essex.

Just down the corridor from the technicians, the Pen Twirler had handed a surveillance report on Massimo Alessi to Mick Dea. In it there were several visits to shops, bars, cafés and a church. The church got Dea's attention for the simple reason that when Alessi left it he wasn't alone. He was followed home and his apartment was being watched. The police team currently sitting around the corner from Alessi's apartment were watching a two-man vehicle parked just down the road from it. They should have been watching the man they had reported into, the man who had entered Alessi's apartment from the rear, the man currently opening the lock on his door and slipping into his hallway. In doing so he avoided the mat on the floor at the door and lifted the receiver from the phone on a nearby table. Gun in hand he crept further and before long the sound of running water filled his ears. He eased towards the bedroom and noted the open door then ran to an en-suite bathroom. Looking through the gap in the door he could see his target soaking himself beyond a steamed glass partition. He also noticed the bathrobe hanging from a nearby wall with the butt of a revolver protruding from one of the pockets. He had been advised to take no chances and now he could see why. It left him with no option. He slipped a silencer onto the end of his gun and prepared. He then kicked the door open, aimed and fired. Alessi was quick to react but not quick enough. The bullet that smashed through the glass slammed into his right shoulder and sent him sprawling in agony. The pain only disappeared when he felt something hard against his skull and that's when it all went dark.

He never knew how long he had been out cold. He only knew that he was still naked and strapped to a chair in his own lounge. Not too far away were two hazy figures dressed in black. When the first one approached and came into focus he saw a sharp lined face of menace that contained tight fair hair and cold blue eyes over a crooked nose and a bitter underslung mouth. When the second figure increased in size it went from black to green and white. That's when Alessi felt the pain in his shoulder once more. The hand now tapping it was smiling.

"Now my son, God is with you now." At that Father John lowered himself into a nearby chair. The figure holding the gun stood beside him. Alessi winced in pain before leaning back in the chair.

"What does Rome want?"

"Rome doesn't know. Let's just say that at St Michael's we only let them know what they need to."

"You are playing a dangerous game, Father."

"Well, I have been playing it for some time now so let me worry about that. What you need to worry about now is living through this day."

Alessi shook his head "Come off it, I am already dead and you know it. I am not going to tell you anything worthwhile so you may as well have done with me."

Father John took a piece of paper from his pocket and unfolded it. He then raised it to Alessi's face. It was a copy of the list he had in his deposit box.

"You have the original of this. It is in code and if you want to know how I know, well that's because my predecessor wrote it. You see this is not a list of where all the money went to, we have known that for years and have dealt with the people accordingly. This is a list of the people that had been on the take here in the UK. Not many people knew about it. Calvi was going to use it as a bargaining chip."

"So why is it so important to you?"

Father John turned the piece of paper over. It was the same list but in addition it had the broken code written below the original lettering. Father John's name appeared at the top."

"Ahh now I understand," said Alessi.

"No you don't," replied Father John, pointing to a name further down the list. When Alessi saw it he started to cry.

It was his close friend Bernardo Cortona.

Detective John Towler felt like shit but he had little room to complain as the only reason he was alive was down to a Boston banker that took the full force of the blast from the device connected to the Vermeer. Tate was dead, Towler's three colleagues had cuts and bruises and he had much of the same along with three cracked ribs and a broken nose. As he sat, all bandaged, before his computer, every move reminded him of how he had been set up. Checking his watch, he put the IT department on alert and then opened his email and winced in pain. A few awkward moves later his screen lit up. It was payback time.

Are you there?
Who wants to know?
A friend of Thomas Magnum and Theo Kojack.

As soon as Towler heard the names of characters played by Tom Selleck and Telly Savalas he got IT to trace the link and a nearby mobile unit was given the green light to move.

How did it all go?
As planned, we got the Vermeer and a few little surprises. So, what is all this about?
The Vermeer was proof that I mean business. In total, we had six buyers.
We?
That can keep, I want compensating and then you will get more. I will keep something back until I know I am totally in the clear.
We have a program.
And it's full of holes so if you don't mind I'll just take the cash.
Cash?
I want six separate payments.
Why six? We only have five buyers left.
The sixth is another little surprise.

Both of Towler's men entered the internet café off the Strand and headed towards the PC they had previously identified as the link. The chair was empty and the monitor facing it was on standby. When one of them checked the CPU he noticed that a portable transmitter receiver had been plugged into the back of it and it was flashing green.

I thought I could trust you Towler, it looks like I made mistake.
You can trust me.
Then why have you sent two of your goons?
Wait.
Bye.

At exactly 04.00hrs on Tuesday 19th May, just six weeks after the robbery had taken place, the Flying Squad assault teams assembled together to learn that today was the day they were going to round up the gang that had been responsible for it. Mick Dea was allowed to listen in on the briefing and it was all grist to the mill. He saw photographs of the targets, listened to tape recordings of them discussing the job itself and watched security footage of them transferring probable proceeds from the heist. There was a summary that mentioned the possibility of flight via the leakage of information and ended with the professionalism expected from the two hundred officers that had gathered. Twelve premises were all going to be hit at exactly the same time, and for a successful result everyone had to know his position, his job and that of everyone else in his team. When a request for confirmation was voiced, it was replied to by a room full of nodding heads. When doubts and questions were asked for, the room remained silent. At 04.30hrs the room was empty. At 05.30hrs every unit had signalled control back at base to report on their state of readiness. Fifteen minutes later they all moved.

Kenny Collins, Terry Perkins and Danny Jones had just met boiler engineer Hughie Doyle at his workshop to transfer three bags of goods from the taxi of John Harbinson before moving onto an address at Sterling Road in Enfield when the police swooped and arrested the three of them. Collins' home in Bletsoe Road, Islington, and the homes of Perkins in Heene Road in Enfield were hit at the same time. They burst through the door of Danny Jones' home whilst Hughie Doyle was arrested at his workshop. A raid was also carried out on his semi-detached home in Enfield. Billy Lincoln was boxed in as he drove his Black Audi A3 along a section of the A10 in Southwark and at the same time officers barged into his home in Bethnal Green. Carl Wood was arrested at his home in Cheshunt, Hertfordshire and Brian Reader was arrested along with his son Paul at their home in Dartford, Kent. They were all taken to Wood Green police station along with the incriminating evidence found at their respective dwellings. Reader had cash, a diamond tester and books on the Hatton Garden jewellery trade. Jones had cash, face masks and an instruction manual on the drill that had been used on the wall of the vault. Collins had jewellery, cash and a money counter whilst Perkins had jewellery, cash, overalls and gloves. The Flying Squad had pinned all four as the ring leaders and it wasn't long before they were each in separate interrogation rooms being grilled by officers. The initial exchanges weren't being taken seriously by one side.

Kenny Collins had to listen to a recording of him and Jones chatting in his car.

Biggest job I have ever been involved in.
And at what cost?
Yeah but it was worth it. I can't wait to see their faces.
"What job would that be then, Kenny?" asked the officer.
"Just had a new kitchen put in," replied Collins.
"Yeah right, and the faces?"
"Norman and Jean."
"Who?"
"Two nosey neighbours of ours."
"Do you expect us to believe that?"
"That's what they said when we told them the cost."
Terry Perkins was shown CCTV footage from Hatton Garden.
"That guy in the hat looks like you, Terry?" asked the officer.
"He looks more like Elton John," replied Perkins.
"He walks like you."
"Like he's just shit himself you mean."
Brian Reader had a set of phone records placed before him.
"Three pay as you go phones, Brian and we can prove they were purchased by you," began the officer. "Now why would you be using them for a short while before binning them?"
"Nuisance calls," replied Reader.
"You what?"
"I keep getting these silly calls from strangers asking all kinds of strange questions. Questions like *'Do you know that your computer is running slow?'* I don't even own one. *'Do you know that if you give Mary three pounds a month she won't have to walk five miles each morning to get clean water?'* Why doesn't she just move closer to the water? *'Do you know that for five pounds a month you could stop a bear from dancing in India?'* I never knew that bears could dance."
"Are you serious?"
"Yes, apparently, they can do the waltz and the Jive but struggle a bit with the rumba. Anyway, I just change the phones but somehow they keep finding me."

Danny Jones had the money-ripping episode with Billy Finch thrown into his face.

"Where did you get the money from, Danny?"

"Harry gave me it."

"Who's Harry?"

"God."

"God is called Harry."

"You know him too?" beamed Jones. "No-one ever believes me when I tell them."

"Tell them what?"

"That he's called Harold but to his friends it's just plain Harry. How long have you known him?"

It was a call that Basil had been dreading.

"You wanted to speak to me?"

"I have been watching the news."

"And?"

"And now I know why you needed the spreadsheet from Mahendra and the keys from Manish."

"Careful now."

"Listen, I took a big risk for you."

"And you were well paid."

"It's not enough."

"Don't even think of holding me to ransom over this, the world is a small place."

"I know what you are and that's why I'm being both reasonable and careful."

"I'm listening."

"I want one hundred thousand pounds in cash and I will hand over my copy of the spreadsheet."

"That's a bit steep."

"I'm not finished. Once I'm clean away I will give you an account number. Once you have deposited another one hundred and fifty thousand into it I will let you have the imprint pad I used for the keys. After that you will never hear from me again."

"And if I say no?"

"If you say no or try anything then a small package will find its way to the Flying Squad."

"Point noted, it will take me a little time to get that amount of cash together."

"I will call at your place in one week."

"Wait—"

"You have seven days so if I were you I wouldn't waste too much time."

And that the call ended.

Basil checked his watch. The week had come and gone and now just minutes stood between him and his expected visitor. From receiving the call, he had made several trips to local markets, banks and to the apartment to make sure nothing could go wrong. He lifted himself onto a stool in the kitchen and waited. On the table before him was a pile of cash, a bag of jewels and a set of keys. He just had time to wipe them down before the doorbell rang. Using a gloved hand, he pressed a nearby release switch and the door slid open. As he lowered his hands the visitor took a seat opposite and focused on the table. He thumbed through the notes and shook his head. "This isn't one hundred."

"It's twenty," replied Basil.

"What the…"

"It's all I could get, that's why I brought the bag."

When the visitor opened it, his eyes lit up. "How much are they worth?"

"One hundred, but even someone like you could get eighty for them."

As a broad grin spread across the visitor's face Basil tilted his head. "I take it we have a deal?" The visitor nodded and produced a memory stick. "And before you ask, yes, it's the only copy I have." He gathered the money and bag of jewels to his side of the table before sliding the memory stick towards Basil's side. He then looked at the keys and picked them up. "Why did you bring these?"

"Because they have an important part to play."

"In what?"

"Your downfall."

The visitor began to frown and was about to speak when a gloved hand clamped over his and began to crush the keys into his fingers. As he cried out in pain another gloved hand clamped over his mouth.

"Nobody holds me to ransom," growled Basil before quickly taking the visitor's head in both hands and turning it sharply to the right. The neck snapped in an instant and the lifeless body slid down to the kitchen floor. He then got to his feet and collected the money and keys and went to the bathroom. After unscrewing the bath panel, he placed the bag behind it and then closed it up ensuring that one of the screw caps was left slightly open. He then left the building for the very last time.

It was Wednesday 20th May and as Mick Dea left his office to go and see the editor of a national newspaper, in the interrogation rooms at Scotland Yard it started to get serious. Danny Jones was shown files that had been extracted from his personal computer. The embedded log files and cookies on his hard drive showed that he had been accessing a variety of websites in search of power drills, forensic techniques, precious stones on the world market and the do's and don'ts of purchasing property in Europe. When Terry Perkins was shown surveillance footage of him with his wife Jacqueline and his daughter Terri Robinson along with her brother in law at her Sterling Road residence in Enfield, his heart sank.

When it was backed up by photographs showing the exchange of large amounts of money Perkins had to stop himself from throwing in the towel. Stubbornly he remained on the ropes awaiting the knockout blow in the shape of a search warrant but it never came. Left with no option he continued to weave his way around the onslaught that followed. Kenny Collins had to listen to more in-depth conversations that he'd had with Jones. This time the discussions had mentioned the address that had been robbed, the time it had taken to breach the wall of the vault and how they intended on spending their share of the slaughter. Brian Reader was shown a series of text messages that he had sent at the start and finish times of the heist as well as photographs of him entering the Hughie Doyle's workshop behind the Wheatsheaf pub. He was then shown a search warrant and a list of jewellery that had been found there.

All four suspects were then given a cup of tea and time alone to think things over before they were gathered together and were led into a conference room and introduced to the only man waiting there. DS Craig Turner dispensed with any formalities and got straight to the point. He landed the required knockout blow that Perkins had been waiting for and backed it up with high resolution photographs of what had been found. He then gave all four of them one last chance.

"When I leave here I'm going to walk down the hall and stand before a few members of the press. I'm either going to tell them that thanks to the co-operation shown by unnamed individuals we have a proven case and will be going to court with it, or I'm going to tell them that very soon I'm going to send a hardnosed gang of thieves away for the rest of their natural lives. Think about it gentlemen and think about it now. We have you bang to rights and if you co-operate you know as well as I do your sentences with be a third of what they should be. So, what is it going to be? Do you want to do an eighteen stretch? Or do you want to be out after six so that you can end your days in freedom?"

All four of them shared a glance before Reader turned back to Turner and nodded. Fifteen minutes later a relaxed Detective Superintendent announced to the world that nine people had been arrested in connection with the Hatton Garden heist. No names were given so editors the world over quickly made funds available so that contacts could be squeezed and reports could be prepared. As far as the scoop of the century was concerned, the race was on.

Yuri Tavlenko and Victor Ramere looked at the six piles of money they had placed on the bed. Tavlenko looked at the list in his hand and put a tick against one of the names on it. "Right, that's *The Independent, The Guardian, The Daily Express, The Daily Mail, The Mirror* and *The Sun* all sorted."

Ramere rubbed his hands. "That just leaves the sports reporter from *The Daily Star* and the sports editor from *The Times*. Who's up next?"

Tavlenko checked the list and then his watch. "*The Times* should be here any minute."

At that there was a knock at the door. Both men nodded to each other, left the room and made their way to the lounge. Ramere removed the cups that had been used in the last exchange and replaced them with fresh ones. Tavlenko opened the door to a holdall-carrying editor of *The Times* newspaper. "Mr. Pinter, you are early."

"I'm not disturbing anything am I?"

"Not at all, please come in. Mr Ramere is also early."

Pinter made his way into the lounge and was greeted with a warm hand and hot cup of coffee. The three men sat down and shared a bit of throw away chat before Tavlenko steered everyone to the business at hand. He then left the room and gave Ramere enough time to receive his bonus. Upon his return, Tavlenko handed over an envelope to Pinter. He in turn opened it to find over one hundred pages of detailed documentation that included photographs, statements, orders, requisitions, laboratory reports and bank statements. Four of the pages were dedicated to the company at the heart of it all. Satisfied that he had his story he placed the documentation into the holdall and retrieved a large white envelope. He slid it across the table and Tavlenko tore away one of the edges and thumbed through a pile of notes. He then placed it to one side and announced, "Gentlemen, I believe that concludes our business."

"Are you not going to count every note?" asked Pinter.

"You did not read every word."

"Point taken."

Ramere got to his feet. "Come on Dave, I'll walk you out."

The three men shook hands once more and parted company. Five minutes after he had left, Ramere returned with an "All clear." At that both men went to the bedroom, gave each other a hug, double checked the money and updated the list. Thirty minutes later there was a knock at the door. They went through the same routine one last time. It began with coffee, went on to small chat and was then followed by an exchange of envelopes. That's when it came to an abrupt halt as one of the envelopes just contained bundles of blank paper. That's when Tavlenko jumped to his feet in shock and Ramere almost had a heart attack. Mick Dea just remained calm about it all. After showing his police registration badge he took a mouthful of coffee and allowed the two men before him a little time for it all to sink in.

SAPPHIRES

As soon as the white transit van came to a halt in the car park of Lenny Bolt's garage in Leatherhead, eight people disgorged from it. Seven of them made their way to the vehicles they had been allocated and found that each of them already had keys in the ignition and a set of registration documents on the passenger seat. Their leader stepped into Lenny's office and introduced himself as Boris before handing over a large brown envelope. Lenny read the note he found inside and then counted the money that came with it. He then nodded, shook hands with Boris and five minutes later he watched eight vehicles head off for Eastern Europe. They included a certain black VW Golf and a black Audi A7 and Lenny was pleased to see them both go.

He put the money in his office safe, shredded the note and envelope, took a sandwich from his bag, poured himself a cup of tea and switched on the TV. He hopped through a few channels that included loose women talking absolute gibberish, bargain hunters that wouldn't know a good deal if it slapped them in the face and a quiz show that made no sense whatsoever. He eventually arrived at a channel where a serious-looking news reporter was reminding his listeners that it was Thursday 21st May and it was a day they would remember for a long time. Behind him police vans swept by as armed support vehicles protected everything on the ground and a police helicopter took care of the skies. The reporter explained it all.

"The destination is Westminster Magistrates Court. There are eight suspects in total and we can now give you their details; John Collins, seventy-four, from Islington; Hugh Doyle, forty-eight, Enfield; Daniel Jones, fifty-eight Enfield; William Lincoln, fifty-nine, Bethnal Green; Terry Perkins, sixty-seven, Enfield; Brian Reader, seventy-six, Dartford; Paul Reader, fifty, Dartford; and Carl Wood, fifty-eight from Cheshunt. It is understood that Judge Tan Ikram awaits them and is expected to hold them in custody for fourteen days as the prosecution has requested that time to complete certain on-going investigations that will have a direct impact on the case ahead. After that all eight will be taken to Belmarsh Prison, a high security building linked to Woolwich Crown Court."

"Will any of them be making statements?" asked the anchor in the studio.

"No, today they are only required to confirm their names, addresses and dates of birth."

"Do we know what the charge will be?"

"A source tells us that it will be conspiracy to trespass the building at 88-90 Hatton Garden with the intent to steal."

"Is that it in total, is it going to be 'The Hatton Garden Eight?'"

Lenny switched the TV off and shook his head at the screen. "Check out the box owners man," he said. "You will find ten times that number."

It was the most relaxed that Gavin Foble had felt in years. The time he had spent with Dr. McKeown had been worthwhile and even though the doctor had warned him that he still carried trapped anxiety and before it erupted he wanted him to enrol into a program immediately, Foble wanted more time to think it over. The bar he chose to think in had begun quiet enough but as the night drew on it had begun to fill with all ages, shapes and sizes. There seemed to be a lot going on but to Foble it had gradually become a blur. He wasn't looking any further than the glass in front of him and the medal he had taken from his deposit box. It consisted of a thirty six-millimetre disc suspended from an ornamental scroll pattern. The obverse bore an effigy of the monarch and the reverse carried the inscription 'FOR DISTINGUISHED CONDUCT IN THE FIELD' underlined by a laurel wreath between two spear blades. It hung from a silver bar wrapped in a thirty-two millimetre ribbon of dark crimson with a navy-blue band in the centre and was known as the Distinguished Conduct Medal (DSC). It was a fine piece and maybe that's why the young loudmouth that spread himself across the bar reached for it. He was already waving it his in hand before Foble realised what the fuss was about. The red mist soon came and as his body began to shake he got to his feet and growled, "Put it back."

"Calm down soldier boy," replied the youth before turning to his mates. "Hey, come and have a look at this, It looks like something you'd get in a box of kids' cereals." Foble attempted to snatch it back but the youth moved to one side and he stumbled across the floor. As the laughter broke out Foble closed his eyes. The images came. One body after another fell before him. "Nooooooooooooo!" he screamed. He heard a cheer and it was quickly followed by, "Where did you get it soldier boy. Ireland, Bosnia, Toys R Us?"

Foble opened his eyes. The images disappeared, the shaking stopped and mind became clear. He stood bolt upright and turned. There were four of them. He moved forward and positioned himself arm's length away from the one with the mouth. "Last chance," he whispered. The youth burst out laughing and Foble gripped the hand that had his medal. As the youth winced in pain Foble punched him square on the chin. He buckled and then collapsed in a heap on the floor. Before he came to rest. Foble slipped the medal into his coat pocket and took a step forward. One of the youths surged forward and when he was within striking distance Foble spun low and with an outstretched leg and swept him off his feet. He hit the floor hard and when he attempted to rise, Foble sent an elbow crashing into his nose. The blood poured and as he rolled in agony, Foble rose to meet the two youths that remained. They both looked at each other and before they could make a decision, it was made for them. A firm hand sent them both sprawling across the bar. They recovered just in time to see an outstretched fist, a badge and the no nonsense copper that was attached to it. Five minutes later Gavin Foble found himself in the passenger seat of a car being driven by Mick Dea.

Belmarsh Prison opened in 1991 and was the first adult prison to be built in London for over a century. Built on a sixty-acre site it houses eight hundred inmates within a building complex of four three-storey blocks with three spurs extending from a central hub. Each spur contains forty-two single and double cells with in-house sanitation. Belmarsh is an all-male prison that is split into five wings. Block one houses prisoners serving long-term sentences, block two is for those serving short-term sentences along with those on remand, block three is for new arrivals, block four holds vulnerable prisoners and those undergoing detoxification and the fifth block is a High Security Unit (HSU) that houses Britain's most dangerous criminals. No-one has ever escaped from Belmarsh and that's why it is classed as one of the most important prisons in Britain.

Belmarsh has seen some very famous visitors over the years and they include such people like armed robber Charles Bronson who has had several spells in Belmarsh. After robbing a post office in 1974 he was sentenced to seven years but due to constant fights with fellow inmates and prison guards the years just kept mounting up as did the locations. One hundred moves and fourteen years later he was eventually released in 1988. After just ten weeks of freedom he was arrested again, and after being involved in several hostage taking incidents he was sentenced to life. He now spends his time writing books and poems and has even been the subject of a movie.

Former conservative politician Jonathan Aitken was convicted of perjury in 1999 and was sentenced to eighteen months in prison of which he served seven. Aitken and his business partner were involved in an arms deal scam with Saudis. Aitken was prepared to let his wife and daughter lie under oath and when found out he pleaded guilty and was eventually booked into Belmarsh for a short stay.

Barry George was sentenced to life imprisonment in 2001 for the murder of TV presenter Jill Dando. She was shot dead outside her home in 1999 and at the time George lived in a ground floor flat nearby. The verdict was considered unsafe by many observers at the time as his guilt rested on a tiny speck of material found on his clothing that may have been gunshot residue. Several appeals and seven years later a cheer went up in Belmarsh prison when he was cleared of any involvement. George has made several attempts to gain compensation for wrongful incarceration but to date they have all failed.

Author and former conservative MP Jeffrey Archer spent a few weeks in Belmarsh in 2001 after he was jailed for perjury and perverting the course of justice over a libel case against *The Daily Star* newspaper in 1987. He was eventually transferred to Wayland prison in Norfolk and wrote a diary about his time behind bars. Archer is living proof that crime does pay.

Singer songwriter, music producer, television and radio presenter and so-called pervert Jonathan King went to Belmarsh in 2001 after being found guilty of indecent assault and buggery. He was sentenced to seven years and his name added to the sex offenders register. He made appeals on the grounds that his sentences were unsafe and although they failed he was released on parole in 2005. He has been arrested and bailed since permeating from investigations into sexual abuse.

Child murderer Ian Huntley was transferred to Belmarsh in 2003 after killing Holly Marie Wells and Jessica Aimee in the August of the previous year. Huntley, a caretaker at Soham Village College in Cambridgeshire was convicted and sentenced to life imprisonment with a recommendation that he serves a minimum of forty years. He went to Belmarsh after attempting to commit suicide by taking twenty-nine anti-depressant tablets. He has spent time in both Wakefield and Frankland prisons and has suffered assaults in both. He is still there and spends most of his time looking over one shoulder.

Abu Hamza, the Egyptian born former imam, known for the hook he has for a hand, was imprisoned in 2004 for preaching Islamic fundamentalism at a Finsbury Park mosque in North London. He spent his days in Belmarsh before being extradited to the United States in 2012 to face charges relating to the support of Al-Qaida.

Great Train Robber Ronnie Biggs was a resident in 2007. He escaped from Wandsworth prison in 1965 and spent the next thirty-six years as a fugitive in Brazil. In 2001 he returned to the UK and resided at Belmarsh until he was transferred to Norwich. He died in 2013.

On Friday 22nd May taxi driver John Harbinson could add his name to the list. For his involvement in transferring the proceeds of the Hatton Garden heist after police found jewellery hidden under floorboards and kitchen units in his house in Benfleet, he appeared before Judge Quentin Purdy at Westminster Magistrates. Although he pleaded his innocence he was remanded in custody and was given a free ride to block three at Belmarsh.

When the car pulled over to the kerb Mick Dea asked his driver to stay put whilst he slipped inside the back of the one carrying the two watchers he had placed on Alessi.

"Anything?" asked Dea.

"No sign of him. As for the car with the two goons in it, well, it's parked just around the corner," replied the officer behind the wheel.

Dea sat in quiet contemplation for a while before speaking asking a question. "What seat is the passenger sat in?"

"You what?"

"Was the passenger in the front of the car or was he in the back. Think and think hard."

"He was sat in the back," answered the officer in the passenger seat.

"Are you sure?"

"Positive, why?"

"There must be three of them."

"How the hell…"

"A driver to get away, a back-up to take care of anything that comes from the rear and someone to work the inside. And he must be the one in charge," interrupted Dea. "Stay here and wait for my signal." At that he climbed out of the car and summoned his driver. He joined Dea on the pavement and then they both headed to the rear of the apartment block. They quickly found the door they were looking for and when Dea reached out, it hit his hand bringing him to an abrupt halt. The friendly face that appeared doffed his cap and walked on by.

"Excuse me, Father," said Dea instinctively before entering the building. As the door closed behind him and his driver it suddenly dawned on him. "Quick!" he shouted before racing up the stairs. Once they were outside the right door the driver drew his revolver. Dea positioned himself opposite it and on a count of three he surged forward and smashed his way into the apartment. The driver leapt over him and took aim at a fair-haired menacing figure that was holding a pistol to the head of a bloodied and broken body that was strapped to a chair. He fired twice and the figure never stood a chance. It just toppled over and ended up in a heap on the floor.

Dea raced over to the chair and gently took the chin of Alessi in the palm of his hand and slowly raised it. "Massimo," he whispered. "Can you hear me?"

Alessi opened his blackened eyes and nodded. He then began to move his mouth but no sound came with it. Dea placed his ear against Alessi's lips. They moved for a moment and then the head dropped and what life was left in the body quickly drained away. Dea stood for a moment and looked at the two dead bodies before him. He then turned to his driver. "Get a cover team over here. Make sure the emergency services only report one body."

"You want those responsible to believe Alessi is still alive?" asked the driver.

"It's the only way I'm going to get to the bottom of it."

"That's heavy stuff, Mick."

"I know, make the call."

As the driver walked away and went on the phone Dea dialled a number on his phone. "Is that car still there? Right chase it, let it get away and make it look good." A brief silence was followed by, "Yes, that's exactly what I said. Call me when you are clear."

The driver returned and nodded. "Where to now?"

"Base," replied Dea. "We need to find where Bernardo Cortona is buried."

After the neighbours, had complained about the stench and the building manager could not be located, it was left to the fire brigade and solid metal backed by brute strength to gain access to the apartment. The dead body found in the kitchen was reported to the police and the bag of jewels on the table brought it all to the attention of the Flying Squad. When it was handed over to the required experts they reported that of the twelve items found in the bag all but one of them were fake. The only item of any worth was a red gold three diamond flower necklace that featured a patented invisible setting of twenty four naturally-mined hexagon shaped diamonds. It was valued at nine thousand pounds and was eventually claimed by its owner, Ralph Cammer. He was a jeweller based at Hatton Garden and he owned box seventy-six, one of the boxes hit in the heist carried out in April. The apartment underwent thorough search and it didn't take long before the items hidden under the bath panel were found. The investigation into the heist took a slight detour by the dead body, the apartment itself and ended with further interviews with members of the Bavishi family. Files were updated and issued and all but one of the Flying Squad officers were convinced they had located Basil, the one that hadn't did his own checks in the apartment before going in search of DI Rearden. When he couldn't be found, he cornered DS Turner with his request. It took three days to obtain the required inspection and results and that's when Mick Dea found himself standing before the entire case team to explain himself.

"As you all know the body in the apartment belonged to forty eight-year old Henry Davis. A one-year lease was taken out on the place eight months ago and was paid in cash. The landlord for the property had no record of the payment and his details have since been passed to HMRC for tax purposes.

"Davis was a freelance accountant that undertook part time work for various business outlets in the capitol and that included the Bavishi family. His accounts have been checked and the sums don't match."

"He was bent," announced one of the officers.

"Yes, but nothing major. There is not one shred of evidence that would put him in the big league," replied Dea. "Now, according to statements taken, he did visit the father in the Sudan recently and in addition paid several visits to the son both at home and at work. That meant that he would have had access to certain sensitive information as well as items of security."

"Like keys," said a figure over Dea's shoulder.

"Like keys," repeated Dea.

"So where are you going with this, Mick?" asked Rearden.

"Guv, this guy is no Basil. He doesn't have the make or the brains to be involved in a heist. He couldn't knowingly set up something like this."

"So you think he was being used?" asked Turner.

"Sir, let's just go through what was found. A bag of dodgy jewels and a dead body. Straight away you would think he was someone that had tried to con someone and then confront him with it and take him out. Now let's just say there is a clever someone involved here. Someone that would leave a genuine clue in the bag that would lead us to a hidden stash of cash and a set of keys. Remember that apartment was clean. The lab reports couldn't find Davis's prints anywhere other than on the jewellery bag, the money and the keys."

"So you think it was staged?" added Turner.

"I know it was," replied Dea as he placed several reports on the table in full view of those present. "These are the lab reports on the clothing found in the wardrobes. They clearly show that although they would fit Davis he never wore them. DNA samples on fibres and tissues found on the garments prove that they belonged to different people. They are just props."

Everyone paused for thought.

"You think Basil turned him?" asked Rearden.

"He may have done, or he may have got someone else to do it. If that's the case, we have to find out what turned him."

Everyone remained quiet for a while longer and then Turner spoke up. "Good work Mick, keep digging on this. As for the rest of you let's keep up the hunt for Basil. It looks like he's still out there and he's probably much smarter than we think. Let's get on it."

As everyone moved away Rearden hung back to help Dea collect up all the paperwork.

"Don't worry," began Rearden. "He won't evade you forever."

"I was close on the Brinks guv until I was pulled off it."

"At the time we needed you to get that child killer, remember? Think of how many young lives you saved when you put that animal behind bars."

Dea threw a wry smile. "Yeah I know but he's within my grasp again, I know he is."

Rearden just nodded.

On Thursday 4th June, all the suspects in the Hatton Garden heist underwent a preliminary hearing that was video linked between Belmarsh Prison and Southwark Crown Court. The charges ranged between conspiracy to burgle, conceal, convert and transfer criminal property. The link was poor and so when Judge Alistair McCreath attempted to set a trial date of 16th November he had his work cut out. It didn't help matters when his case guidelines were interrupted by automated messages. It also didn't help when some of the suspects began to play to the gallery. Terry Perkins kept inviting people around for tea. Kenny Collins kept complaining that it was the worst hotel he had ever stopped in and was going to take it up with his tour operator when he got home. Danny Jones kept ending every question with 'This is Danny Jones, for Sky News, Belmarsh old folk's home.' As Judge McCreath ended his proceedings with a sigh of relief, Mick Dea began his with a knowing nod. He was sat in an interview room at Scotland Yard and before him were Ralph and Amanda Wilson. They were separated by a table that contained a bundle of files. The recording equipment was up and running and as Dea had classed it as an interview and had obtained the consent of those present, no legal aides were in the room.

Dea slid a piece of paper across the table so that Ralph and Amanda could see it. They found themselves looking down at a birth certificate of a baby girl that was born on Monday 17th August. Dea then added another one. It was a certified death certificate for the same baby.

"I remember this," muttered Amanda. "When I held Faith in my arms that day I thanked God for how fortunate I was and at the same time I said a prayer for that poor little soul and her mother."

"Is that what you thought, Ralph?" asked Dea looking across to her husband.

"Well it was a shock," blurted Ralph.

"It was for everyone else, but not for you." Dea let the words sink in and when Ralph began to go red and start to shake he placed another sheet of paper on the table. "We checked the parents out. The father was Peter Ross, he died of a cocaine overdose in 2013. The mother was Beverly Fallon, she went the same way the following year." Another piece of paper was added to the pile. "The administrator at the hospital that day was Steven Carrow. He was sacked from his position in 2013 over alcohol related incidents. He got divorced, lost his property, and has dropped off the radar. He could be living rough somewhere or he may even be dead. We are looking for him as we do have a few questions to ask him. Now that would shock you wouldn't it, Ralph?"

As he continued to shake, Amanda frowned at him and turned back to Dea. "Could someone please tell me what the hell is going on here?"

Dea leaned forward onto the table and folded his arms. "We have been investigating the birth of your child. I have records from the hospital, case files from Mr. Holt and we have managed to put a few statements together. We now know that you two are not the biological parents of Faith. Your DNA doesn't match and neither do your blood groups. We do know that they do match the little baby girl that died in that hospital."

"Oh, my God!" shrieked Amanda before bursting into tears.

Dea continued. "We can prove that the files of the administrator had been tampered with and according to the audit procedures in place at the time some key documents went missing and needed replacing. They were such things like, inspection logs, birth registers and treatment reports. Am I getting close, Ralph?" Dea asked. As Amanda broke down Ralph lowered his head into his hands.

Dea went on. "Those babies were swapped. Someone replaced tags and altered certain records as well as removing others in such a way as to lay blame elsewhere. A crime was committed and I am going to prove it." He paused for a moment and watched as two people began to crack at the seams. "I can see that this has been a little traumatic for you both," he added. "So let's have a little break before we go any further."

Dea got to his feet and made his way to the door. As he opened it a tearful voice asked, "What was her name?"

"What?" replied Dea.

"The baby girl, what was her name!" cried Amanda."

"Hope."

That's when Amanda became inconsolable.

On Monday 24th August, the Hatton Garden Safe Deposit Company put up the closed sign on its door for the final time. After the irreparable damage the raid had caused to its reputation they were left with no option but to call in the liquidators as the business became insolvent. As the Bavishi family that owned it were forced to endure the heartache of losing the business, Juliette Roux thought she was about to lose her daughter. Louise Roux was seventeen years old and every one of them had been a struggle. She came into this world with a faulty heart and defective lungs and although she had surgery to repair it, life was never going to be fair with her as far as physical activity was concerned. She never could find that extra yard to win a race or that additional surge of power to secure a game point. Then there was the medication and the annual check-ups. Louise wasn't a complainer, she was an endurer. Although her medal cabinet was empty her love locker was full. She had the best mother anyone could ever wish for and a close family that was always there with the hugs and kisses.

It was supposed to be a girly day with mother and daughter spending some quality time together full of serious shopping and idle gossip. Three hours in and Louise began to feel faint. When she collapsed in the middle of a busy mall and started to turn blue all hell let loose. Screams and panic were quickly followed radio calls, phone calls, paramedics, an ambulance and a frantic transfer to Great Ormond Street Hospital. It was their specialists that had worked on her heart and lungs at birth and so they were the obvious choice.

Juliette and family spent an agonising two hours pacing corridors outside an operating theatre before she was introduced to Professor Roger Shepherd, the surgeon tasked with saving her daughter's life. He was an elderly man that came with grey hair a soft voice and a warm smile. He held her hand and explained that although Louise was stable she was still a concern. Shepherd went through it all slowly and carefully. As far as Juliette understood when her daughter was born and surgeons corrected the scarred aortic valve she had, they also inserted two stents into her defective airways to assist breathing. One of those stents had just eroded to a point where it had lodged itself into her gullet. That meant that her airways had begun to collapse and in essence she was being throttled by her own heart. Shepherd explained that although it had become a lethal cardiac condition he had it under control as he had the best people to deal with it once they were sure Juliette's body could cope with the associated trauma. Once Shepherd left for theatre, Juliette and her relatives drank tea and prayed for the best. Just along the corridor from where they were sat an elderly gentleman got up from his seat and went for a stroll outside and made a single phone call to his boss in Knightsbridge. That's when the wheels on the bus no longer went round and round.

On Friday 4th September Brian Reader, Terry Perkins, Kenny Collins and Danny Jones all admitted taking part in the Hatton Garden Heist. William Lincoln, Hughie Doyle, and John Harbinson all denied the conspiracy to burgle charges whilst Carl Wood and Paul Reader had declined to enter a plea. Wood was on dodgy ground and he knew it. Young Reader was going to walk free in three weeks but was unaware of it, his father had seen to that. The heist was headline news once more and although it made for fascinating reading it didn't get much column width in *The Boston Herald* that Dwight Shunter was reading. There was a story that did and once he had confirmed the death mentioned in it he went for a walk. It took him just under one hour to find a suitable internet café and after logging into an available PC he made an aching detective sit up straight.

Are you there, Towler? It's Fred.
I hear you.
You should have told me the truth about the banker.
Sorry, I was under orders.

Anybody else hurt?
A few walking wounded but we are all on the mend.
You don't listen.
I'm listening now. All I need to know is, do we have a deal? After what went down there won't be any more tricks, you have my word on that. I need to get these people.
Ok, but it's a new deal. I want a one-off payment. For that you get five names. Then when I'm in the clear you will get the little surprise.
I will need time to get it sanctioned.
You have twenty-four hours.
How much do you want?
Two million dollars.
That's a little extreme.
It's nothing compared to the value of the paintings. Speak to the insurance companies concerned. I'm sure they will have no problem with it.
And what's in this for me?
The little surprise. I will give you the location of two dead bodies.

Towler went all tense. This was it. After all these years, he had been searching for Carl Benner and Rick Mason, the two men at the heart of the robbery, and now he had the confirmation that they were dead. If he could get to them then he could use what clues had been buried with them to crack the whole case widen open once more.

You have twenty-four hours.

Towler read the sentence several times before he managed to type;
Deal.

As soon as the connection was broken a technician seated in the bowels of the Secret Intelligence building at Vauxhall Cross, passed a copy of the exchange to his section chief. From there it went to a safe house near Scotland Yard. Two hours later a certain Face Puller was hauled off the street and bundled into a vehicle. One hour after that he was let go and Mick Dea had two uninvited guests to lunch.

As they chatted Shunter went to a local market. Using cash, he purchased two chipped mobile phones with one hundred pounds' worth of credit on each. The phones would be registered to a deceased cocaine addict. The credit would come from the ghosted card of a local car dealer. He would discover it when it was four weeks too late.

At Belmarsh Prison, Danny Jones returned to his cell and continued with a letter he had addressed to Sky News reporter Martin Brunt.

It came as a bit of a surprise as this is a prison within a prison. We are not killers, paedophiles or terrorists. It was a commercial burglary. We haven't had no visits and it took almost five weeks to get our mail as they say they are short staffed. It's all wrong as I can't see some of this so-called gang getting through this. Let me tell you Dads Army are like super sportsmen compared to this gang. One sentenced has a heart condition, aged 68. One has cancer, he's 70. Another, 75, can't remember his name. Then there is a 60-year old with two new hips and knees. Just for a laugh I wrote to the Archbishop of Canterbury to get his take on it all and he just replied to say that although he couldn't help us he would say a prayer for us all in his next church service. He also added that he was sorry to hear that I had got mixed up in it all and finished his letter by remarking that being famous must seem like a pretty poor reward.

Speaking about rewards I want to give back my share of the Hatton Garden burglary and the police were ok with me showing them where I buried the loot but the authorities here at Belmarsh won't release me. What a load of bull. They obviously don't want it back. I am the only person in the world that knows where it is hidden and all I want is to do the right thing and give it back. Can you help me with this and mention it on TV. Maybe that will make them see sense.

God bless.

Danny Jones.

Just a hole in the wall, nothing more.

Hatton Garden Jeweller Emil Wiener shook his visitor by the hand and ushered him to the seat situated on the opposite side of his desk. After asking his secretary to hold all calls he looked down at the report that the visitor had sent to him some three weeks ago, and then pushed it across the desk.

"I believe this is yours?" offered Wiener.

"I believe it is," replied Mick Dea.

"What are you going to do with Karl Brant?"

"That depends."

"On what?"

"Are we dealing with a John Demjanjuk or an Oskar Groening here?"

Ivan Demianiuk was born in the Ukraine and during the Second World War he was drafted into the Soviet Red Army and spent most of his military service as a guard in the Sobibor extermination camp in occupied Poland. He went on to become a prisoner of war himself at the hands of the Germans, and once he had served his time he emigrated from West Germany to the United States of America. In 1958 he was granted citizenship and that's when Ivan Demianiuk became John Demjanjuk. He lived the quiet life as an auto worker until the Israeli authorities caught up with him in 1986. For the next two decades he became part of a lengthy investigation and on two occasions he was deported to Israel to stand trial for war crimes. Appeal followed appeal and as Demjanjuk was under constant suspicion no country wanted to house him and so he became a stateless person. That all ended in 2009 after new evidence from holocaust survivors was passed to the German authorities. He was deported to Munich and formally charged with just under thirty thousand counts of acting as an accessory to murder. In 2011 he was convicted pending appeal but he died before the appeal could be heard. That meant he went to his grave as an innocent man.

Born in Lower Saxony, Oskar Groening was a child to proud nationalists, and due to his fascination with uniforms he spent most of his young life in the Scharnhorst and the Hitler Youth. He eventually became a bank clerk and when war was declared he joined the Waffen-SS. His paper-shuffling skills earned him a desk job at the Auschwitz concentration camp. His duties included registering the possessions of the doomed including clothing, shoes, valuables and currencies so that it could be sent to Berlin. Although he was never actively involved in the extermination processes at the camp he did bear witness to it all. During his time there he put in two transfer requests and both were turned down by his superiors. In 1944 when Germany was heading for defeat he was shipped to the Belgian Ardennes where he served until his capture. After the conflict was over, Groening returned to Germany and was reunited with his wife. They had two children together and lived a comfortable life. She spent her days as a housewife and he worked as a wages accountant in a glass factory. In 2014 state prosecutors caught up with him and charged him with accessory to murder of some three hundred thousand Hungarian Jews and aiding the advancement of the Nazi economy with his bookkeeping and transfer of funds. In 2015 he was found guilty and sentenced to four years in jail. When he went in he was ninety-three years old.

"His real name is Otto Faber," began Wiener. "He was a bookkeeper at Bergen Belsen." He then passed over a sheet of paper to Dea. On it was the photograph of a proud looking young man in an SS uniform along with his personal details.

"Are your people on their way?" asked Dea.

"No."

"So you know that he's dying?"

"Yes."

"He told you?"

Wiener shook his head "Instinct."

"Instinct," repeated Dea.

Wiener lowered himself into a chair. "Mr. Dea, I have seen and heard many terrible things in my life. I have listened to the choir of madness and watched the ballet of death as human beings fought for a single breath of air. I have watched them die and then have to endure the indignity of tipping their ashes into pits and rivers. I have seen individuals kicked to death, heard their limbs break one by one. I have seen people lined up against a wall and shot just because they made a simple mistake or upset someone. You could say I have seen a lot of death and do you know something? We all have a certain look in our eyes when we know it is coming. Karl Brant has that look."

"Why did he come to you?"

"I spent some time at Bergen Belsen. He brought me a list that contained two people he had helped to escape from there. He wanted to know what had happened to them. He must want to go to his own grave with a clear conscience."

"So, there isn't much time then?"

"For what?"

"To see if there is a case to prosecute him."

"Mr. Dea, he has a whole ledger. Can't you spare me the time to try and get it from him? He could destroy it and then where would I be?"

"Have you confirmed that the extract he gave you was genuine and not fabricated around two names?"

Wiener opened a desk drawer and passed it over. Dea looked at it for several moments. There were twenty-five names on it. Two of them had the family name of Wiener. When he got to them and looked up the old man before him had tears in his eyes.

"They were my parents," he whispered.

On Friday 16th October after a tip-off from a landlord that owned industrial units overlooking the O2 Arena, detectives found the three lock-ups that had been rented by Basil. The landlord had only visited the site to see if an extension to the agreement was needed when he came across the concrete slabs and deposit boxes. As forensic teams began to crawl all over it not too far away Danny Jones was escorted from Belmarsh Prison to Edmonton Cemetery in North London. Once there he took the officers to the grave of a relative by the name of Sidney John Hart. Buried there were two small white bags stuffed with jewels. Jones was asked about the haul and confirmed that it was the remainder of his share. Police knew that he was lying, as after information received, they had visited the same cemetery just three days previous and found three blue and orange bags of jewels under the slab of Sidney John Hart, his father in law. When it was reported in to the team at Scotland Yard they had a laugh about it just before piling into the office of DI Mark Rearden to say their goodbyes, burden him with a pile of useless presents and take the piss out of him. He did manage to make a small speech and it was well-received. The offer of free beer in a local boozer had something to do with it. Thirty minutes later the drink was flowing, well-wishes were being exchanged and hands were being shaken. After mine-sweeping around the room for a while, Rearden found an empty seat near Dea and filled it. Both men shook hands once more.

"I thought you were stopping until the end of the tax year? asked Dea.

"I couldn't wait that long, Mick," replied Rearden. "I'm getting itchy feet. You know how it is. If something needs doing, why put it off?"

"Well you've earned it."

"And so have you."

"What?"

"My job. My proposal to have you replace me has been sanctioned by those upstairs. It will be rubber stamped in a few days. After that the office is all yours."

"I don't know what to say."

"Don't say anything. Besides you could be cursing me in a few weeks."

Dea laughed. "What. More than usual you mean?"

"I hope I didn't overdo it with the cases you are on at the moment. How are you getting on with them by the way?"

"They are all interesting for sure but there doesn't seem to be a link anywhere."

"Right, I also noticed that you have just returned a load of old case files back into the archive. Wasn't there anything of worth in them?

"Not really. All the open avenues had been walked several times. I walked them all again and came to the same dead end."

At that a young police constable threw her arms around Rearden and gave him a kiss. "Come on old timer, the girls want to say goodbye."

Rearden and Dea clinked glasses. Rearden went to get covered in lipstick and Dea went home. He made tea and sat in front of the television for a while and was about to call it a night when there was a knock at the door. He opened it to an elderly lady supported by a young man that would be identified as a grandson. They chatted for fifteen minutes before Dea was handed a plastic sleeve that contained the tattered remains of a charred scrapbook on the understanding that he would not mention it to a living soul. He agreed, contact numbers were exchanged, goodbyes were said and the door was closed. Dea made himself more tea and returned to the sofa and slowly began to open the plastic sleeve. He didn't know it yet but Angela Davis, the daughter of Sean Murphy, had just opened another avenue.

Basil had just gotten closer.

On Wednesday 28th October, Judge Christopher Anthony Kinch chaired a follow up meeting in his chambers. Present were D.S. Craig Turner from the Flying Squad, security box owner Catherine Taylor and her current partner Raymond Teller, an oil executive out of Texas. Those gathered had met back in June 2015 shortly after the robbery had taken place in Hatton Garden. Back then Catherine had advised the police that her box number 524 had been emptied of jewellery and to support her claim she had purchase invoices, letters of confirmation and photographs of the thirty-one pieces that had been stolen. Since then the police had spent the four months that followed collaborating the information that had been supplied and found it all to be genuine. Miss Taylor was thanked by the Judge for the co-operation she had shown and then invited to sign a statement and declaration of authority that had been prepared by the Flying Squad. Once complete, pleasantries were exchanged and Kinch found himself alone with Turner.

"Extraordinary affair, wouldn't you say?" remarked the Judge.

"She's some woman alright," replied the D.S.

"What?"

"She's been married four times. She's seen off two diamond merchants, a banker and a property entrepreneur. She's followed that with a string of partners that have included lawyers, brokers, fashion designers and the odd…" At that Turner shook his head. Kinch finished the sentence with "Oil executive." He then smiled and opened the file on his desk.

"So Detective Superintendent, where does that leave us with status of the haul?"

"The original total was fourteen million of which four million has been recovered. Now that we have clarified the loss of Miss Taylor at seven million that leaves us with a delta of seventeen million."

"But as it stands we can only go to trail based on the original total. Otherwise we would get an objection from the defence and that would mean a postponement pending the agreement on renewed dates. Is that what the Metropolitan Police force wants?

"Certainly not, that's why we pushed though the addendum on the case file."

Kinch checked the folder. "According to this you have submitted a request for a confiscation hearing against those that will eventually be convicted of the crime."

"Yes, I believe we now have sufficient grounds to hold them accountable for the increase in the losses sustained."

"And you will be looking for a sentencing review against what co-operation you receive?"

"Normally it would be a long shot in them offering anything up as they are old school criminals but when you take into account the health factor we just might get a result."

Judge Kinch checked his diary. "Ok, we will be going to trial in November and so sentencing should be in the first quarter of 2016. If you take into account possible delays and challenges to rulings of law we could be looking at the fourth quarter of 2016 before we can initiate this."

"That works fine for me. I'm not the one holding the time bomb."

"Quite," replied Kinch before adding his signature to the file.

U. S. DOLLARS

Father John lowered himself onto an available bench opposite Westminster Cathedral and marvelled once more at its splendour. He would have loved to step inside but today wasn't a day for that. Ever since he got the note from Alessi he hadn't been able to settle. He expected him to be dead. He checked his watch. 'Never mind,' he thought. 'You soon will be.' His phone buzzed. The message said *Figure approaching*. Father John never looked up. He felt the bench creak under the additional weight. He then slowly nodded and without looking over remarked, "So you are still alive?"

"Why wouldn't I be?" replied a voice.

Father John shook and looked across to newly promoted Detective Inspector Mick Dea. In gloved hands, he was holding a small wooden box that still had segments of dried mud across it.

"Just before Massimo died he asked me to look under the headstone of Bernardo. This is what I found." Dea opened the box to a sealed plastic bag. From that he withdrew a red velvet pouch. He opened that to a tied bundle of documents.

"We have some sort of list that looks like it has some hidden meaning and I'm sure you know what that is. We also have a variety of currency and a photograph. And last but not least we have an envelope entitled *To Whom It May Concern*. It makes for some fascinating reading."

"What does it have to do with me?" asked Father John.

"Quite a lot," replied Dea. "I think Massimo wanted to meet his maker with a clear conscience. He admits his involvement in many crimes and in particular the murder of Roberto Calvi. He also mentions your association to it."

"You can't prove anything."

Dea picked up the photograph and stretched out his arm. "Recognise anybody."

Father John took hold of it and when he tried to pull it close he felt the resistance from Dea. He leant forward and then the black and white still, came into focus. It was a typical family gathering. Calvi was at the heart of it all. On the right-hand fringe of the picture stood a young priest. Father John's eyes widened.

Dea pulled the photograph away.

"I can prove that all these documents are Calvi's as they have his fingerprints on them. They also have prints from Bernardo and Massimo and now they also have yours."

"You can't…"

"I can't what, Father? I can't make this thing stick? Maybe you are right with that as God only knows what devils you have on your payroll. But I tell you what I can do. I can give this to the Calvi family. I can ensure that the Vatican hears about it all." Dea went silent and looked on as Father John began to shake. He then collected all the documents and returned them to the box. As he got to his feet Father John shot up to his.

"Wait! We can come to some arrangement."

"Whoever conceals his transgressions will not prosper, but he who confesses and forsakes them will obtain mercy," replied Dea. "*Proverbs*, wasn't it?"

Father John was lost for words.

Dea shook his head, walked over to him and leant forward so that their faces were almost touching.

"Don't bother praying to your god, not even he can help you now."

As both men parted company the two figures watching it all from the safety of a car were politely asked to move on by two uniformed officers. When Father John got back to his church the first thing he did was make a secured phone call to Rome. When Mick Dea got back to his office the first thing he did was tear up an envelope that contained a few pieces of blank paper. He then spent the rest of the day pouring over the burnt scrapbook that Angela Davis had given him. When he had finished he was left looking at four pages of scribbled notes. They contained the names of some of the biggest crooks London had ever seen. Dea stared at them for a while before adding certain robberies against each one. He then added the dates of each robbery. After that he went back to two handwritten notes that had survived the fire. It was obvious who had written the first one but the second was a mystery.

He was about to give up when a secretary walked in with a document she needed signing. It was a request register for files that had been taken out of the archive. He noticed that his signature was littered all over it as well as a few well-known others. He signed the continuation section of the register and was about to hand it back when something caught his eye. He quickly flipped through all the pages of it just to confirm what he had seen. He then checked one particular signature against the mystery note. He stood bolt upright and thought about the Brinks Mat case. He then thought about the task he had been given on the Hatton Garden heist. Pretty soon his mind began to race and alarm bells started going off. He grabbed the phone and dialled the office that his researchers were situated in.

"All of you in here now. I've just found what we have been looking for."

On Friday 13th November after five months in custody Hughie Doyle was granted bail under curfew. Three days later he was back in Woolwich Crown Court in South East London to face charges along with other members of the gang. Judge Christopher Anthony Kinch was in charge of it all. The jury consisted of six men and six women. The prosecution was represented by QC Philip Evans. Carl Woods' council was Nick Corsellis, William Lincoln was represented by Mark Tomassi, John Harbinson was being taken care of by Philip Sinclair and Hughie Doyle was pinning all his hopes on Paul Kelecher. When all four of the accused pleaded not guilty the prosecution opened their case. They had CCTV footage, items recovered from the searches, recordings of exchanges between the gang members, mobile phones records and the evidence from security guard Kelvin Stockwell.

The exchanges in the court were quite drab and those watching from the spectator's gallery did get to smile on four occasions. When Hughie Doyle was asked as to why he had a book on diamond cutting by D. Sawdon if he had no interest in it. He replied that he also had a book on fly fishing by J.R. Hartley but he had no interest in that either. Carl Wood was asked if he had sleepless nights over all the debt he was in. He just shook his head and said that he left the sleepless nights to the people he owed it to. He also added that he didn't mind being in constant debt as it meant that he always had people interested in his health. Taxi driver John Harbinson was asked about the array of books he had and the constant journeys he had taken around Hatton Garden. He told the prosecution that he was thinking of going on mastermind with Hatton Garden as his specialist subject. Those listening that were old enough to remember Fred Housego couldn't contain themselves. It gained them and Harbinson a stern rebuke. William Lincoln was asked about his fascination with the fish market and he replied that it gave his life a porpoise. When he was reminded that he could go to jail and in doing so could lose his partner he just shrugged his shoulders and replied, "Well, there's plenty more fish in the sea."

Three people watched Mick Dea hand over all the research and reports he had on Dwight shunter. Two were British, one was American, and all three were secret service. It was the latter that ensured the required instruction had also been signed by all parties.

"So, what happens now?" asked Dea.

"We have all the required assets in place already. He will be with us real soon," replied the American. He never waited for the reply. If he had still been listening as he walked out of the office he would have heard Dea whisper, "You must be joking."

Using the first mobile phone Dwight Shunter made six calls. The first five calls lasted fifteen minutes each. They all began with the same phrase, continued on with a bank account and a clear set of instructions and ended with a warning. The sixth call was to a certain FBI Detective.

"John Towler."

"Hello John Towler, you are speaking to Fred."

"I don't know anyone by that name."

"How about the names Jim Rockford and Steve McGarret. They should be the last two names in your file for the Isabella Stewart Gardner Museum."

"Yes they are."

"Write this number down."

Towler did.

"You have one hour."

When the line went dead Towler took forty-five minutes to obtain a confirmed trace to an apartment situated on the Strand, London and ensured that a local team was on location. A further fifteen minutes was spent on a ghost transfer of two million dollars into a UK-based bank account.

Shunter contacted his bank for a balance check on two accounts. Once he had the figures he immediately transferred the whole amount of the first into an offshore account in Jersey. He then transferred the whole amount of the second into an onshore account in Boston. Once confirmed he made a further six calls. The first five lasted just five minutes each and although they were cordial they were also final. The sixth call had him back with Towler. Exactly four hours later five addresses across America were raided by FBI agents. The first team raided the home of an airline executive in Atlanta, Georgia in search of a Manet. The second team raided the residences of a CEO from a prominent motor company in Detroit, Michigan in search of three works by Rembrandt. The third team hit the home that belonged to the president of one of the biggest media companies in Denver, Colorado on the trail of a stolen landscape by Flinck. The fourth team went for five works by Degas that were supposedly purchased by a lawyer in Philadelphia and the fifth team surprised a cattle baron in Texas when they approached him about an Eagle and a Chinese Gu. Although all five suspects owned several pieces of art, they all had the required invoices and certificates of ownership for them all. None of them had any of the pieces that were stolen from the museum in Boston.

The team that knocked down the door to an apartment on the Strand, London found nothing but a mobile phone. It was switched on and as soon as one of the agents swiped the screen a pending text was sent. Towler got it two minutes later. It took ninety minutes for a recovery team to reach the co-ordinates contained in the message. That's when a car was pulled from the River Thames with two dead bodies in it.

When Towler received the information he just put his head in his hands.

When Dea heard about it he just shook his head.

Shunter watched it on a TV screen in a departure lounge at Heathrow airport before boarding a flight to New York.

On Thursday 24th December D.S. Craig Turner learned that the forensics teams that had been encamped at the lock-ups opposite the O2 arena for several weeks had come up with nothing to assist the investigation. Totally dejected he thought the day couldn't get any worse until he was about to leave his office at Scotland Yard and his secretary introduced him to Mr. John Ryder, a representative from the Home Office. When Turner tried to question the approach he was handed a letter that was on notepaper headed by the address 10, Downing Street. After quickly reading it Turner retreated into the office with Ryder and closed the door.

"How can the squad be of help?"

"What do you know about an organisation that goes by the name of Combat Action 213?"

"They are a racist neo-fascist group that was established on April 28th 2005, exactly sixty years after the death of Bernito Mussolini. It is believed that the two in their title refers to the second letter of the alphabet being 'B' and as the thirteenth is 'M' then the group carries his initials. I believe they are listed in the proscription of the Terrorism Act 2000."

"That's correct," began Ryder. "As you are aware they still have several branches scattered across the UK from which they promote their anti-Semitic and homophobic ideology."

"But I thought they were low key now, online propaganda and the odd anti-immigration rally."

"They are but they do have supporters."

"Locally?"

"Afraid not, they are being funded by such groups as the Italian Fascist League (IFL, the American Nazi Party (ANP), the Socialist Reich Party (SRP) in Germany and the Racial Volunteer Force (RVF) in Belgium which has links to the UK-based Combat 18."

"Ok so Neo-Darwinism is alive and well, where do I come in?"

Ryder handed over a file. "They had a box in Hatton Garden that was under the name of a deceased jeweller and contained some two million pounds in eight different currencies."

"And obviously, it was one of the boxes that was hit."

"Correct."

Turner slumped down into his chair. "Is there any end to this?" he questioned out loud.

"As you can imagine, Her Majesty's government has a vested interest in what can be retrieved and accordingly a specific investigation will be set up in conjunction with yourselves once we have something to go on."

"Right," replied Turner before shaking Ryder by the hand and ushering him out of the door. He then picked up the phone and made a call to Judge Kinch. Another addendum to the case file was discussed as well as the information act and clearance protocols. Ten minutes after that Turner was in a local bar on the first drink of many.

Mohamed Al-Fayed handed his visitor three letters. The first was from Great Ormond Street hospital giving thanks for the sizable donation they had just received. The second was from Louise Roux and detailed the recovery program she was currently following. It was the fourth such letter Al-Fayed had received from her and he had begun to treasure them. The final letter was from Buckingham Palace and carried the insignia, seal and signature of Her Majesty Queen Elizabeth II. The letter was formal and although it was full of procedure and protocol, room was made to say thank you for returning a document that rightly belonged to the family of a departed king. They all made for fascinating reading and once Mick Dea had done so he handed them back.

"Is there a case to answer?" asked Al-Fayed.

"Not to me," replied Dea. "The theft, if you can call it that, wasn't carried out within my jurisdiction so there is nothing I could do about it. Unless of course you wish to pursue the matter?"

Al-Fayed smiled and shook his head.

"I thought so. In addition to that the item in question has been returned to the rightful owner, and as it comes with an approval that doesn't get much higher, then I think we can safely say there is no further intervention needed."

"I agree."

"I can only hope it helps to build a few bridges."

Al-Fayed looked to a photograph that took pride of place on his desk. It was a picture of two people in love that were never going to be allowed to realise it.

"I can only hope and pray," he answered.

At that moment, a phone buzzed and Al-Fayed was informed that his next guests had arrived. Dea brought things to a close and thanked his host for all the help he had given. Al-Fayed thanked Dea for the understanding he had shown. The door was opened and when Dea crossed it he saw two women with apprehensive looks on their faces. One of them remained motionless and waited for a sign to move. The younger couldn't contain herself. Ignoring what protocols were expected she ran into the room and threw her arms around a beaming Al-Fayed.

"Hello Princess," he whispered.

On Wednesday 13th January, the jury at the Woolwich Crown Court retired for the verdict. When they returned the next day Lincoln and Wood were both found guilty of conspiracy to commit burglary and conspiracy to conceal, convert and transfer criminal property and would remain in jail. Although Doyle was found guilty of conspiracy to conceal, convert and transfer criminal property he was granted bail and was allowed to walk. He did so with Harbinson who was cleared of all charges. As for Perkins' daughter, Terri Robinson, and her brother-in-law Brenn Walters, who had pleaded guilty to the same charges as Doyle, they were advised that their sentencing would take place on Wednesday 9th March.

Back at Scotland Yard, Mick Dea received the news just has he was about to step into an interview room that contained Ralph and Amanda Wilson. It had been a few weeks since they had last spoken. That was when Dea had let them go on the understanding that he was giving them both one final chance. During that time, he had officers monitoring their movements and so expected today's meeting to be the final one.

As soon as Dea lowered himself into a seat Ralph Wilson pushed an envelope across the table. "In there you will find the missing logs, registers and certificates."

"So, what are you telling me?" asked Dea.

"I swapped the babies. I know it was wrong and I know that's not a justifiable answer but at the time I was desperate."

"You said 'I'."

"Yes. Amanda had nothing to do with this."

Dea looked across to Amanda and she just sat there with a distant look on her face. Her eyes were red, her skin was pale and she looked like she had not had a decent night's sleep for some time. He turned his attention back to Ralph. "Did you keep the documents in the safe deposit box?"

"Yes."

"Why?"

"I thought that maybe one day Faith may learn of her true identity and if that was the case then I would come clean."

"Or maybe if you were caught you could use them as a bargaining tool. Either that or you could use them to lay the blame elsewhere."

Ralph didn't respond.

"I noticed that the death of her parents came as a shock to you. Was it because one of your plans had just gone up in smoke?"

Ralph shook his head. "If it wasn't for that bloody robbery."

Dea got to his feet. "Ok, let's get you some legal representation in here so we can do this by the book." He then looked to Amanda. "You are free to leave." She rose to her feet and followed him out of the room. When the door closed behind them both she paused. "What will happen to him?"

"He will be charged and held in custody pending trial."

"Is he looking at a jail sentence?"

"Probably."

"How long?"

"Depends on the judge and on what advisement he gets."

"It's all my fault," blurted Amanda. "I was the one that wanted the baby."

Dea held her arms. "You are not to blame. He knew what he was doing."

"And where does that leave me?"

"With a beautiful daughter that's worth fighting for. You are going to fight for her, aren't you?"

"Until my dying day."

Basil poured himself another glass of white wine and looked out across a golden sandy beach which ran to deep blue waters that rippled beneath a cloudless sky. He toasted the scene and remembered the risks involved in it all. He also questioned its worth. The English newspaper that lay open before him was full of pictures of those celebrities that the world had said goodbye to in 2015.

The actress Anne Kirkbride, who had played Deidre in Coronation Street for as long as he could remember, departed in January. She was quickly followed by Geraldine McEwan, his favourite Miss Marple. The following month saw farewells to Leonard Nimoy, best known for being Mr Spock in Star Trek and the new romantic pioneer that was Steve Strange. March saw the passing of the author Sir Terry Pratchett and Free bassist Andy Fraser. In April it was the turn of soul singer Ben E King and ventriloquist Keith Harris. Basil gave thought to the fluffy green duck that was Orville and smiled. May saw the deaths of author Ruth Rendell, and the Hot Chocolate front man, Errol Brown. Two acting legends passed on in June. The first was Sir Christopher Lee and the second was Ron Moody. Egyptian actor Omar Sharif had his final curtain call in July as did legendry crooner Val Doonican. The following month saw the surprised passing of TV favourite Cilla Black and Minder star George Cole. Novelist Jackie Collins came to her final chapter in September and the same month was a wrap for director Wes Craven. Irish-American actress Maureen O'Hara slipped away October as did Coronation Street actor Peter Baldwin. November was *Till Death do us Part* as the actor who played its main character, Alf Garnet, went silent. Basil could just picture Warren Mitchell going off on one. Then there was *The British are Coming* Oscar winner, Colin Welland. As for December we were finally being served by actor Nicholas Smith and saw the final ace of spades dealt by Ian 'Lemmy' Kilmister from the metal band that was Motorhead.

The pictures were accompanied by all the usual sound bites. They led the way, they lived life to the full, and they will go down in history and will never be forgotten. Basil gave another toast. This time it was to himself.

It all began on Horse Guards Parade. That's where twelve hundred members of the public and the representatives from every UK newspaper and TV channel watched a battle re-enactment with a difference. The participants were all serving soldiers and the uniforms they wore covered units going back one hundred years. The crowd looked on in pride as those on the field reminded them of power, glory, and dedication. When the guns eventually went silent those combatants that had escaped with their lives, retreated from theatre. Twenty bodies remained still. After a moment of calm an elderly woman dressed in a nurse's uniform took to the field. She stood before the fallen and raised her arms up to the sky. The soldiers rose up once more and stood in an orderly line. The nurse turned away and when she began to walk, they all followed. They left the parade ground and made their way down Whitehall. The crowd left their seats and followed. Photographers took pictures and reporters looked into cameras and reminded the nation of what was happening. The twenty soldiers were wearing the uniforms of comrades that had either been lost in action or had succumbed from the trauma they tried to carry after it. Gavin Foble was one of those soldiers. He was wearing the uniform of Barry Randall.

They marched down Whitehall to a deafening round of applause. When they turned onto Downing Street they were met by a sea of veterans. The tears flowed. The march ended at the steps of number ten. That's where Prime Minister David Cameron was handed a petition from Mary Randall. They chatted for a while. He promised to do everything in his power to help the cause. She thanked him on behalf of her son and all those that had paid the full measure for the sake of others.

When the PM disappeared from view, Mary Randall stepped into the middle of the street and stood before a bank of microphones. She read from a well-rehearsed speech and everybody listened. She mentioned, in detail, the injustice that had been shown in all circles towards those young men that had given so much and asked for so little. She asked for recognition, she asked for help, and reiterated the many ways in which people could do so.

Mick Dea watched the proceedings on a TV set hanging from a wall in the canteen at Scotland Yard. He noted the emotion in Mary's voice as well as the medal that hung from the chest of 3 Para's Gavin Foble. He also remembered the website that had been mentioned.

On Wednesday 9th March at Woolwich Crown Court, the Hatton Garden gang appeared before Judge Christopher Kinch QC. Before handing out the required sentences he told them and a packed audience that the crime committed was in a class of its own and would probably go down as one of the biggest in British legal history. At the same time, he did remind everybody that it was a crime and that the theft and damage inevitably caused significant financial and economic loss on an unprecedented scale.

Billy Lincoln, Kenny Collins, Danny Jones and Terry Perkins received seven years. Carl Wood was sentenced to six years. They were each advised by council that they would only serve half of their sentences and as they had already spent ten months in custody they would only be behind bars for another two and a half years. In addition, they were also told to expect to face protracted asset recovery proceedings which could end with them losing everything they own. Terri Robinson and Brenn Walters were sentenced to eighteen months' imprisonment suspended for two years. Hugh Doyle got twenty-one months' imprisonment suspended for two years. He was so relieved he shook hands with every member of the jury and offered to fix their boilers for them.

As the five members of the gang that received custodial sentences were led beneath the courtrooms the public witnesses to it all broke into spontaneous cheering. The clapping that accompanied helped fill the room with a chorus of delight tinged with a hint of sympathy.

The siren was on, the lights were flashing and Mick Dea was racing through one red light after another. Besides him, in the passenger seat, was a very worried Emil Wiener. The call he had received from Karl Brandt had not been a good one. The voice was strained, the conversation was short and the instructions were direct. The race to Brant's apartment in Hatton Garden took thirty minutes and when both men got there they were met by paramedics. They were in attendance at the request of the man that was holding Brant by the hand whilst having his ear adjacent to his lips. After joining the scene Mick Dea and Emil Wiener were introduced to Dr. Francis Prello. He kept the exchanges brief before guiding Wiener into the seat he had vacated. Everything went still and then Wiener reached out and took hold of Brant by the hand and gave it a gentle squeeze. The German's eyes flickered and opened. That was followed by a strained smile. As his mouth began to move Wiener leaned in close.

"Did you find them?"

"Yes, the mother lived for another fifty years. The daughter is still alive. She is married and has a daughter of her own. Do you want us to tell her?"

With tears in his eyes, he just nodded.

"We can bring them to see you?" offered Wiener.

"I'm afraid it's too late for that," replied Brant.

"You must hang on."

Brant went still for a while and then whispered, "Did you find them?"

"Yes, the...." that's when Wiener stopped. That's when he realised that Brant was not repeating himself and was referring to his parents."

"Yes, I found them a long time ago with the help of some friends."

Brant gave a knowing smile before turning to his doctor and nodding. He then turned back to Wiener. "Find them all and tell them I am sorry."

Wiener was going to answer but felt the hand in his suddenly go limp. He looked at Brant and saw that although he had gone, the face, although still, had a peaceful look about it. He got to his feet, kissed Brant on the forehead and said a small prayer for him. When he turned to walk away he was met by Prello with an outstretched hand. In it was a ledger.

"He wanted you to have this. He said it was from a time he wanted to forget."

Wiener took hold of the book. "It was from a time too painful to remember."

On Monday 21st March at Woolwich Crown Court, Brian Reader, the oldest member of the Hatton Garden gang was jailed for six years and three months for the conspiracy to commit burglary. Due to his continual ill health he appeared via video link from Belmarsh Prison in a wheelchair. Judge Christopher Kinch reminded those present that Reader had previously pleaded guilty to a crime in which he was satisfied that Reader was rightly described as one of the ringleaders. He addressed Reader personally when he said, "I don't place you above the other conspirators and I don't place any great weight on the nickname 'the Master' which at the time of the police recordings may have been used with a degree of irony."

Reader just listened to it all. He never showed any signs of pity or remorse as he was past caring now. He was suffering, and in old traditional thief style, he was doing it in silence. A recent stroke had left him with pains that tortured him at will. Along with that, the septicaemia and the cancer, Reader had enough going on internally not to be bothered by what was happening on the outside. He contented himself with the fact that he had been given a life and there wasn't much about it that could be classed as hum drum. He basked in the thought that his name was going to go down in history. He knew that whatever happened in the courtroom the final chapter in his life still had plenty of pages to fill.

As the judge rose to leave he took one final look at the man he had just sentenced. He saw the pain but at the same time he also noticed a glint of satisfaction. He knew he had just put away a career criminal for his final time and although he knew that it was the right and proper thing to do, something just didn't seem right.

When Yuri emerged from the water on the French Riviera he could see Victor making his way back to their sunbeds. He looked out across the clear water and along the line of fine hotels and smiled. He liked being here. He liked the people, he loved the food and enjoyed the weather. That's when he gave a quick thought to the winters he had endured in Moscow and shivered. "No more," he said to himself. "From now on this is your life."

As he made his way out of the water he noticed the young waiter that had served him the evening before. The waiter waved and smiled. Yuri nodded and smiled in return. When he reached the sunbed, Victor threw him a towel. "I saw that."

"He was just being friendly."

"He was hitting on you."

"It's not like you to be jealous."

"I wasn't when we had no money but you have some value now."

Yuri smiled and kissed him on the lips.

Victor laughed and handed him a pile of English newspapers. Every one of them had the sporting scoop of the year. Yuri thumbed through the headlines and thought of all those editors that would be cursing him right now. Placing the papers down, he tossed a bottle of sun tan lotion over Victor and positioned himself face down on the bed.

"When are we going to introduce the next step?"

Victor picked up the bottle and began to rub its contents across Yuri's skin. "What's the rush? Let's just enjoy it for a while. There is plenty of time."

"You know something?" nodded Yuri. "I never thought we would get away with this."

"We nearly didn't. I still can't work out where that cop came from."

"I still can't work out why he let us go."

"Maybe it has something to do with the one hundred thousand pounds he took off us."

On the morning of Friday 1st April Mary Randall took delivery of a surprise package that she had to sign for. Intrigued she immediately rushed back into her kitchen and tore it open. Inside there was a small typed note that carried no name. It mentioned her website and the cause she held so close to her heart. It also mentioned the contents of the package and the respectful request for anonymity. Mary Randall then counted out twenty-five thousand pounds in cash and broke down.

Amanda Wilson received two packages. The first was from her solicitor Michael Holt. In it were adoption documents and a letter that said all the right words. The second contained a note along with a stack of money. After holding Faith in her arms for a moment she picked up the phone and made a phone call. When it ended, she made preparations to go to the bank and Michael Holt made preparations for the defence of Ralph Wilson.

As Juliette Roux stared at the package before her and was lost for words, Louise had to make the agreed phone call. The receiver called her 'Princess' and after listening to what she had to say he too was lost for words. It took him some time before he could advise her that he had not sent the package in question. When the call ended Juliette and Louise spent the next thirty minutes in a shocked silence and then just gave up trying to work it out. Mohamed Al-Fayed spent it pacing up and down his office before it suddenly struck him. He then poured himself a drink and toasted British justice.

When Emil Wiener was handed his package, he thought of Karl Brant, but as he had assisted with his burial and finances, he quickly dismissed the idea. He pondered over the note and money for quite some time before summoning one of his sons. He gave him the task of banking the money whilst he made a call to a friend at the Foundation for the Benefit of Holocaust Victims in Israel.

"What the bloody hell is that?"

When D.I Mick Dea looked up from his desk he found D.S. Turner standing there.

"Take a seat Guv, you are in for one hell of a shock."

Turner lowered himself into a seat.

Dea opened the plastic sleeve and using a pair of tweezers he slowly took two hand-written notes away from the charred pile that filled it. He turned them both around and slid them across the desk. He explained what they were and then Turner looked at the first one and read it out loud. It rang to a few paragraphs and ended with "Be lucky, I'm still getting away with it, your old mate 'B'". He then turned his attention to the second one. It was just one line and Turner read it out for clarity. "We are doing one last job, wish me luck, 'B'."

Dea picked up eight folders and waved them in the air.

"Why didn't you want me on the Hatton Garden job?"

"I did want you on it," replied a surprised Turner. "But Mark said he needed you for a specific task."

Dea slapped the folders on the table. "That task was eight red herrings. It was the eight boxes that had been damaged during the heist but their contents had not been touched. I was tasked with finding what connected the dots."

"Dots? You mean what connected them to the empty box that used to contain money from the train robbery of '63?"

"Yes, and that's where I went wrong. I should have been looking for the person that selected those boxes. You see it all goes back as to why did the gang only did seventy-three boxes."

"Because of inside information."

"Yes, that murdered accountant, Henry Davis, he had visited the old man that owned the depository shortly before the heist took place. He had access to all kinds of information and if someone knew that then he could have been bribed into helping out."

"Yes, but whoever did that would also have to have inside information on the depository itself or it wouldn't be of much use."

"So, let's say they had visited the place in a public capacity and a professional one."

Dea pushed a piece of paper across the desk. "That is a list off all the people that owned a box at the time of the heist. According to the investigation the lads did, sixty-two of those people don't exist. Our man could be any one of them." Dea then passed another sheet over. "That is an audit report that was carried out on the depository as part of a safety check the squad undertook after the depository was robbed in 2002."

"Yeah, I remember that. The Bavishi family had only owned the place for a year when that so-called dealer Philip Goldberg conned everyone and then did half a dozen boxes. We got the call when the owners complained that their locks had been disturbed and their boxes had been glued shut."

"You will note the names of the audit team."

Turner nodded and gave special note to one of them.

Dea passed over more pieces of paper. "We have the extracts from his log books along with his time records. They are attached to specific crimes. We have November 1983 and the Brinks Mat robbery, July 1987 and the Knightsbridge Security Deposit robbery, February 2006 and the Securitas deport robbery, August 2009, the Graff jewel heist and then Hatton Garden in 2015. When all of those took place, he was off shift but he was part of the investigation team on all of them. When I got close to the inside man on the Brinks Mat he had me moved."

"So, you think it's the same inside man?"

"I'm sure it is."

Turner looked down at the two hand-written notes. "So, who is 'B?"

"The first one is Bruce Reynolds," began Dea before passing across a report that contained the signature of his predecessor. He then drew Turner's attention closer to the lettering. "Look at the handwriting, look at how the words are formed. I have had it confirmed. They are a match.

Turner was about to speak but Dea continued on.

"In addition to that, the note had a thumb print on it. I've had the boys in the lab check it against some samples we had here. They also got a match."

"My God!" exclaimed Turner. "You don't think Mark Rearden is Basil."

"No, but I do believe he's involved and has been playing a very clever game. Remember this all started for me with the Ulsterman link on the train robbery of '63. It was believed that he was postal worker Patrick McKenna and we now know it was Sean Murphy. The latter set it all up that way. Now, as for today, according to all the informants that have been squeezed this Basil character is some sort of clinically-minded techno freak that has been mentioned on other jobs. Rearden was on those jobs. There has to be a link between the two of them and the only way we are going to find out is to speak to Rearden."

"Ok, I will speak to my opposite number in the 'Policia Nacional', we need to make sure he's still in Spain." As soon as Turner left the office Dea made a call of his own.

When Mark Rearden tied his boat off against the yacht and stepped onboard he was met by a lovely tanned blonde creature that glowed around a bright white bikini. She handed him a glass of champagne and ushered him to a seat on the lower deck. As he looked out over a crystal clear stretch of the Mediterranean she went to get the man he had arranged to meet. He appeared on deck a few moments later. They shook hands.

"Basil."

"Hello Mark, sorry about that, just had to take an urgent call. Good trip?"

"Very nice."

Basil looked over to the boat. "You just making sure?"

"Yeah, no-one knows I'm here. Old habits and all that."

"A man after my own heart. When are you moving on?"

"As soon as we have concluded our business."

"Take a seat, I will be back in a moment."

As Basil retreated Rearden's gaze was averted by a vision on the upper deck. A two-piece bikini had just become one. He hesitated for a moment to take in the glorious form on view before lowering himself into a seat. 'It's not a bad life' he thought to himself as he looked out over a clear horizon that shimmered under a scorching sun and closed his eyes.

He heard the footsteps approach. "We may have a slight problem," boomed Basil.

"What's that?" replied Rearden, not opening his eyes.

"They have the scrapbook and on one of the documents they have your print."

"That will be easy to explain away. I could say it did it whilst reviewing the file."

"But they have records to prove you have never had the file."

"Right, I'll think of something."

"I already have."

"What?" questioned Rearden, opening his eyes to a shadow that reflected a raised arm.

Basil brought the palm of his hand down onto Rearden's neck with such force it snapped in an instant. As the body went limp Basil grabbed both of its legs and toppled it over the side and into the sea. He watched it disappear and then he loosened the rope that had attached the boat. As it drifted away he looked around. It was all clear. He wandered to the upper deck and lowered himself face down onto a sunbed. The vision near him picked up a bottle of lotion and began to rub the contents over his back. He picked up one of the mobile phones that were nearby and made a single called to Scotland Yard in London. The call lasted just five seconds.

It was all the time he needed to say, "It's done."

ZIRCON

Yuri Tavlenko walked out of a nightclub on the French Riviera and was expecting to meet Victor. Instead he was confronted by two Russian agents from the FSB. They rammed a syringe into his neck and bundled him into a car. Three days later he opened eyes and found himself in a rundown warehouse overlooking the River Volga at Volgograd in Russia. He was interrogated, beaten to death and then his body was dumped in the Volga. Victor Ramere fled from France and is believed to be in Portugal. The FSB file on him is closed.

Ralph Wilson was sentenced to four years in prison. He is expected to be released after eighteen months. Amanda has never missed a visit.

Although Gavin Foble left the army he still keeps in touch with Dr. McKeown so that they can have the odd chat when the need arises. He spends the rest of his time working with Mary Randall campaigning for the rights of veterans. He now wears all of his medals when attending official occasions.

Massimo Alessi is buried in a cemetery in north London. On every anniversary of his death fresh flowers will appear on his grave courtesy of the Calvi family. Father John returned to Rome and has never been heard of since.

Juliette Roux lives in London with her daughter Louise. Juliette lives the quiet life and cherishes every moment. Louise is in fine health and when she's not at dance classes or at the gym she still finds time to write letters to Mohamed Al-Fayed.

Dwight Shunter eventually left Boston and settled in Florida. That's where he met Jenny, the widow of an investment banker. They got married and now spend their time managing the orchard they purchased.

Karl Brant was cremated and his ashes were scattered over the rose garden that belongs to Emil Wiener.

Sean Murphy was the Ulsterman.

Printed in Great Britain
by Amazon